GÓMEZ
the god

Order this book online at www.trafford.com
or email orders@trafford.com

Most Trafford titles are also available at major online book retailers.

Print information available on the last page.

ISBN: 978-1-4269-2610-5 (sc)
ISBN: 978-1-4269-2611-2 (hc)
ISBN: 978-1-4269-8665-9 (e)

Library of Congress Control Number: 2010903951

Trafford rev. 03/11/2021

www.trafford.com
North America & international
toll-free: 844-688-6899 (USA & Canada)
fax: 812 355 4082

Comments from the Cast

This book introduces a new icon of Latina Womanhood, Carmen Salazar. Beautiful, vivacious, clever and witty, Carmen is at once the embodiment of all that is Latina, and at the same time a True Original. My only criticism of this book is not enough Carmen!

Carmen Salazar

In a city with a long Mexican-American history, it is surprising how few books do a good job portraying the Latino community of Los Angeles. Here, in this book, are the people you don't see on the 6 o'clock news: your mom and dad, your brothers and sisters, your aunts and uncles, the family next door. Oh, and if you are an Hispanic-American living in LA, there's one more person you'll find in this book—you.

Councilman Eddie Morales

I don't know if this book is a great book; but it is a good story, and I liked it.

Humberto Sánchez

If every life has a defining moment, for me that moment began in April of 1988—the day 'Gómez the god' showed up—and ended on a magnificent, impossible evening in October. I will never forget the people with whom I shared those days. I love them more than words can express.

Alex Morales

I only read it because I have nothing better to do.

Mrs. Estella Cortez

For Carolina

The Villa

GÓMEZ
MR & MRS. SÁNCHEZ
STAIRS
OUR HOUSE
MRS. CORTEZ
PATIOS
MR. AGUILAR
TÍA CARMEN
WALKWAY
GRASS
LOCKE AVENUE

Spring, 1988
El Sereno, California

A Memorial

I met Gómez on the day we buried our father. It was a Monday, the day after Easter, and we had just arrived home. Many of the guests had already come from the cemetery, and every parking spot on both sides of the street was taken. My mom double-parked in the street below our house, and as we climbed out of the car she barked out orders.

"Rosa! Find Tía Carmen. Eddie! Do me a favor! Act like a man today and let your father rest in peace. Alex! I'll need you. Meet me in the house!" Then she drove off to find a parking spot.

My little sister Rosa hurried up the stairs to our house, but my big brother Eddie and I hesitated on the sidewalk, neither of us wanting to face the crowd assembling on our front lawn. There were six houses in our little villa, one on each side of three terraced lots, each house identical in shape and size to the others, each with a small lawn that bordered the stairs. Ours was the second house up on the left. Above us was the vacant Nuñez house—the old man had moved out last month—and below us, closest to the street, was Mr. Aguilar. Across from Mr. Aguilar was my Tía Carmen, above her was Mrs. Cortez, and above her, on the top right, were Mr. and Mrs. Sánchez.

Reluctantly, Eddie and I started up the stairs. We knew we'd be smothered by sympathetic guests—we'd been through it at the cemetery—

and we dreaded it. Just to delay the inevitable we stopped halfway; but our respite was short-lived. Up the walkway stormed my mom, holding the hem of her black dress in her left hand as she waved her right like a mad conductor. "Alex! Nuñez's house is open. Make sure the bathroom has toilet paper, and soap, and a clean towel. Eddie! Go down the street and see if there are any parking spaces on Carnegie. Hurry!" Eddie ambled down the stairs, I continued up to Nuñez's house, and my mom, continuing her ascent, yelled, "Rosa! Where's your Tía Carmen?"

I walked up to Nuñez's with a roll of toilet paper and two hand towels. The front door was open so I pulled on the screen door and stepped inside. There was a large tarp spread across the hardwood floor, and near the back wall stood a ladder with a paint tray on it. Who was painting Nuñez's living room? I heard a sound like a flute and followed it to the bathroom door. It was open a crack; I pressed my hand against it and pushed.

What the—? The toilet paper slipped from my slack hand and rolled—in slow motion it seemed—toward the toilet where an old man sat, his pants down around his ankles. I looked up. There was a wooden flute near his lips.

The stranger looked at the toilet paper next to his feet and then gradually lifted his eyes, backtracking the paper trail until our eyes met. They were wolf-eyes: gray, deep, entirely in the moment.

He lowered the flute and smiled. In a voice deep and rough, like he'd smoked a million cigarettes, he said, "Thank you, lad" in a tone so casual it was like he'd been expecting me.

I didn't speak. With his eyes holding mine, he reached down for the toilet paper. "Son, could you excuse me for a moment?" He cleared his throat. "There's business to which I must attend." As I backed away he added, "Don't go away! I'll be just a minute!"

I was in such a daze I forgot to close the door. Looking around the living room for somewhere to put myself, I saw an old record player against the wall and plopped down next to it. Soon I heard a flush, and a few moments later the old man appeared.

Except for his light brown skin, his head was dominated by shades of gray: bushy silver eyebrows arched above gray eyes; wavy silver hair flowing back from his forehead; and cloaking his jaw a Hemingway beard—silver with dark gray highlights. White overalls covered his bare chest—also overgrown with silver hair—and his shoes, Jack Purcell's, were also white, except for the laces, which were red, matching the red bandana tied around his neck.

Approaching me he smiled and said, "There's only one valuable thing in this house and you found it!" He gestured toward the towel in my hand. "Say, may I use that?" After drying his hands he extended his arm. "Rise, my fortuitous friend, and let's be introduced!" He lifted me up with one huge hand, then bowed his head slightly. "I am Gómez."

The seconds ticked by. He waited expectantly for a reply, but I couldn't find my tongue. Releasing my hand, he waved his arm toward the wall and said, "You've probably noticed I've been doing a little painting . . . ."

With his attention directed away from me I had a sudden urge to flee. Shifting my eyes to the door, I tensed my muscles to back away, took one last glance back, and—damn! The old man was looking right at me! He nodded his head. "Perhaps later, son," he said softly.

Slowly pulling myself away from his unblinking gray eyes, I silently backed out of the living room, through the open door—and *ran*.

*****

"There's a man in Nuñez's house."

"What?" My mom stopped slicing a cabbage and cocked her head sideways in that funny doglike way of hers. A strand of black hair slipped out of its tight bun. Still clutching the knife, she brushed back the errant lock with her right hand. "Alex, what'd you say?"

"There's an old man in Nuñez's house. When I walked in he was using the bathroom."

"Ayyy! What's this world coming to? A bum just helps himself to Nuñez's bathroom. On the most important day of your father's life, a bum just moves into Nuñez's house. What's next, eh Carmen? When I go to the market, will I come home to find a band of gypsies in our house? 'Oh, *perdóneme*, señora, we thought you had moved out. The window wasn't locked.' Ayyy!"

My Tía Carmen was washing fish fillets in the sink. "I wish some gypsy would break into my house." She wiggled her butt, stressing the threads of her jeans beyond the manufacturer's suggested limits. "I'd punish you good!" She slapped a fillet with a loud whack. "What, Señor Gypsy, still not sorry? Then I punish you again! You're a *bad man*, but I'm more than you expected, eh, my love?" She turned sideways to my mother, mischievous hazel eyes glinting through bronze curls, and placed her hands beneath her large breasts, pushing them up. "*Much* more than you expected, no Señor Gypsy?"

"Carmen!" my mom hissed. "Don't you ever stop thinking about men?"

"Of course; when I'm worrying about you."

My mom let the comment drop, then put her hands on my shoulders and turned me around. "Alex, take me to the gypsy."

We made our way through the crowd in the living room, my mom graciously answering each condolence as we passed by. "Yes, well, I don't know if he was a *great* man, but he did the best he could" . . . and onto the porch—"The children are fine, thank you" . . . and into the yard—"No, there's nothing we need, but thank you" . . . and finally to the stairs and up to the old Nuñez house.

Without knocking she opened the screen door. A song was playing on the record player —*"Nessun Dorma"* I discovered later—and Gómez was standing on the ladder, slapping the paint roller against the wall, bellowing out words I didn't understand.

I looked at my mom. She appeared to be deciding between righteous anger and good manners. Opting for good manners, she said, "Excuse me, sir."

No response.

She stepped inside and I followed. "Sir! Excuse me."

Still no response.

She spread her feet, planted her 5'3" and 125 pounds, and leaned forward. "Hey you! What are you doing here?"

Gómez's head spun, wolf-eyes flashing. For a second my mom wavered, but righteous anger asserted itself and her brown eyes took on a dark, menacing look. When I turned back to Gómez I was shocked to see those hungry wolf-eyes had shifted from my mom to *me*. Instantly I was paralyzed with fear, and just when I thought my legs might buckle, he changed. The wolf-eyes vanished, and suddenly he was grinning, looking just as cheerful and merry as a Mexican St. Nick. He hopped off the ladder and swallowed my hand in his giant paw. "Amigo!"

After an enthusiastic, shoulder-separating handshake, Gómez turned back to my mom. "Please excuse my bad manners, señora! You must be this fine boy's mother." He extended his arm. "I am Gómez. It is a pleasure to meet you."

"Yes, I'm sure." My mom put her hands on her hips. "What are you doing here?"

Finding a sudden use for his dangling hand, Gómez gestured toward the partially painted wall behind him and said graciously, "I am painting, señora."

"Yes, I can see that. You're a painter, then?"

"At the moment, señora."

"And when you are not a painter? What then?"
"Many things, señora."

"Yes. Such as . . . ?"

"Sometimes I am a gardener; sometimes a carpenter, or a mechanic; many things, señora."

"I see, Mr. Gómez; you're a jack-of-all-trades. That's fine. But what are you doing here, on the day of my husband's funeral?"

Gómez began to answer, then stopped. He reached back for the ladder; it was too far away and his arm fell awkwardly, causing him to stumble slightly. "I—I am sorry, señora." Regaining his balance, he looked at me, then turned to my mom. "I didn't know. Now I understand—the people in your yard: guests—many guests." He tilted his head to the left: "bathroom—extra." Extending his arms he said, "Please señora, *mi casa es su casa*."

Screech. "*Your* house?"

"Uh, no, it's Mr. Johnson's house. I am renting it."

"I see." Pushing aside that same pesky lock of hair, my mom gathered herself and said, in a voice less than contrite, "Forgive me, sir. Please, come over later; we're having a barbecue. Alex can introduce you to your new neighbors. Good day, Mr. Gómez." She turned and reached toward the door.

As the screen door banged shut Gómez whispered, "It is just 'Gómez,' señora." Then he turned his gray eyes on me. "Well, I suppose we ought to clean up this mess, eh son?"

*****

There were already more than fifty people at my father's Memorial, with at least three dozen packed into our little house. Tío Julio, my mother's brother, sat in one of two matching stuffed chairs; his wife, my Tía Estella, sat in the other. Whenever they came over the first thing they did was claim those chairs. They wouldn't move for hours for fear someone would steal their chairs; and, with lots of kids around, they always had someone to fetch things. The only service a kid couldn't do for them was relieve their bladders, yet I never saw them get up even for that. They must've had very large bladders.

There was one more chair in the living room—my father's recliner. It was empty. Even in his absence everyone knew better than to sit in that chair.

On our lawn were two large round tables, each surrounded by eight white folding chairs. On Mrs. Cortez's lawn were another four tables, and on my Tía Carmen's lawn were two more. With seating for sixty-four guests my mom was still afraid someone could be left standing, so she sent me up to Gómez's for permission to use his lawn, if needed. He agreed. "Let's get the chairs now, lad, so it's all ready just in case."

As we were pulling chairs from the truck, Gómez said, "Son, your father must have been a very popular person: so many people have come to honor him."

"He knew a lot of people. He was a teacher."

"Really? That's a fine profession." He stopped to rub his Hemingway. "What subject did he teach?"

"Math; at *Our Lady of Guadalupe*."

"A math teacher," Gómez mused. "I always liked math too: precise, predictable, everything adds up."

"He was also the Dean. If you got in trouble, you saw my father."

"Math teacher *and* Dean. Uh-oh."

With a chair in each of my hands and four in each of Gómez's, we soon had his lawn filled. When we were done, Gómez sat down and invited me to join him on the retaining wall that separated our property. Together we surveyed the activity below us.

In our little villa, each house connected to the central walkway by a concrete path. The front door opened onto the path, and to the left, as you looked out, was a small patio. On ours, Mr. Aguilar had just begun grilling fish and *carne* on his oil-drum barbecue. On the lawn, perpendicular to the patio, was a long table covered in a white bed sheet. As the tortillas came off the grill, my cousin Mariano put them in a folded towel to keep them warm. Next to the tortillas sat a bowl of pinto beans with shredded Mexican cheese on top, a large bowl of Spanish rice, and another large bowl of green salad.

The scene absorbed Gómez. He rubbed his Hemingway, eyes moving from table to table. "Bottled salsa," he said at last.

"What?"

He turned his head and looked at me intently. "Bottled salsa; on each of the tables is bottled salsa. Why don't they just pour ketchup on their food?" He walked away a few paces and then returned to his chair.

"Alex—may I call you Alex?"

"Sure."

"Alex, a Mexican should *never* serve bottled salsa. In the old days, a host serving this bottled puke would've been sacrificed to the gods—if the gods would've accepted such a poor gift. No self-respecting Mexican should defile his body with that *pico de* puke. If the gringos want to eat it, well, I suppose that's fine. But frankly, I think I'll just ban it from my world altogether." He waved his hand as if to make it so, and sat back down.

I think he wanted to sit there all night, unmoving and silent, just to make his point. Out of courtesy I was respecting his silence, but I was getting hungry, and I was just about to speak when he said, "Well, a feast like this should not be spoiled just because of one mistake. Besides, your mom has made a great effort to honor your father."

He stood up and placed his hands on the small of his back, turning his head slowly left, then right, as if he were considering each side of an argument. Resolved: "There are two things we need here. First is salsa. Is there a *taqueria* nearby?"

"Sure. 'My Taco.'"

He winced. "'My Taco.' Hmmm . . . well, all right. The second thing is music. In my world there is music. I know," he said as if anticipating an argument, "this isn't a party. Still, there is music appropriate for every occasion. Would you please put my record player on my patio? When I get back I'll put some music on."

When Gómez returned we poured eight bowls each of *salsa verde* and *salsa rojo* and placed them on the tables. He excused himself to put on a record—Beethoven—then we went down to my yard to fill our plates. We ate in silence, our legs dangling over the retaining wall as evening descended and the chords of "Moonlight Sonata" filled the air.

Eddie appeared on our walkway and headed toward the food table with that cocky swagger of his. Just as Gómez was about to swallow the last bit of taco he saw Eddie—and stopped. The wolf-eyes didn't blink once as they followed Eddie's progress from the stairs to the food table.

"Son, over there, grabbing a plate, who is that?"

"Eddie. He's my brother."

"Your brother?"

"Yes. My older brother."

Eddie circled around some guests who were moving too slowly and went straight to the front of the line.

"What is he like?"

"He doesn't take shit from anyone."

Gómez seemed pleased by that description. He nodded to himself and smiled. "Yep. That's what I thought."

Drinking tequila out of Coke can and smoking a cigarette, Eddie joined us a short while later. After introductions the three of us sat on the edge of Gómez's retaining wall and watched the people below us, candles flickering in the gathering dark.

Gómez motioned to a table. "Who is the young woman cleaning up and chatting with everyone?"

"Her?" Eddie pointed with his chin. "That's Tía Carmen." Sounding like a TV Mexican, he said, "She's a fiery one, señor, and worth one hondred pesos: that's what all the soldiers say. But tonight, to honor my padre, you can have her for feefty pesos—feefty pesos! What a deal!" He wagged his forefinger at Gómez. "That's tonight only. Tomorrow it's back to one hondred pesos for the lovely Carmen Salazar!"

Gómez said nothing, and in the silence Eddie's laughter sounded like a braying donkey.

"I like her," Gómez said softly. He pointed to a table on Mrs. Cortez's lawn. "Who are the three people sitting there?"

"That's Mrs. Cortez," I blurted before Eddie could answer. "She lives across from us. She's with Mr. and Mrs. Sánchez. They live across from you."

Gómez watched them silently for a few seconds, then said, "Mrs. Cortez is uncomfortable; she only speaks when she's spoken to." He leaned forward, resting his chin on his folded hands. "She looks at the children playing over there, but she doesn't see them." He turned toward me. "Alex, you said '*Mrs.* Cortez.' Where is Mr. Cortez?"

Eddie, still speaking like a TV Mexican, pointed his gun-finger into his mouth and answered, "He blew his brains out, señor. Very messy."

Gómez seemed to ignore Eddie's answer. He continued looking at the table, and minutes passed before he spoke again.

"They don't talk to each other."

"Eh señor?" drawled Eddie, following Gómez's eyes. "Oh, the Sánchez's? Ain't you heard of telepathy, man? The Sánchezes don't need no mouths to talk, they use their minds—like Spock." I laughed. The comparison of the Sánchezes to Mr. Spock on *Star Trek* just struck me as funny. Gómez was silent.

Eddie fired up another cigarette and said, "Señor Gómez, lemme break it down." He waved his hand towards the remaining guests on the lawns below us. "This is my kingdom, and these are my people. The man who lived in your house— Nuñez, was a drunk and a gambler. His daughter took him and his shit a few weeks ago. Señor and Señora Sánchez are aliens pretending to be simple peasants from the old country; it is obvious now, no? Mrs. Cortez I told you about; Tía Carmen too. Mr. Aguilar, the cook, is a bachelor—an *old* bachelor, and you know what that means, eh señor? And my *madre* is playing the grieving widow. Do you understand now, señor?"

"Thank you, Eddie. I understand you well."

The party was winding down; only a couple dozen neighbors and family remained. Even Tío Julio and Tía Estella had given up their chairs and departed.

Eddie stood up shakily. "It's time, Alex; time to say goodbye to our father." He raised his Coke can. "Dear father, there are so many things I never got to tell you, and now it's too late. Even though you're gone from this world, I hope you can hear me—in Hell, where I pray you roast forever. For every time you hit Alex or mom, may Satan stick a pitchfork up your holy ass. As for every time you hit *me* padre . . . well, I'll take care of that when we meet again."

He drained the Coke can. Then he took a final drag on his cigarette, flipped the butt on our lawn, and jumped down from the wall.

Gómez and I looked at each other. Then we watched Eddie as he disappeared down the stairs.

The Garden

"Goddammit, Alex!" Eddie threw his pillow across the room. "Turn off the radio!" I didn't know what the hell he was talking about, and told him so, but then I heard it too. Horns—loud. Then drums—boom! Boom! BOOM! It was *really* loud, and it was coming from outside.

I sat up in bed and lifted the window. There was Gómez, standing on the stone retaining wall, the sun glowing on his face. From his record player came a crescendo of horns and drums. It was quite a sight.

Eddie climbed on my bed and looked out. "Jesus Christ, our new neighbor's insane!"

Gómez became aware of us and gestured to join him. "Good morning, amigos! Come on over; it's a beautiful sunrise!"

"I have a better idea, old man," yelled Eddie. "Go stick your head in a toilet!"

Gómez smiled. He probably didn't hear Eddie.

Eddie pulled our window closed and fell into his bed; in a minute he was asleep again. But not me—I got up to see what our crazy new neighbor was up to next!

"Good morning, Alex!" hailed Gómez as I scaled the retaining wall. Today his overalls were blue, strapped over a gray sweatshirt cut to short sleeves, again with the red bandana tied around his neck. He held a shovel upright in his hands, twirling it carelessly on his right boot.

"You like 'Sunrise'?"

I turned around to look at the rising sun. "Sure."

Gómez smiled. "I seldom miss one. But I was referring to the music, 'Sunrise,' by Richard Strauss."

"Oh, is that what that was. I thought someone was beating my head with a hammer."

The smiled lengthened. "It was a bit loud then, hmmm?" He stopped twirling the shovel. "Yes, it was. But that song demands to be played loud." He lifted his eyebrows apologetically. "And I can't refuse it."

He pushed the shovel into the grass and said, "When I first heard it I thought, 'If there is music for the dawn, this is it.' A herald of the sun, that's 'Sunrise'; and you don't tell a herald to be quiet, do you?" It was more of a statement than a question.

"I guess not." Sometimes it was hard to figure what Gómez was talking about. "So, what're you doing?"

"I'm planting a garden." He grunted as he lifted the first shovelful of dirt. "But this is special—" He looked at me expectantly, and after an unfulfilled pause added, "—it's a salsa garden!"

He stopped and leaned on his shovel. "After you went home last night, I was sitting out here thinking about this and that when it dawned on me—a salsa garden! Look, over here we'll have chilies—yellow chilies here, serranos there. Along here we'll plant *tomatillos;* over there, cilantro. But we'll also need green onion, yellow onion, and garlic." Gómez frowned and rubbed his Hemingway. "Hmmm, getting a bit crowded. Well, we'll start with the chilies—the most important ingredient." He handed me a spade.

We began to tear up a patch of grass on the southeast side of his lawn, about ten feet long and three feet wide, extending from the porch to the retaining wall. Gómez shoveled up large clumps of grass, which I broke down with the spade.

We hadn't even worked up a sweat when Gómez exclaimed, "Bolero!" He put down his shovel and disappeared into his house. In a minute he reappeared with an album and his record player. "What a lucky garden you will be!" He placed the album on the turntable. "Alex, this garden will be blessed in the most perfect way: we'll soak the earth with the fertile genius of 'Bolero.' Before planting a single seed we'll first plant the blueprint for life, captured in music by my friend Ravel."

Gómez put the record on and we went back to work. At first I was wondering what happened to "Bolero"—I couldn't hear anything—but after a little while I began to notice the melody; well, actually I became aware of the rhythmic sweeping of Gómez's head and the beat of his shovel as he inserted it into the ground, *then* I became aware of the soft, methodical rhythm of "Bolero." I could hear it clearly now, and like Gómez I began to move to the enchanting beat. Up with the spade, down with the spade, lay the spade down, bend over the ground, grab the grass, shake it loose. Up with spade, down with the spade . . . *doom dada doom, da da da da da da, doom dada doom, da da da da da daaa, da da da da da da da da, da da da da daaaaa.*

Now the music is louder. Gómez's movements are exaggerated; his shaggy head swings in great arcs. Down goes his shovel into the yielding earth, back goes the blade, out comes a clump of dirt, over it comes to me. Down, back, up and out.

My head swings back and forth, too. I look at Gómez; he smiles. Our heads swing in mirrored reflection. *Doom dada doom!*

Horns soar, beckoning as they rise. Soon they are overtaken by the surging melody and wove into a new theme, richer and broader, like a multi-colored tapestry of sound. But it doesn't last, for even now an intrepid band of violins are breaking free and springing ahead. And so it goes: bold instruments launch themselves skyward, dauntlessly driving the music ever higher, ever louder. I reach for another clump and shake the dirt from the grass; it may be the first time I've ever *really* looked at a blade of grass. It isn't just green; it's shades of green fused together. And the texture: glossy and smooth in the center, rough on the sides, edges like knives.

The drums pound out the primal beat. Gómez and I are in perfect concert. Then suddenly the finale—bass drums groan, a burst of horns—and it's over.

"Wow," said Gómez. He dropped his shovel and looked around. All the grass was gone: only dirt remained, dark and glistening.

"Alex, I think this ground has been blessed!" He crouched and picked up a clod. "What do you think?" He threw the clod at me and it bounced off my chest. I got down on my knees to pick it up, inspecting it closely. "It looks blessed to me!" I yelled, throwing it back at Gómez.

"And this one?" Gómez said, throwing another.

"Blessed!" I said as I flung it back. "And this looks blessed too!"

The next thirty seconds was a whirlwind of whirring arms and flying dirt. Every particle in that little patch of earth must have changed position a dozen times. Gómez and I finally rolled on our sides, spent with laughter. Our clothes were covered in chocolaty dirt, as were our faces and hair. Gómez sat up on one elbow and said, "I may have to put 'Bolero' away! Or write on the box: 'Caution! Dangerous! Not to be used while planting salsa gardens!'"

I heard the faint sound of a screen door clang, followed by my mom hollering, "Alex!"

"Up here!"

"Alex! What are you doing? You're filthy!"

"I'm helping Gómez plant his salsa garden."

Gómez stood up quickly, as quickly as his old joints would allow, and in a vain effort to look presentable, he began the hopeless task of dusting off his overalls. My mom watched him, and when he finally raised his eyes to her, she shot him a glance that said, *So you're responsible for this, you corrupter of children. I have my eye on you. From now on when I see you, I will visualize this moment and you will know that I know.* That's what the look said, but the words were, "Good morning, Mr. Gómez." Then, shifting her eyes to me: "Alex." She shook her head slowly to emphasize her disappointment. "Breakfast is ready. Come in and clean up."

Considering my mom left for work without any specific orders against seeing Gómez again, after breakfast I headed back up to his house. "Hey Gómez!" I looked at his lawn. A new swath of grass on the east side of his pathway was chewed up. "What're you doing?"

"After our first success I thought, 'Why stop here?' This little patch isn't nearly large enough for a complete salsa garden. I'll put the chilies over there—they deserve their own spot, and over here will go the *tomatillos*, the cilantro, the onion—oh, and garlic! Hmmm, yes . . . ." He surveyed the little plot of land. "The garlic will have to go with the chilies; I think they'll get along just fine. What do you think, Alex?"

I wasn't accustomed to giving my opinion—on anything. In my house kids weren't asked, they were told. It was a harmless question, "What do you think, Alex?" Nevertheless, my mind locked up and all I could do was give a non-committal shrug.

A shrug was affirmation enough. "Yes, that will do just fine. Now, what music . . . . I'm thinking something subtle. Robust was perfect for chilies, they're the star of the salsa: hence 'Bolero.'" Gómez rubbed his Hemingway. "These other ingredients though, they require something different: something subtle; simple, integrated, if you know what I mean. 'Trois Gymnopédies,' I think. Alex, do you agree?"

"Uh, sure."

For the rest of the morning we worked in the garden. After brief, one-sided discussions, I'd put on another selection: Stravinsky, Tchaikovsky, Bach and others.

We were so engrossed in preparing our soil—turning it over and "letting it breathe," as Gómez said—that we didn't notice Mr. Sánchez watching us from the walkway. He was standing there, dressed the way he usually dressed: baggy, white cotton pants, a red Pendleton shirt, and an old Panama hat.

Gómez was the first to see him. "Mr. Sánchez! Good morning!" He wiped his hands on his overalls. "It is a pleasure to meet you! I'm your new neighbor." Approaching Mr. Sánchez he extended his right hand. "Gómez is my name."

Mr. Sánchez looked down at Gómez's dirty paw, then put his hands in his pockets. "You're digging up the grass," he said, matter-of-factly.

Gómez turned briefly to survey his work. "Yes, I am doing that—that and more! I'm planting a salsa garden."

"Does Mr. Johnson know you're digging up the grass?"

"No, I didn't tell him I was replacing this worthless grass," Gómez gestured to his yard, "with a salsa garden." Gómez, who was much taller than Mr. Sánchez, peered down at him with an earnest look on his face and said, "Mr. Sánchez, have you ever had real, homemade salsa?"

"Yes, I have," answered Mr. Sánchez, a bit of defiance in his voice. "In Oaxaca, in the mountains, when I was young, my grandmother made salsa. The hottest chilies are from Oaxaca."

"Hmmm, I didn't know that." Gómez put his hand behind Mr. Sánchez's shoulders and invited him forward. "Please, let me show you what I have in mind. Over here," and he led Mr. Sánchez to the narrow strip of dirt parallel to his house, "is where the chilies will be—yellow chilies and serranos. But there's room for more! Jalapeños maybe, or those chilies from Oaxaca. Mr. Sánchez, do you have any?" A pirate asking for the whereabouts of buried treasure wouldn't have been more eager for an answer.

"No, I don't. Anyway, it wouldn't do you any good even if I did. It's the climate that makes them so hot. Everything is hot in Oaxaca, most of all the people. It is said that our chili—the *rocoto,* which is the hottest in the world—was made by the gods to cool the blood of the Oaxacan people."

Gómez listened with rapt attention. "Those must be very good chilies, indeed. Would you mind seeing if you can locate some? I'm sure they wouldn't be as good as homegrown, yet still I would like to try some. Would you mind, Mr. Sánchez?"

Mr. Sánchez bent down and grabbed a small handful of soil. He looked at it carefully as he rubbed it between his fingers. "I'll ask around."

"Thank you," answered Gómez solemnly, matching Mr. Sánchez's mood. "Now, over here we'll grow the rest of the ingredients." Gómez led Mr. Sánchez across the upturned dirt. "*Tomatillos*—I'm in the mood for *salsa verde*, and yellow onion, green onion, garlic and cilantro. Ahhh, cilantro . . . how I have missed you," he said wistfully.

"Mr. Gómez, the chilies should be grown over here, not the cilantro. Chilies need a full sun. Put the cilantro, onions, garlic, against your house, facing north; the *tomatillos*, over here with the chilies."

Gómez rubbed his Hemingway. "Hmmm, I see your point." He looked at me and said, "Well, we better get busy. We need to irrigate our garden, and I'd like to start looking at plants, too. Is there a hardware store around here, Mr. Sánchez?"

"There's a Builder's Emporium over on Main Street; they'll have irrigation supplies. They also have plants, but not many. Not sure where there's a full nursery."

"Okay, then we'll start with Builder's Emporium." He put his hands on the small of his back and said, "By the way, Mr. Sánchez, it is just 'Gómez.' My name, there's no mister." Then turning to me: "Say, Alex, would you like to come with me?"

It took us about two hours, but it went very fast. Gómez looked at things differently, and he said things I'd never heard before. For example, when a cop drove by he said, "Alex, when the people have strayed from The Way, they make codes of honesty and conduct. Lao Tzu said that." I had no idea what he was talking about, but it didn't matter; it's been etched in my memory ever since.

Later on, we came upon some *cholos* hanging out. As we moved through their company, Gómez looked at each one, nodding his head in silent greeting. The last one was sitting on a stone fence, idly chipping concrete out of the wall with the tip of a knife. Gómez stopped.

"Excuse me. My name is Gómez and I am new to your village. Can you tell me if there is a nursery nearby?"

The *cholo* didn't answer—he didn't even lift his head. One of his fat buddies stepped up. "Whattaya want with a nursery, man?"

"I'm planting a salsa garden."

The fat *cholo* laughed. "You came to the right place, man; we're gardeners too. But we don't grow no salsa. We just grow weeds." That got a few chuckles from his buddies. Then he said, "Hector, we got competition." That also got some laughs, but the *cholo* named Hector wasn't laughing. He wiped his knife on his pant leg and said, "Ain't nothin' here." Then he resumed chipping out concrete.

We left, and after a minute or two Gómez said, "In my world, people don't take drugs. When you're engaged in life, you need your wits. Drugs just make you stupid."

A block later he added, "And there aren't any street gangs. In my world, the young men and women are a *necessary part* of the society. They're looking forward to the roles that await them: farmers and craftsmen, merchants and soldiers, statesmen and poets, mothers and fathers."

On that walk he must have prefaced half a dozen statements with, "In my world . . . ."

When we returned home, we began installing our "drip irrigation system." After three hours we had all the water lines laid out, with little misters perched along the crest of each furrow, and the timer attached to the outdoor faucet.

It was about 5:30 in the evening; Gómez and I stood on his walkway inspecting our work. We were both gratified, but for me it was probably the first time I had worked all day on a project in my entire life. Mr. Sánchez came over and inspected our work, too. He placed a hand on the tubing, and beginning at the timer, followed it up and down each furrow. When he was done he asked, "Does it work?"

"Well, I *think* it will," Gómez answered, "but the truth is, I've never done this before!" Gómez laughed and Mr. Sánchez smiled wryly.

I had the honor of turning on the faucet for our test run. Instantly, several thin water-jets burst out of the connection.

"Just as I thought," said Mr. Sánchez as I quickly shut off the spigot, "the diameter of the hose is too narrow. It'd take at least a one-inch hose to handle that much pressure."

Gómez listened to Mr. Sánchez, hands placed in the small of his back, eyes moving back and forth from Mr. Sánchez to the irrigation system. He got on his knees and looked over the hookup for several seconds. "Silly me," he said, "Plumber's putty. Mr. Sánchez, you're right. The pressure is too great for a connection that isn't properly sealed. How much putty do you think we would need?"

Mr. Sánchez knelt next to Gómez and ran his hand over the connection. "If it works at all," he pronounced, "not much; just a dab squeezed over the threads. But make sure it dries before you turn on the water."

"Yes, I think you're right. Well, it looks like I am off to the hardware store again."

"You *could* do that," said Mr. Sánchez. "That would take about forty-five minutes to walk there, about five minutes to locate the putty, maybe another five checking out, another forty-five minutes back. An hour and a half is a lot of time to invest in a squeeze of putty. Or you could walk down to Aguilar's and ask him for some of his. That would take about twenty seconds of walking, about thirty minutes of questions, thirty minutes to inspect your system, and thirty more minutes of advice. So, you break even on the time, but you'd save on the putty."

Gómez had begun smiling part way through Mr. Sánchez's speech. "Mr. Sánchez, my good fortune never ceases; to have a neighbor such as you! Would you mind making my introduction?"

"Come with me." He took a step forward, then abruptly stopped and placed a hand on Gómez's shoulder. "But it would be best not to ask any questions. Each one will add another ten minutes to the estimate."

I went with them, and while Mr. Sánchez was correct that Mr. Aguilar had some putty, his estimations were way off. It had been dark for some time when they applied the putty to the spigot.

"Now, let that sit all night," said Mr. Aguilar, wiping his hands with the handkerchief he always carried, "and in the morning you can turn on the water. It'll be fine by then."

Eddie showed up, took a quick look at our work, and said, "Dirt." He flicked his cigarette and hopped over the wall.

We ignored him. "Well, Alex," said Gómez, "by tomorrow evening Salsa Garden will be planted."

"Gee Gómez, I have school tomorrow; it's Wednesday."

"Hmmm. Well, this is *our* project, so we'll just have to wait until the weekend. No problem; I'll do some research on salsa gardens. Yes, of course! That's the next step anyway!"

*****

On Saturday morning I was again awakened by "Sunrise." Eddie groaned and mumbled, "I'll kill that sonuvabitch." Gómez didn't play it during the week, out of courtesy I guess, although now that I think about it, it made more sense to play it during the week when everyone got up early. Gómez the alarm clock!

Gómez met me at the wall and gestured for me to sit. "Alex, Mr. Aguilar is driving us to Anderson's Nursery, but before he shows up I need to discuss something with you. I've done some reading about growing vegetables, and I've spoken at some length to Mr. Sánchez and Mr. Aguilar. Although my personal inclination is to grow all the vegetables from seed, we could also go with seedlings. Tell me your thoughts."

"What's a seedling?"

"A small plant; seeds are planted in a greenhouse, take root, and become seedlings. When they reach a certain size they're sold." Gómez leaned back, supporting himself with braced arms. "So, what do you think?"

This time I wasn't so thrown off by an adult asking my opinion. I didn't introvert too much, and my mind didn't freeze up. You treat a kid like an adult, next thing you know, he's acting like one. After some back-and-forth dialogue, I said, "So it would take at least two months to grow everything; that's if we use seedlings. If we start from seed, then more like three months, maybe even longer. It's April now. That takes us to the middle of July."

"Exactly."

I nodded.

"One more thing, Alex; Midsummer Day is June twenty-third. I thought it would be fun to have a Midsummer's Eve feast, featuring, of course, our homemade *salsa verde.*"

"A party! Sounds great, Gómez."

"Yes—but more than a party. A fiesta! A celebration of life! A toast to friends, family and fortune. There will be food and drink and music and dancing!"

"And *carne asada* tacos smothered in the world's greatest salsa!"

"*Bueno!*" Gómez tousled my hair. "But, still we have the question of seeds or seedlings. Alex, you decide."

I rubbed my chin. "Well . . . seeds are good because we're starting from scratch—like raising them from birth." Gómez listened intently, his gray eyes sometimes shifting to my mouth as if he wanted to catch each word as it took shape on my lips. "But I think seedlings. It'll be like adopting plant orphans!"

Gómez laughed and pushed himself off the wall and into my yard. "Well thought and well said! Seedlings it is."

We saw Mr. Aguilar exit his home and start up the stairs, hailing us as he came. "Gómez, you ready to go to Anderson's?"

"Yes, Mr. Aguilar, we're ready. Let's go, Alex. Wait! Is it okay with your *madre?*"

I walked into my house. Rosa was watching cartoons, without sound so my mom wouldn't know, and I could hear my mom and my Tía Carmen talking in the kitchen. As I entered, Carmen said, "Alex, I was just thinking of you. Come here, *corazón*."

She guided me into the chair next to her. "Alex dear, this mystery man, Gómez, what do you know about him?"

"He's a lunatic," my mom butted in as she walked over to the sink. "A con man, or worse, a con*vict*; I trust him as far as I can throw this stove."

"Yes, yes, Maria," said Carmen, her eyes never leaving mine. "Now *mijo*, this *lunático* Gómez, has he ever mentioned a wife?"

"And," my mom butted in again, pointing at me with an empty coffee cup. "I don't like you hanging out with him, Alex. Play with your friends."

"I don't have any friends."

"Yes, you do."

"No, I don't."

"What about Wilfredo? He's a nice boy. Play with him."

"He moved, mom; over a year ago."

"Oh. Well then, what about those boys I saw you playing with at school a couple of weeks ago? You were playing tag."

"That wasn't tag, mom. They were trying to steal my Ninja Turtle; the one Eddie gave me."

"Why didn't you—"

"Maria, please!" interrupted Carmen. "This is *my* conversation; have your own when I'm gone." She cupped her hand under my chin. "Now *mijo*, listen to me. Gómez, has he ever mentioned a wife? Or a girlfriend?"

"No tía."

Carmen leaned back and dropped a sugar cube in her coffee, stirring it with one long fingernail. "Are there any pictures in his house of a woman?"

"Tía?"

"Wedding pictures? Vacation pictures? High school prom?"

"No tía."

"All right, let's try a different angle. Does he have a boyfriend?"

"Carmen!" My mom banged her empty cup on the counter. "That's enough!"

"Alex?" continued my tía. My mother's command was temporarily suspended, like an old movie scene where the action is frozen while two characters discourse privately. Carmen's eyes held mine.

"No tía."

"All right, Maria Lena," Carmen relented. The spell passed and my mom became animate again. The walls themselves seemed to exhale. "This 'no, tía' and 'yes, tía' is going nowhere, anyway. Alex dear, what *can* you tell me about the mystery man?"

"Well, he's planting a salsa garden. We're planting it together—"

"Just as I said," interrupted my mom, "the man is here a week—less than a week!—and he tears up the lawn to plant a garden. Does he ask Mr. Johnson? No."

Carmen waited for my mom to finish, then continued to question me as if my mom hadn't spoken. "Go on Alex."

"He likes music."

"Good, Alex. Mmmm . . . what kind of music?"

"Classical music."

"Exhibit two," my mom cut in. "Playing music at six in the morning? Not *playing*, Carmen—blaring!"

"Overruled, *mi hermana*. I like my men eccentric." She winked at me. My mother snorted.

"This is good, Alex; you're doing good. Now, I have another question: Have you noticed anything unusual about him? Does he have scars on his chest? Does he recite poetry when he thinks no one is listening?"

"He says funny things sometimes."

"Yes?" Carmen leaned forward. "What funny things, *mijo*?"
"He says, 'In my world . . .' a lot."

"More. Tell tía more about that."

"He'll say something like, 'In my world people respect each other. It's okay to be different.' Stuff like that."

"Ooooh, I like that."

My mom sat down and put her hand on my tía's arm. "Carmen, listen to me. Doesn't that just fit the profile of a lunatic con man? Any drugged-out-60's-hippie-con-artist could have said the same thing. I bet he got that from Charles Manson."

Carmen didn't even look at my mom. "What else does he say, Alex dear?"

"Like a few days ago, we saw these *cholos* and he said something like this: 'In my world there are no gangs. People are valuable. Everyone has a place.' Things like that."

"Now Maria, that's not hippie bullshit. He sounds like a philosopher to me."

"He sounds like he thinks he's God. And that makes him not just a lunatic, but a dangerous lunatic." She stood up and walked back to the sink. "What do we know about this man? Nothing! Where is he from? Nowhere! Is he married? Does he have children? Who knows! He doesn't have a job, so how does he pay for the roof over his head? Tell me that."

I needed to get out of there—Gómez and Mr. Aguilar were waiting for me! "Mom, Mr. Aguilar wants to know if I can go with him to buy some plants. I'll be back in an hour."

My mom, preoccupied washing her coffee cup, said neither "yes" nor "no." I took it as a "yes."

I got up to go, but Carmen grabbed my hand and whispered, "Aguilar, huh? Didn't know you two were hanging out."

I smiled and ran out of the house.

*****

Gómez tortured the salesman at Anderson's with so many questions that even Mr. Aguilar left us to wander through the aisles. "How much distance should there be between each plant? Are there any particular soil requirements? What garden pests should we watch for?" On and on.

It turned out that it was too late for garlic, which must be planted in winter, but we were able to pick up the rest of our plants. Personally, when it comes to shopping I have my limits. Gómez though—if he was going to plant a salsa garden, then he was going to know all about it and do it right.

We arrived home around eleven and started right in—well, almost right in. First, Gómez went inside to find the right music for the occasion. He handed me an album. "You can't go wrong with Bach."

We would begin by planting serrano, jalapeño and yellow chilies along the back rows, away from the house. Mr. Sánchez came over as we began. "Yep, exactly where they should be; more sun means more fire."

I carved out a little hole in the ground and stuffed in a serrano seedling.

"Eeee! No! No! No!" yelled Mr. Sánchez. I nearly jumped out of my skin. "That's not how you do it! Here—" He grabbed my hand shovel. "You have to make a hole six inches wide, eight inches deep, like so. Then, you fill it with mulch. Where's the mulch?"

"*Dios mío!*" exclaimed Gómez, "we forgot the mulch! Mr. Sánchez, do you think they have it at Builder's Emporium? Alex and I could just walk there."

When we returned a couple of hours later, pushing a shopping cart filled with mulch, Mr. Sánchez was nowhere in sight, but the entire garden had been prepared: twelve neat little circular holes precisely spaced on each of the five rows, each hole no doubt six inches wide by eight inches deep.

"Mr. Sánchez," mused Gómez, "I knew he was a farmer at heart."

Mr. Sánchez came out of his house. "*Hola amigos*! I was just taking a break." As he approached, he bent his left hand down, palm flat, as if he was caressing a row of barley. The knees of his white cotton pants had large brown spots on them.

Gómez put a hand on Mr. Sánchez's shoulder. "I'm wondering—why keep *any* grass over here?" He gestured to the west part of his yard. "Our Garden is too small. Maybe we should tear up the *whole* yard. What do you think about this: there, on the west side of this pathway, five rows—the top row: jalapeños; the next row: serranos; the middle row: yellows; the next row: yellow onions; the last row: green onions. Mr. Sánchez, what do you think so far?"

"Go on."

Gómez took a stick and drew a crude outline of his property. "We'll have a row of tomatillos—two rows! Three rows!" He gestured emphatically with his right hand. "And two rows of cilantro!"

Mr. Sánchez nodded thoughtfully. "I agree."

"Alex?"

"I agree."

"Well," said Gómez, reaching for his shovel, "we've got some daylight left. Let's break out 'Bolero' and start digging."

We didn't go crazy on "Bolero" this time, but like the week before, my body moved in unison to the rhythm, and glancing at Mr. Sánchez, I saw his movements were following the same cadence. Gómez winked. Doom dada doom . . . .

By the end of the third playing of "Bolero" we'd finished tearing up the lawn. Mr. Sánchez's baggy pants would never look white again.

"Mr. Sánchez," I said, "your pants are ruined."

"Not ruined," he replied, looking down at his legs, "broken in."

We were resting on our tools, enjoying our achievement, when I saw my mom and Rosa looking up at us from our yard. Not good. For all we knew my mom had been standing there for an hour, which is what she wanted us to think.

"Alex." Flat even tone means I'm in trouble. Rosa put her hands on her hips, like my mom. "Alex," she said, echoing my mom's voice exactly.

"Mom," I replied in kind.

"What's going on here?"

"We're making the garden I told you about."

"Uh-*huh*."

"Mrs. Morales," Gómez said, bowing his head slightly.

My mom looked at him briefly, then without moving her head, she shifted her eyes. "Mr. Sánchez, are you part of this?"

"Si señora."

"I see. Alex, dinner will be ready at six. Please see that you are clean." She grabbed Rosa's hand and headed inside our house. Rosa turned her head, her eyes never leaving us as my mom dragged her along.

Gómez exhaled. "Whew. I can start breathing again."

Mr. Sánchez chuckled nervously. My mom could have that affect on people.

"Well," said Gómez, "we made some progress today, eh amigos?"

We all nodded.

"I suppose we should clean up," continued Gómez. Then suddenly his eyes got wide. "I nearly forgot! The Dodgers are on TV tonight!"

Baseball

I washed up and had dinner, and then at 6:30 asked if I could go to Gómez's to watch the baseball game. "I don't think so, dear. Not tonight."

Then I did something that just a week before would've never entered my mind. I asked, "Why not?" It just popped out. My mom was shocked.

"Don't sass me," she rasped.

I had crossed the line, but at that moment it seemed harder to cross back over than to just keep going. "I'm not sassing you mom. But tell me why not."

She glanced over to my father's chair, and I followed her eyes. My father had always been the "no parent." The ultimate "no parent" pronounces their verdict without explanation and will tolerate no questioning of authority once judgment has been delivered. My father was a "no parent" without equal.

Once, when Eddie was ten or eleven, he asked my mom if he could go out after dinner and play with some of his friends. She wanted to say "no," but she didn't have a valid reason, so she deferred to my father, who was seated in his recliner reading the evening paper. Eddie approached him and said, “Papá?” My father lowered his paper and, without warning, slapped him in the face. Eddie stumbled backwards, but kept his feet. I looked at my mom; she was shocked, but she didn’t say anything. Eddie stood there in the middle of the room, the left side of his face inflamed, tears in his eyes. Then the unthinkable occurred—my father re-crossed his legs, fluffed out his paper, folded it over, and continued reading as if nothing had happened.

Now that my father was gone, my mom was the “no parent,” and I could feel her reluctance to wear the hat that my father had worn like a South American dictator. With both of us still looking at my father’s chair, I pressed on.

Mom, it’s the Dodgers.

I don’t think it’s a good idea, Alex.

It’s okay. I’ll be home early.

I don’t want you out.

Mom, I’ll be right next door. It’s closer than Tía Carmen’s.

That’s not the point.

What is the point, Mom?

My mom pulled her eyes from the chair and gave me a stern look.

The point is that tomorrow’s a school day and I want you in the house.

Mom, his house is twenty feet away from my window. If I wanted to go to Tía’s you wouldn’t mind.

That’s different; she’s family. He’s a stranger, and he’s strange. I don’t trust him and I don’t like the idea of you spending so much time with him.

Tía Carmen likes him.
Your tía is crazy.

My tía is crazy but I can go to her house. Gómez is strange but I can't go to his house.

Don't get smart with me, young man.

Here we were again. Both of us recognized my father in her words. It was like he was there, his evening paper folded across his knee, about to declare judgment. She pulled on a piece of her apron and balled it up in her hand as her eyes moved nervously from me to the chair and back again. The first to speak would lose.

Your Gómez is a grown man. He probably has things to do and would prefer to be alone.

Mom, he asked me if I'd like to come over. He said watching baseball is more fun with friends. He even asked if you would like to come over. All right, I embellished the truth a little bit.

Did he now? Mmm-hmm. Well, no thank you. I haven't time to watch grown men run around like boys. You win, Alex, you can go watch the baseball game. But I want you home by nine, and I'm walking you up there and telling this Mr. Gómez myself.

The front door was wide open, the screen door closed. I knocked, but the TV was on and he probably couldn't hear me. My mom folded her arms.

"Gómez!" I yelled.

"*Hola*!" he hollered from his kitchen. A moment later he appeared in the living room wearing a red apron.

"Mrs. Morales, it is nice to see you again." He pushed the screen door open. "Please, won't you come in?"

"My son would like to join you for the Dodger game."

"Why of course, Mrs. Morales. Alex is always welcome."

"I want him home by nine."

"Certainly, Mrs. Morales."

"Now Alex, that means I don't want you coming in at nine-fifteen and telling me you didn't notice the time, or you just couldn't pull yourself away, or any other excuse. Do you understand?"

"Yes mom."

"And I will guarantee he is home by nine, Mrs. Morales," added Gómez.

I sat down at the kitchen table, one of those Formica ones with a pink top, and Gómez went back into the kitchen, opened the refrigerator, and said, "Because we Mexicans appreciate baseball *and* good food—guacamole!" With a flourish there appeared on the table a bowl of fresh dip and tortilla chips.

The TV, an old black-and-white portable, took up the end of the table. "Who's playing?" I asked.

"The Dodgers and the Atlanta Braves."

"Who do you like?"

He furrowed his eyebrows. "The Dodgers, of course." Absurd question.

"Why?"

He popped open a root beer and poured it into a tilted glass. As he watched the foam rising to the rim he said, "Well, I'll tell you." When the foam settled down, he filled up the rest of the glass and handed it to me, then did the same for himself.

"This story begins when I was about your age." He turned down the TV volume. "Back then the Dodgers were perennial losers. Well, not losers really, but they were always overshadowed by the Yankees, and fact was, they hadn't won a pennant in twenty-one years. But in 1941 the Dodgers won the pennant! And their opponent in the World Series? The mighty Yankees, who had won the American League by seventeen games! This was the first 'subway series' between the two New York teams.

"It was game two, and I was sitting in a bar where my father was playing pool. At another table were two men listening to the radio. I could barely hear it, and I wasn't familiar with baseball, but I couldn't take my eyes off those two men who lived and died with every pitch. These were *real* Dodger fans. They argued with the umpire, they pounded their fists on the table and flailed their arms, they swore and yelled and danced a jig, and in the course of two hours they exhibited every human emotion known to man, and maybe a couple of new ones, too. I'd never seen anyone so wrapped up in something like these men were.

"In the second inning my father sent me out to the car to get some cigarettes, and while I was gone the Yankees scored a run. In the bottom of the third it happened again: I went to the restroom and the Yankees scored another run. When I sat down, I noticed both men were looking at me. During a radio commercial, one of the men leaned over and whispered something to his friend, then stood up and approached my table.

"'Son, would you like a Coke, or maybe a Dr. Pepper?'

"'No sir.'

"'Peanuts?'

"'No sir.'

"'Are you hungry? Can I get you a sandwich?'

"'No sir.'

"Then he pulled up a chair next to me. 'Son, permit me to speak plainly.' I looked at my father, but he was concentrating on the pool game. 'Me and my friend, we're Dodger fans, and we noticed that when you leave your chair the Yankees score.' He reached into his pocket and pulled out a quarter. He set it on the table and said, 'Would you mind staying in your seat until the game is over?'

"And I did. After a while I was afraid to even change position! Lord, my butt was sore! In the sixth the Dodgers took the lead and never gave it back. When the game ended, those men hugged each other like long-lost brothers.

"The man who spoke to me before approached my table again, and looking down at me said, 'Son, there are days in a man's life he will never forget: the day your first child is born; the night Louis beat Schmeling; and today, when the Brooklyn Dodgers defeated the New York Yankees—at Yankee Stadium!' He put another quarter on the table and said, 'Thank you, son.' That's the day I became a Dodger fan, and over the years I became a baseball fan too!"

There we were in Gómez's kitchen, conjuring up the ghosts of Dodgers past, and not ten miles away were today's Dodgers, about to embark on one of the most magical seasons in baseball history. I leaned back in my chair and put my hands on my head. "Wow. I see why you like the Dodgers."

Gómez nodded vaguely, his blank eyes betraying that his mind was still in 1941.

As I waited for him to come back, my conscience made a sudden and unexpected appearance. I'd have to tell Gómez the truth.

"I've never played baseball."

Gómez lifted an eyebrow.

"And I don't understand it."

He nodded thoughtfully. "Yep, it was the same with me."

"Really?"

"Really. I never played baseball as a kid; not once. A little stickball, yes; but actual baseball, with teams and bases? The first time I played I was in my 20's. As far as understanding baseball, *fully understanding it*, well who does? It's not checkers, baseball; it's chess.

"The basics can be learned easily enough, probably in a few games. Strategy can be learned over weeks or months, but what makes baseball unique is that once you know everything about how to *play the game*, you arrive back where you began, with one man, separate but not alone."

I looked at the TV. The Braves were taking the field, but the camera was on a Mexican player in the bullpen. Apparently he was important; the camera stayed on him for a long time.

"Who's that?"

"That, Alex, is the country of Mexico wrapped in a Dodger uniform"—Gómez laughed—"like a burrito."

"What's his name?"

"Fernando."

"Oh, I think I've heard of him. Fernando Valenzuela?"

"Lord, even his name is perfect. It rolls off the tongue like poetry."

"Who's pitching for the Braves?"

"Tom Glavine."

"Is he good?"

"Too early to say; it's only his second year. Let's see what he does tonight against the Dodgers." He turned the sound back on. The first Dodger batter was Steve Sax, the second baseman, and he singled to center field on the first pitch of the game.

"Watch out for Sax; he's always a threat to steal second." The Atlanta pitcher was thinking the same thing, throwing over to first base twice. Two balls to the batter, and then he threw over to first base again.

"Balk!" yelled Gómez, and the umpire agreed; Sax moved over to second base. "Way to go, Saxie! See Alex, just the threat of Sax stealing a base has unnerved the pitcher and caused a mistake."

Alfredo Griffin got a base hit to center field and Sax scored. Gómez raised his hand for a congratulatory slap and I happily complied. "Dodger baseball, amigo! When you have an opportunity—attack! If you have a chance for a run you go for it!"

Kirk Gibson was the next hitter. "This guy, he's a difference-maker. In all of baseball there's only a handful, maybe just one or two at any given time; he's one of them." After Gibson struck out, Gómez shrugged. "Baseball is life. Sometimes you give it your best, but your opponent, he's giving it his best, too."

Between innings Gómez talked baseball. "Jackie Robinson is of course remembered as the man who broke the color barrier, but what is forgotten about Jackie is that he changed the way the game is played. Not since Ty Cobb in 1915, 1916, had a player terrorized the bases like Jackie. Talk about living lightning! He was one player you hoped *didn't* hit a home run. A home run—you trot around the bases, it's over. But a base runner like Jackie on first base? He scared the hell out of the other team: Is he going? Is he not going? He's going! He's . . . safe! A scary sight—Jackie Robinson running the bases."

Valenzuela was ready to pitch. "Watch how he lifts his eyes when he pitches."

Sure enough, on his first pitch he paused halfway through his delivery, glanced to the sky and then continued with the pitch.

"Is he praying?" I asked.

"Heavens no! Athletes praying to God—that's the most pathetic sight in sports. I mean, if you're talking tribal gods, fine: it's me and my god against you and your god and may be the best god win. But if you believe in the One God, why would he favor you over your opponent? Have we advanced at all in the last 2,000 years? Are we just a bunch of cavemen driving Cadillacs? No Alex, he's not praying. He's *Fernando*—what's to pray for?"

"Then why does he do it?"

"No one knows. Let's watch; maybe we can figure it out."

Both of us were watching Fernando's eyes on every pitch. I said, "Maybe he's looking up to heaven to see if God's watching."

Gómez laughed. "That could be it!"

Between innings I asked Gómez if he was any good at baseball. "To tell you the truth, I've never actually played baseball. I played softball; and I was better than good."

"No you weren't," I teased.

"No, I was," countered Gómez. He was looking directly at me, and there was no kidding in those wolf-eyes. "I was a natural hitter, and I built on that. No one I played with could hit the ball as far as I could."

The next batter was John Shelby, who struck out looking. Gómez sighed. "This Atlanta pitcher, Glavine, he's got a head for the game. Shelby didn't get a single good pitch to hit."

Mike Davis stepped up to the plate. "Davis could be key this year." The first pitch was in the dirt, but Davis swung anyway. "By that I mean he could be a key reason *our whole season goes up in smoke!* C'mon Davis! Discipline, man!"

After the commercials the Dodgers were on the field and the camera zoomed in on Fernando. Gómez pointed a corn chip at him and said, "Some people compare Fernando to Babe Ruth."

"Babe Ruth—I've heard of him. He made a candy bar."

"Yep, and he was the greatest player to ever play the game. Like Fernando, he started as a pitcher, with the Boston Red Sox, and he was the best pitcher in the American League. The problem was he was also a great hitter, like Fernando. When the Red Sox sold him to the Yankees, the Yankees made him a right fielder so he could hit everyday. There are a lot of similarities between Fernando and The Babe. It's like Fernando is the Mexican reincarnation of Babe Ruth."

Fernando had begun pitching to the first batter, Dale Murphy. "But do you know how Fernando resembles The Babe the most?"

I thought about it for a few moments. "Were they both left-handed?"

"Yes. But that's not what I had in mind." Gómez scooped up a small mountain of guacamole and tossed it in his mouth. "They're both fat!" He pushed out his stomach. "Like me!"

"Well, I wasn't going to mention it, but he doesn't really look like a baseball player."

"Exactly! Take off the uniform and he's just a chubby Mexican, sitting on the porch eating tacos and drinking beer. But here he is, the best pitcher in all *America del Norte*. Bless that boy!"

Fernando got Murphy out, as well as the next two batters. "Say Alex, I haven't seen Eddie around lately."

"Me neither."

"Has he been staying out late?"

"Yeah, I guess so. I'm asleep before he gets home."

Gómez nodded his head slowly. "Eddie's at an important age. He's making choices now that will affect the rest of his life."

After seven innings the Dodgers held a four-run lead and were about to add to it, when Rosa came to fetch me home. I sensed someone at the door and when I looked, there she was, standing behind the screen, silent as a ghost.

"Rosa's here to get me. I guess I can't be trusted. Is it nine o'clock already?"

Gómez leaned back to see the clock. "No, it's only 8:50; she's early." Then he got out of his chair and walked towards the door. "Rosa, *mi corazón*! Come in, darling!"

Rosa swung the door open and bounded into the room. "Hello, Mr. Gómez."

"Rosa, it's just Gómez, but I'll tell you what: because you make me smile when you say 'Mr. Gómez,' you just go right ahead and keep calling me that."

Rosa answered with a casual "Okay" as she walked over to the kitchen table and sat down. She folded her hands together and turned her attention to the TV.

Gómez followed her to the table. "Rosa, do you like baseball?"

"Yes," answered Rosa, without taking her eyes off the TV.

"Do you like the Dodgers?"

"Yes."

Gómez looked at me and winked. "Do you like the Braves?"

"Yes."

"I see. You like the Dodgers and the Braves. Lucky you! They're both playing tonight!"

All of that meant nothing to Rosa, as indicated by her silence.

"Alex, I think Rosa is saying she likes TV and she doesn't care what's on it!"

"Well, we don't watch much TV in our house. Our father let us watch only a few things: baseball wasn't one of them."

"Mr. Gómez," interrupted Rosa, "I want a chip."

"Of course, dear. Would you like some guacamole with that?"

Rosa wrinkled her nose and shook her head.

The Dodgers had scored two runs and were threatening to score more, but Gómez said, "Alex, I think you better go home now. We don't want to break the rules on the first night, right?"

"No, I guess not. You think the Dodgers'll win?"

About an hour later I heard Handel's "Hallelujah" for the first time.

*****

The next morning I was once again awakened by 'Sunrise,' but this time it was playing low and I only became aware of it when I recognized it had no place in a dream about getting separated from one's parents at Disneyland.

When I arrived at Gómez's house, he and Mr. Sánchez were drinking coffee and discussing the project. "Well, let's get started," said Mr. Sánchez abruptly. I got the impression that Mr. Sánchez felt I didn't quite belong in adult company, and Gómez seemed to read my mind. He immediately turned to me and said, "Alex, we were just going over today's plans—we're picking up the plants! But we need a car so I'm going down to impose on Mr. Aguilar again."

I had a sudden idea. "I bet my tía could help us." Off I went before anyone could suggest otherwise. Knowing my tía as I did, she'd welcome this opportunity with wide-open arms.

Carmen leaned against her door frame, smiling like the hidden lioness when the fleeing gazelle turns in her direction. "Well, I'll think about it, *mijo*," she said. "I have plans too you know, and I just can't drop everything because someone needs a ride. Is it my fault they don't have a car? Am I responsible for everyone around here?"

I listened patiently, waiting for her to finish her rant and give her assent. I knew she wanted to pester Gómez with questions and pierce the veil of "the mystery man."

"Anderson's is about fifteen minutes from here. We already know what we want; we'll just run in and grab the plants—it'll be quick. We also need to drop by Builder's Emporium. But if you don't have time for that, it's okay; we can walk there."

"That depends on if I get bored," she smiled.

"We're ready to go when you are, tía!" I yelled as I ran off.

Thirty minutes later Carmen appeared on the walkway. She was stunning. She had on a floral skirt, a hot pink blouse tied at the midriff, and gold hoop earrings. Her thick brassy hair had been artfully arranged in the carefree "lion's mane" style.

I looked at Gómez. "Oh, my," he said in a low voice. Mr. Sánchez had a dreamy look on his face, and I bet nowhere in that dream was there a Mrs. Sánchez.

Carmen tilted her head to the right in a movement that said, "Boys, that's enough now." Then she raised her left hand and bent her index finger twice in the "come hither" command of her sex. It wasn't until Mr. Sánchez missed the first step on the stairs and plunged into Gómez that Tía Carmen's spell of enchantment was broken. She laughed, and as she turned toward her red '73 Camaro her skirt swirled to catch up to her hips. "This way, boys," she trilled.

When we reached the street, Carmen extended her left hand to Gómez, who deftly cradled it in his right palm and, bending slightly at the waist, said, "Words race to my tongue, señorita, pushing and shoving amongst themselves like schoolchildren; but I dismiss them all, for no words of mine could describe a lady so fair as you." And with that he placed his lips upon her hand, soft as a whisper.

My tía swooned, briefly, but quickly regained control, exaggerating her swoon and lifting her eyes as if overcome by Gómez's manners. "My, my, Señor Gómez," she said, "a gardener *and* a poet."

"Just a gardener," he replied. "May I open your door, señorita?"

My tía was speechless—for about five seconds.

What do you do, Señor Gómez?

Please, señorita, Gómez is name enough for me.

All right. Gómez, what do you do?

I'm retired, señorita.

Retired from what?

Retired from work, señorita.

Oh, retired from work. From woooork . . . of course! Where did you work, Gómez?

Many places, señorita.

Oh. Here in L.A.?

Here and there.

Uh-huh. Any place in particular? You know, where you stayed for awhile, put down roots, swayed in the breeze, watched the baby trees grow up?

Señorita, it is you who has the word-gift.

Ay, señor, if only you were as good with answers.
Señorita?

Nothing, Señor Gómez.

Gómez, señorita. Just Gómez.

And so it went, round and round, from our house to Anderson's, from Anderson's to Builder's Emporium, from Builder's back home. Mr. Sánchez and I sat in the back, ignored like chaperones on a teenage date.

Around one o'clock we returned, the trunk of the Camaro filled with baby plants and mulch. "Well boys, the pleasure was all yours. Hurry now. I'm late for the beauty parlor."

We all climbed out, but Gómez leaned back into the passenger side window. "Señorita, I suggest you cancel the appointment with your beautician, for she is not an honest person, and your money with her is wasted."

"Señor?"

"You already have what she cannot sell; what cannot be bought."

"Can you speakee English?"

Gómez dropped his eyes briefly to gather his thoughts. "Many women are pretty, señorita, but few are beautiful. One doesn't become beautiful at a salon—as if beauty could be made with paints and powders. One *is* beautiful. It comes from the inside and radiates out, illuminating the eyes, the hair, the skin. You are a beautiful woman, señorita. Efforts to improve upon such beauty would be as vain as efforts to obscure or diminish it."

My tía listened to Gómez, and then turned her gaze to the windshield, her eyes looking through the glass as if it wasn't there. She called me to her window and cupped my chin in her hand. "*Mijo*, you listen to Gómez. Here is a man who knows how to speak to a woman."

*****

For us it was up to The Garden and a day full of work. With Wolfgang Mozart directing us from the record player, faster than a speeding violin we laid the chilies along the first three rows of West Garden. When we were done we were oddly moved—Mr. Sánchez most of all. Gómez asked him if he wouldn't mind saying a "Benediction to the Chilies." It seems ridiculous now, laughable even, looking at the three of us talking to those baby chilies, but at that moment, softened up by Mozart and feeling a sense of camaraderie, well, a benediction seemed not only normal, but necessary.

"My little chilies, welcome to our Garden. Three of your race, the jalapeños, the serranos, and the yellows, are represented here today on this small plot of land in a country far from the land of your fathers. This is not Oaxaca, and only one of the mountain people is before you now, but this is a good land, with fine soil, and we are three humble but willing farmers who pledge to keep the ancient covenant between our races."

Gómez and I looked at each other with what-the-hell looks on our faces. Gómez's lips moved soundlessly as he searched his mind for an acknowledgment equal to the benediction. He gave up and simply said, "Shall we?"

We continued with the yellow and green onion. We had just stood up to inspect our work when Mrs. Sánchez appeared like a beneficent angel, carrying a tray of sandwiches, chips, and lemonade. Just moments before, food and drink were the furthest things from our minds. Now, nothing was more urgent than sitting down immediately and devouring that lunch.

Gómez, ever the man-of-manners, insisted on properly introducing himself. "Mrs. Sánchez," he said, vainly dusting the dirt from his overalls, "please excuse me for a minute." He dashed into the house to clean up, leaving Mrs. Sánchez holding the lunch tray as if she were in a video put on "Pause."

He reappeared about thirty seconds later, still wiping his hands on a dishtowel. Seeing Mrs. Sánchez alone on the walkway, the tray in her hands, he cast a reproachful look in my direction and hurried to her side. "Please, let me take that from you." He passed the tray to me. "Mrs. Sánchez, it is my great pleasure to meet you at last." He extended his hand, and Mrs. Sánchez played her part by placing her right hand gently in his.

"Mr. Gómez, I have heard so much about you from Humberto." She spoke in a measured tone, neither friendly nor unfriendly.

"Your husband has been a great aid to us, Mrs. Sánchez, and please, there is no 'Mister'; it's just 'Gómez.'" He let go of her hand and smiled.

"As you wish . . . Gómez." She raised her right hand and placed the first two fingers on her chin. "But is 'Gómez' your first or last name?"

Gómez tilted his head in a playful way. "First name, last name, middle name, it is all just 'Gómez,' señora."

"Very well. And for my part, 'Isabella' will do." Mrs. Sánchez answered with all the warmth of a mannequin.

Mr. Sánchez abruptly ended the introductions. "Isabella, thank you for lunch." He stepped around Gómez toward the sandwich tray.

Mrs. Sánchez slowly moved her head one-quarter turn to look at her husband and answered flatly, "You are welcome, Humberto. When you are done please bring home the dishes."

Mr. Sánchez grunted an acknowledgement, and with no further thought for her he grabbed a sandwich and drink. "Gómez, shall we sit on the porch?"

Gómez looked at Mrs. Sánchez as she stood stone-still, her eyes on her husband. "Isabella, would you care to join us for lunch? I could bring out a table."

Mrs. Sánchez didn't even look at Gómez. "No thank you, señor." Still looking at her husband, she added. "I'm not hungry."

Whatever was going on with Mr. and Mrs. Sánchez was beginning to dull my appetite, and Gómez's sunny disposition was starting to eclipse too. However, when Mrs. Sánchez turned and walked away there was nothing left to do but sit down on Gómez's porch and dig into those sandwiches.

"Ummm," said Gómez, "corn chips. I haven't had a corn chip for . . . well, it's been a long time. And imagine that, not just a corn chip, but a Wampum!" He put one in his mouth and crunched with unrestrained pleasure. "Man, that's a corn chip!"

After lunch, we were all too stuffed and too contented to get up and toil in The Garden. We hardly had the strength to hail Mr. Aguilar when he walked up the stairs. "I expected to see you boys working," he said with a smile, "not napping."

"Mr. Aguilar," answered Gómez, pushing his silver hair off his forehead, "if we were in a civilized country *everyone* would be napping now. We wouldn't be sitting on a hard concrete patio, feeling guilty for letting an hour of sunlight pass without lifting a shovel. No, we'd be stretched out in long hammocks in the cool shade, our hats pulled over our eyes." Gómez unwrapped his legs and stretched them to their full length. "As the cares of the world fall away I drift into a dream. It is evening in my little village; a young girl walks by my side . . . ."

"Hey Gómez!" Mr. Aguilar said, kicking the sole of Gómez's shoe, "that sounds like my dream!"

"Mine too," added Mr. Sánchez.

"My friends," sighed Gómez, "that is the dream of any man who has walked the promenade in his youth."

Mr. Sánchez stretched his legs out too. "My village was a very small village," he said softly, "two hundred families, more or less. In the center of the village was a pond. Long ago our ancestors dug out the pond and lined it in river rock. It wasn't big—about the size of two soccer fields. Around the pond was a path sheltered by trees. In the summertime, in the evening, the whole village was at the pond. Children would swim; old men sat in chairs, smoking and drinking and playing card games; mothers and grandmothers sat on benches near the small children, knitting or mending clothes. But the young men and the young women, they would walk the pond. I must have walked the pond a thousand times. Sometimes when I wake up in the morning, I just lie in bed and think about those days walking the pond."

"Holy Cow, Sánchez!" said Mr. Aguilar. "You've just said more words in the last thirty seconds than I've heard you say in three years."

"I'm only saying a small part of what I could say." Mr. Sánchez drew up one knee and plopped his arm on it. "There were many adventures walking the pond, many stolen kisses in the shadow of a tree; dreams dreamed, promises made—promises broken."

"Is that where you met Isabella, Mr. Sánchez?" asked Gómez.

"No, señor, I had known Isabella all my life. As I said, it was a very small village and everyone knew everyone. But that is where I gave her my promise."

"What did you promise, Sánchez, to bring her to East L.A. and live in a rented house?" Mr. Aguilar snickered softly, but no one joined him. I was offended by his sarcasm; Mr. Sánchez just ignored it.

"I promised her the same thing that every young man promises, on every promenade, in every village. I promised to place her above me." Mr. Sánchez stood up to resume planting The Garden. Gómez and I and followed him.

*****

Later that day we had a lemonade break, courtesy of Mrs. Cortez. Once more Gómez went through his man-of-manners routine, racing into the house to wash his hands before greeting Mrs. Cortez.

"Mrs. Cortez! Thank you for the lemonade! And how are you today?"

"Very well, Gómez, and you?"

"Quite well. As you can see, I took your advice."

"Yes, I can see that." She stood in front of each of us so we could remove a glass from the tray.

"What do you think?"

"It looks like a dirt garden. Not much to look at, but not too much trouble either, like my husband Frank."

Now it was Mr. Sánchez and I exchanging what-the-hell looks. Since the incident with her husband, none of us in our little villa had much to say to Mrs. Cortez. What do you say to a woman whose husband killed himself?

I asked Gómez, "How long have you two known each other?" I took a swig of the lemonade—aaaghh! No sugar; just water with sour lemon juice!

"Well, Mrs. Cortez, how far back do we go?"

"It's hard to remember, really. Last Tuesday, I think."

"Yes," nodded Gómez, "I believe it was Tuesday." He took a long drink. "Alex, Mrs. Cortez was kind enough to lend me a stick of butter. Although Mrs. Cortez, I have to confess, when I was done with it the butter was in no shape to be returned; all stuck to the bottom of my frying pan."

"Well then, I don't know how you're going to repay me, because all I wanted was my stick of butter back. Not some other stick—the *same* stick. That's only fair." She smiled crookedly.

"I see your point, Mrs. Cortez."

"How could you miss it? And Mr. Johnson won't miss the point when he sees what you did to his lawn." She placed the tray on the sidewalk and abruptly returned down the stairs to her house.

Mr. Sánchez tossed the contents of his glass onto the dirt. "Loco," he said.

Gómez smiled. "She's a character, all right."

I was perplexed. "Gómez, what did you mean when you said you 'took her advice'?"

"Mrs. Cortez is the one who said we should rip up the whole yard."

"You're kidding."

"'Halfway is half-done,' she said."

An hour or so later, Mr. Sánchez tossed his shovel aside. "And all done is all done." As evening descended on the wings of Albinoni's "Adagio for Strings in G Minor," the three of us stood on Gómez's walkway surveying our accomplishment. We had done it. The Garden was planted.

*****

When I entered my house I heard my mom and Tía Carmen talking in the kitchen.

Manita, I nearly fainted!

Carmen, I've seen you 'nearly faint' in the presence of a man more times than I can count.

Escucha mi hermana, I really did almost faint.

Because this Gómez praised your beauty and devoured you with his eyes? Boys have been devouring you with their eyes since you were fourteen.

Twelve, manita; since I was twelve. But that's the point, he wasn't devouring me—it was just the opposite. It was more like he wanted to memorize every detail. And Maria Lena, have you ever heard words like that?

Those words were just a line. Come on, Carmen, he's probably said the exact same words to a dozen women. Two dozen! Three dozen! Maybe those lines are a family heirloom, passed down from father to son for generations, like a good hunting rifle.

What, you don't think I can recognize a line? I've heard a thousand lines, and I recognized every one for what it was: bullshit. Because it doesn't matter how you package bullshit; you can wrap it in pink velvet and tie it in a silk bow and call it grandma's fruitcake, but it's still bullshit. What Gómez said wasn't like that.

So, what are you saying? That this Gómez loves you.

I wouldn't say that, sister. Maybe, maybe not.

This gypsy has the gift, Carmen, and that's all the more reason not to trust him. So, what's next, are you going to invite him to your bedroom? Maybe you could arrange pink rose petals on the sidewalk in the shape of arrows.

Maria, I think maybe it's you who is obsessed with sex. Actually, I hadn't even thought of it. Well, that's not exactly true; of course I thought of it. But it seemed like a step down, if you can believe that.

Salsa Verde

The weeks leading up to the Midsummer's Eve party passed as fast as a Fernando fastball. During the weekdays, Gómez and Mr. Sánchez fussed over the plants from dawn to dusk, and as soon as I came home from school I joined them. On the weekends all three of us tended The Garden from sunrise to sunset.

Over time, Gómez developed a standard music program for the plants. The mornings always began with "Sunrise," although at a lower volume. I could still hear it, but Eddie slept right through it. Ravel's "Bolero" was often next, to reinforce the blueprint laid down at The Garden's conception. The rest of the day featured Bach, Beethoven, Mozart and Tchaikovsky, while evenings included Debussy, Satie, Vivaldi, Gershwin, and always and without fail, Pachelbel's "Canon in D," which is my favorite classical piece and will be forever associated with summer evenings spent with dear friends. And many evenings included a Dodger game, followed, if we were fortunate, by Handel's "Hallelujah."

Although Gómez, Sánchez and I were regulars in The Garden, most of the residents of our villa were frequent visitors. Mrs. Sánchez, who had been working part-time at the public library since Mr. Sánchez was laid off, always made a brief appearance on the weekends to bring us sandwiches, tuna fish usually, sometimes chicken or egg salad, but always Wampum corn chips. Gómez's lavish praise of Mrs. Sánchez's lunches never diminished, and it appeared to me that Mrs. Sánchez was thawing—at least a little. Sometimes she would actually smile at Gómez's accolades, although in a grudging, Mona Lisa sort of way, and conversations between Mr. and Mrs. Sánchez seemed to have taken on a civil, almost pleasant tone.

Mrs. Cortez also continued to bring us afternoon drinks—something none of us looked forward to. Many times she served her infamous unsweetened lemonade; sometimes she served up tap water—not iced or chilled, just tap water. One day she served vodka and water. The look on Gómez's face when he swallowed the drink still makes me smile.

"Mrs. Cortez, you really outdid yourself today! This water's got some bite!"

"What's that?" answered Mrs. Cortez, absently.

"The water, it's got some kick. *Muy caliente.*"

Mrs. Cortez tilted her head to favor her good ear. "Gómez, are you speaking English?"

"I'm trying to."

"Well, try speaking a little clearer. My husband Frank had the same problem. But in his case it was because he drank too much."

"I'll try harder," answered Gómez, suppressing a smile.

"Good man." Mrs. Cortez turned and walked away in that uniquely abrupt manner of hers.

Mr. Aguilar was a weekend visitor too. He never worked in The Garden, but he did shuttle us to the hardware store or nursery many times. It was odd how Mr. Aguilar didn't entirely fit in. I believe he wanted to be a part of our little group, and there was certainly no effort to discourage him. It was like something held him back.

Of course my Tía Carmen was a frequent visitor and boy, did Gómez and Mr. Sánchez light up when she arrived. Well, Gómez lit up. Mr. Sánchez's response was more of a subdued glow, like a table lamp covered in a dark cloth. When my tía entered The Garden, Mr. Sánchez would immediately busy himself in some activity, the most minor things suddenly requiring his full attention. And I think Carmen delighted in his agony. Maybe she just needed to keep her claws sharp, and Mr. Sánchez was her whetstone.

"Humberto," she said in a husky voice one evening, "would you come here, please?"

Mr. Sánchez was busy inspecting one of the drip lines. His attention didn't waver.

"Humberto," she repeated, "are you ignoring me?"

His body stiffened a bit, but his attention remained fixed. Carmen walked right down the furrow and stood in front of him; he would've had to be blind not to see the yellow and green slippers directly beneath his eyes.

"Humberto, I think I have something in my eye. Can you look for me?"

"Si, señorita," choked Mr. Sánchez. He stood up, his head only slightly above Carmen's bountiful breasts, and looked into Carmen's right eye.

"Do you see anything, Humberto?" cooed Carmen.

"No señorita."

"Closer dear, I'm sure there's something in there."

Mr. Sánchez craned his neck closer. The poor man; a tiny stream of sweat was running down his reddened cheek. "I'm sorry, but I don't see anything in there."

"Oh all right; I think it fell in here anyway." She daintily pulled on the elastic neckline and peeked into the crevice between her breasts. Mr. Sánchez obediently followed her gaze. Suddenly the neckline snapped back into place.

"Mr. Sánchez! You weren't looking down my . . . . Shame on you, señor!"

Poor Mr. Sánchez. He dropped to his knees like a sack of potatoes, his eyes fixed on that wholly fascinating drip-line. Given a choice, he probably would've never moved again.

Carmen looked over to Gómez, who shook his head in mock rebuke. My tía smiled and made a small curtsey. Gómez acknowledged her with a bow of his head, then followed her with his eyes as she gracefully lifted her hem and stepped onto the walkway. As she drew near he whispered, "Don't be concerned; I'll carry him back to his wife later."

"Let him walk," answered my tía as she passed him. "It would do him good to get some blood flowing in his limbs, eh señor?"

Another frequent guest was my sister, Rosa. Gómez absolutely adored her, and when she came over he dropped everything. Rosa had an unpretentious candor that Gómez admired. Gómez might say, "Rosa! You look lovely today," and she would reply, "I know." She was Cleopatra in a five-year-old body.

Eddie also visited The Garden, but infrequently, and his candor was of a different type. One evening he came up to Gómez's while we were sitting on the patio.

"So," he said, as he entered the yard with one of his new *cholo* friends, "how's 'The Project to End World Hunger' coming along?" He laughed and the *cholo* smirked.

"In another few weeks," answered Gómez, "we will have enough for a hundred."

"Señor, that's a little short, no?"
"Well, it's just about right for a party, but not nearly enough to save the world."

"Don't feel bad, señor. Hey, 'from humble beginnings,' right?"

"Yes," answered Gómez. "Say Eddie, maybe you could help us expand our enterprise."

"Me, señor?" Eddie fumbled in his pockets, looking for a pack of cigarettes. Unable to find any, he tapped his friend on the chest, who handed him his pack. Eddie took one, tamped it on his wrist, and lit it. His eyes followed the trail of smoke as he exhaled.

"Me, señor? I don't know. My responsibilities are so vast. Sure, life in your little world is simple and good, but outside of this paradise . . . ." He pretended to look thoughtfully into the distance as he took another long drag on his Camel. "It's a wicked world, señor."

"You're right, Eddie. I've seen some of that wickedness."

"Then you comprende, señor. There are bad men out there: drug dealers, señor, and killers and rapists and hombres *muy* bad." Eddie pointed at Gómez with his cigarette. "Just the other day there was a robbery at the liquor store. In our own hood two *banditos* wearing ski masks took fifty-seven dollars."

"And a six pack of Corona," added the *cholo.*

"Eddie, maybe the good citizens of our town should seek some protection."

"Si señor, maybe they should. There are so many bad men, and the police are so few. Hey! I got it!" Eddie slapped his buddy on the back. "We could call in the Texas Rangers. Hell, *we'll* be the Texas Rangers! We could wear badges on our chest, and the bad men, when they saw us, they'd run for the hills!"

Mr. Sánchez, who had been quiet during the dialogue, said softly, "In my village we had a way of handling that problem."

"Eh, Sánchez?" mocked Eddie. "How'd you do that?"

"Once the offender had been identified, and confessed, he would be sentenced to *tiempo cómo muerto*—'time as a dead person.' For a week, or a month, or even longer he was treated as if he wasn't there. Of course he couldn't work, so he would have to scavenge for scraps of food. Those who spent even just a little time as dead men were men changed. Some actually became important people in the village."

Gómez was impressed. "Mr. Sánchez, I've never heard of this before."

"And you'll never hear it again," added Eddie. "Alex told me about your Mexican mountain-people jungle bullshit, Sánchez. This ain't Mexico. America is a different kind of jungle."

Gómez ignored Eddie's comments and continued to question Mr. Sánchez. "At any given time how many people were 'dead'?"

"Usually there was no one. It was a very serious thing, Gómez, and as painful to the living as to the 'dead.' I can only remember maybe six of them, and that's over eighteen years."

Eddie was unimpressed. "I gotta piss." He swung open the screen door; his buddy followed him in.

Gómez whistled. "Incredible. Over eighteen years there were only half-a-dozen crimes?"

"Well, there may have been more crimes, but no more than five or six convictions. Like I said, it was a very serious thing."

"Mr. Sánchez," I asked, "what happened to those who were dead for a *long* time?"

"In my life, there was only one. His sentence was for six months. It started in the spring to avoid bad weather. But, there was a sudden snowstorm and he was found dead just a couple weeks later. It was very sad."

"What had he done?"

"He shot a neighbor's prize bull. In a small village like ours, a prize bull made you a wealthy man."

Gómez was thoughtfully rubbing his Hemingway. "Mr. Sánchez, what happened when a man's sentence was up?"

"He had a birthday party."

Gómez slapped his knee. "A birthday party!"

"Yes, and let me tell you, you've never seen such a birthday party. Imagine the celebration if a member of your family died and then one day suddenly came back to life."

"I see!"

"When I was sixteen, one of my cousins came back from the dead. The party was magnificent! So much food! And music and laughter and tears! He'd been dead for one month."

Eddie, walking through the door, drawled sarcastically, "What was his big crime?"

"One evening he was shepherding a neighbor's flock, when some boys from another village came out of the woods behind him. Eight boys, all about sixteen—my cousin was thirteen. One of the raiders fired a shotgun, and my cousin ran. Three sheep disappeared—stolen probably. The owner blamed my cousin for his losses. At the trial, my cousin offered no defense. He said he didn't know what came over him. He heard the blast and the next thing he knew he was running down the sheep path."

Mr. Sánchez stopped talking; even Eddie didn't interrupt the silence.

"He was acquitted of any wrongdoing. What was he supposed to do? Stand up to a bunch of thugs? But my cousin wouldn't accept leniency; he was supposed to protect the sheep and he hadn't. Although he'd broken no laws, all the men understood. His sentence was one month."

Gómez whistled. "I've never heard anything quite like that."

"What became of your cousin?" I asked Mr. Sánchez.

"A few years later he died. He was in the capital city one day, buying food in the marketplace. A car backfired, startling a woman on a balcony above him. She bumped into a potted plant; it fell and hit Pedro on the head. He never even knew what happened."

Eddie exploded in laughter. "Holy shit!" He laughed and slapped his hands together. "Dead—just like that! Hey Sánchez, maybe you should go to Sunday school and teach the kids. 'And kids, don't forget: God rewards you if you do good.'" Eddie laughed again. "Carlos, I think we've had our lesson for today." He slapped the *cholo* on the back and added, "Let's go rob a liquor store."

We didn't say goodbye; none of us felt like talking. It was quite a story, despite the ending. Finally, Gómez broke the silence. "Alex, I haven't seen your mom lately."

The truth was, he hadn't seen my mom for three weeks; not since she'd come over for that first Dodger game and laid down the law. My mom was the one person in the villa who *didn't* visit The Garden. To her, Gómez was a lunatic, and lunacy wasn't encouraged. Still, I didn't want Gómez to know what she thought of him.

"Well, she's been busy."

"I'm sure. It isn't easy being a single mother. But, it would be good for her to take some time off. To be fun, life requires some exclamation points every once in a while."

"You mean like a vacation? Just the other day my tía said she was thinking of going to Hawaii, and my mom said she'd probably never take a vacation for the rest of her life; or until her children are grown and she's too old to care."

"Well," answered Gómez, "a vacation would be nice—who wouldn't want to go to Hawaii?—but there are lots of ways to get exclamation points without even leaving the city. The Dodgers, for instance; in the summertime almost every day ends with an exclamation—unless we lose, in which case we look forward to tomorrow!" Gómez laughed. "That's baseball: there's always tomorrow."

Coincidentally, that night my mom went with me to Gómez's house. I had gradually started coming home later and later: one night 9:05, the next night 9:15 when Hershiser was in a tight jam in the seventh inning and I couldn't pull myself away. My mom's prediction was coming true, but in a mood of clemency she chose to confront Gómez and me rather than simply revoke my baseball privileges altogether.

She rapped on the door. Gómez hollered from the kitchen, "Alex, come on in!" When I reached for the screen door my mom put her hand on my shoulder. A few seconds later Gómez came around the corner. "Alex . . . ?" Then he saw my mom at the door, her battle mask on.

"Mrs. Morales!" He wiped his hands hastily on his apron and opened the screen door. "It is a pleasure to see you again!"

"Mr. Gómez, do you recall Alex is to be home by 9:00?"

"Yes," answered Gómez. No doubt he intuitively understood, as most men do, that the best way to navigate the wrath of a woman is to give short, agreeable answers.

"And this was a condition to him watching the games with you?"

"Yes señora."

"And did you agree to this?" My mom was going to stretch this one out.

"Yes."

"Well then, Mr. Gómez, how do you explain Alex's coming home after 9:00?"

"Hershiser, ma'am."
My mom laughed despite herself. "What?"

"Hershiser, ma'am."

"I heard what you said," she said, incredulously. "I just didn't understand what you meant. What's a 'Hershiser'?"

"Hershiser is a pitcher on the Dodgers, mom."

"Mrs. Morales, please, come inside so I can explain." He put his hand on her elbow and gently eased her forward. In her confusion my mom didn't have the resolve to stop him.

Gómez pulled out a kitchen chair and seated her. "Mrs. Morales," he said, sitting next to her, "here is what happened. Alex and I were watching the Dodgers play the Cubs—Chicago Cubs. Orel Hershiser was pitching for the Dodgers. Through six innings he was nearly unhittable, but in the seventh inning he ran into some trouble: a bloop single to right, a ground ball to third that squirted off Guerrero's mitt; in other words, flukes, accidents—but suddenly we're in trouble. Nobody's out, we are only winning by one run, and the heart of the Cubs order is coming to the plate."

Gómez looked intently into my mom's eyes, searching for any indication that she understood. Her face was stone.

"I confess," continued Gómez, "that it did occur to me it was getting close to nine o'clock. I knew Alex should go home. He couldn't see the clock from his seat, but I could, and I should've told him." Gómez concluded his summation with outstretched arms. "I just couldn't bring myself to abandon Hershiser. Our Dodgers needed us."

My mom shifted her eyes from Gómez to me and back to Gómez. "You felt if Alex left your kitchen table and came home it could affect the outcome of a baseball game at Dodger Stadium."

Neither Gómez nor I responded. She looked at me, but I couldn't meet her eyes. She looked at Gómez, and he couldn't meet her eyes either. He stroked his Hemingway.

"Mr. Gómez?"

Gómez opened his mouth to speak, but nothing came out.

"Mr. Gómez?" my mom repeated. "Do I have it right, or have I misunderstood you?"

This was not going well. The seconds ticked by. Finally, Gómez lifted his eyes. "No, Mrs. Morales, I don't think you misunderstood."

"And did I understand correctly when, just a few weeks ago, over there, at your front door, you promised me Alex would be home at nine o'clock without fail?"

"Yes, Mrs. Morales."

"Well, what am I to do?" She released her eyes from Gómez and fixed them on me. "Alex?"

I shrugged my shoulders.

"Well, neither of you seems to have much to say about this. I guess it'll be up to me to decide." She stood up to leave. "In the meantime, I trust you will be home tonight by nine?"

Was I going to come out of this alive? "Yes mom!" She was walking toward the door when Gómez found his tongue.

"Mrs. Morales?"

My mom stopped. "Yes, Mr. Gómez?"

"Hershiser. He got out of that jam in the seventh inning."

A puzzled look and a tilted head encouraged Gómez to continue. "After that he struck out the next three batters—in a row."

"I see. That's a good thing, right?"

"Yes, a very good thing."

"Well, goodnight, Mr. Gómez." She continued toward the door.

"It is just 'Gómez,' señora. My name—it is just 'Gómez.'"

She turned again. Her brown eyes softened. "Goodnight, Gómez." There was a hint of a smile; then she was gone.

Gómez came back to the table grinning. He swung a pretend bat and said, "Gómez hits a line drive to the gap!" Pumping his arms furiously he strutted around the table. "It's rolling to the wall! Gómez rounds first and heads to second, he slides—he's safe! A double for Gómez!"

"A double? She could've cancelled the whole season! That's a home run!"

"A home run?" Gómez's eyes twinkled. "Let's not get carried away! Besides, the official scorekeeper says it was a double."

"Who's the official scorekeeper, you?"

"Si. It's my house. You can be the scorekeeper in your house."

I turned on the TV. The Dodger pitcher, Tim Belcher, was finishing his warm-ups on the mound. Gómez lifted up a grocery bag from the floor and put it on the table. "In 'Take Me Out to the Ballgame' the verse goes, 'Buy me some peanuts and Cracker Jack . . . .' All these years I never really thought about it, but the other day it dawned on me: what the hell is a 'Cracker Jack'?" He handed me a box of Cracker Jack.

They were good! Popcorn and peanuts with a caramel coating. Gómez threw one up in the air and caught it with his mouth. "Fun food!"

Meanwhile, the Dodgers were off to a rough start. The first Pirate hitter, Barry Bonds, hit a single. The next hitter singled him to third, and the third hitter, Andy Van Slyke, hit a three-run homer. Just like that, we were down three runs. Then the next hitter, Bobby Bonilla, singled to right. Things might have gone from bad to worse if the next man, Sid Bream, hadn't hit into a double play.

Gómez caught another Cracker Jack. "When Sid played for us he did the same thing. Nice to know some things never change."

When the Dodgers came up, Gómez proclaimed, "Alex, I think we're going to have to do something extra tonight. Our announcers, Vin and Ross, they're good reporters, they know the game—hell, no one knows the game like Vin Scully—but they don't *act* like Dodger fans. It's up to you and me to bring the boys back."

"Whattaya have in mind?"

Gómez leaned over and turned off the volume. "Listen; you'll know what to do."

Gómez became Vin Scully, I was Ross Porter, and what followed went something like this:

Vin: *Well, Ross, we're looking at the wrong end of the horse tonight, aren't we?*

Ross: *Yep, we sure are, Vin.*

Vin: *Let's see what Sax can do to change the view a little bit. He spits into his hands, squeezes the bat, and steps up to the plate. Okay, Saxie, the comeback starts with you—ball one. Has Sax hit against Dunne before?*

Ross: *Uhh . . . .*

Vin: *Line drive to left! A single for Sax! Here come the Dodgers!*

Ross: *Wow, Sax gave that ball a whuppin'.*

Vin: *He gave it a spankin', that's for sure. My dear old dad couldn't even spank that hard—here comes the Dodger center fielder, Mike Davis, to the plate.*

Ross: *Your dad, did he use his hand or a belt?*

Vin: *Neither. He used a switch. For those young viewers who don't know what a switch is, it's a thin tree branch, about three feet long, with a lot of whip in it—Davis is ready. Ball one, outside.*

Ross: *There's Dunne's curveball. If he can't break it off more than that he's in for a long night. A switch, huh? Must've hurt.*

Vin: *Like a son of a gun—Strike one, slider on the outside corner. But the worst part was the waiting—Dunne's shaking off the sign from the catcher. I think he wants to come back with that slider again, Ross. Here's the pitch and Davis hits a blooper down the left field line. It falls in for a hit! Sax is going for third! The throw . . . he's safe! Davis goes to second! The throw . . . safe at second! Go Dodgers!*

Ross: *Well Vin, lucky is better than good; that was one ugly swing. He looked like he was trying to hit a piñata. Speaking of hitting, you said the worst part was the waiting.*

Vin: *Nothing worse, Ross. My dad would go to his room to get that switch and he wouldn't come back for five minutes. He had a secret place for it and it took him that long to dig it out—here comes Gibson. He's got that look in his eye, Ross, like he's going to do something special.*

Ross: *They're going to walk him, Vin.*

Vin: *Put the tying run on first? Doesn't make any sense; it's only the first inning. But that's fine with me. The more Dodgers on base, the more runs we get. You're right, Ross. He's putting Kirk on. Ball one. Gibson is seething! Look at that scowl. Well, I wouldn't want to face Gibson either. Here comes ball two.*

Ross: *Y'know, the intentional walk is the one thing that baseball could do without. At the very least they could just put the runner on without making us wait through four balls.*

Vin: *Change the game at your peril. Next thing you know, players won't trot around the bases after a home run. They'll say, 'Why bother? What am I going to do, forget to touch first base? Take a wrong turn at third?'*

Ross: *Good point, Vinnie. And besides, if the game was sped up too much maybe they'd only need one announcer, not two. Wonder which one of us would go—there's ball four. Gibson trots to first.*

Vin: *And here comes the Pirate skipper.*

Ross: *He's bringing the switch, Vin.*

Vin: *I feel for the kid, Ross. One time, when my parents weren't home, I went to their room to find out where my dad hid that switch. Under their bed was a foot locker. You'll never guess what I found in it.*

Ross: *The switch?*

Vin: *Good guess, Ross. Along with the biggest bullwhip you've ever seen.*

Ross: *Gee, Vinnie, all that time you were getting off easy.*

Vin: *I came to the same conclusion.*

And so it went. Watching baseball is fun, but *announcing* a ballgame? It's like being in the game. And what a game! We scored five in the fourth, one in the fifth on Marshall's second home run, and four more in the sixth. By the time nine o'clock rolled around we were leading fourteen to five, and it was only the beginning of the seventh inning! Gómez was convinced that our taking over for Vin and Ross was the reason for the Dodger comeback and, following the logic of those two old men in the bar so many years before, he insisted that we continue announcing each televised game until they lost. You never mess with a winning streak—even a one-game winning streak.

I was home by nine and in bed by 9:05, but I couldn't sleep. Finally I heard what I was waiting for: Handel's "Hallelujah." It was sweet dreams that night.

Over the next few weeks I was usually home by nine, but occasionally I didn't make it. However, for some reason my mom's attitude on the subject had softened. Instead of giving me 'the look,' or revoking my Dodger privileges, she would simply say, "Close game?" Usually the answer was "yes," but sometimes I couldn't leave because we were putting a whuppin' on someone and I didn't want to miss it. Either way, my mom seemed to be okay with it.

Her tolerant attitude reached a new level when one day she said, "Alex, who are the Expos?" I told her what I knew: they were a team from Montreal.

"My store manager gave me some tickets. Would you like to go the game?"

I was almost too stunned to answer.

"Carmen's never been to a game, and since he gave me four tickets I thought I'd invite her too."

"Who else are you inviting?"

"I don't know. I don't think Eddie would want to go. Rosa would get bored. I don't know."

"Gómez!" I yelled. "He'd love to go! He's never been to a Dodger game! In his whole life he's never been to a game."

"You can ask him if you want."

I ran up to Gómez's. He and Mr. Sánchez were in West Garden, Mr. Sánchez on his knees inspecting a plant. Gómez put a finger to his lips. "He found a small caterpillar," he whispered gravely. "We're checking to see if there are more."

I waited. Mr. Sánchez looked up at Gómez and said, "Clean."

"Well," responded Gómez, "I guess we better look over all the chilies."

"The chilies and the tomatoes, everything," Mr. Sánchez added.

"Okay. Alex, would you mind looking over the onions? And cilantro? I'll look over the tomatillos; Mr. Sánchez will look over the chilies."

"Okay, but what music is appropriate for caterpillar hunting?"

"Handel. If there are any bug demons, 'Messiah' will drive them out." I went inside and loaded up Handel.

Over the next hour, we searched every inch of every leaf. We found four caterpillars on the tomatoes, but that was all. Gómez and Mr. Sánchez seemed satisfied there wasn't an all-out invasion of The Garden. The sun was beginning to go down and we were sitting on Gómez's patio when I remembered my mom's invitation.

"Gómez, my mom has tickets to the Dodger game Saturday."

Gómez's eyes widened. "Alex, that's great! Your first Dodger game! Who are they playing?"

"The Expos."

"Good team; that should be a good game. Let's see, who will be pitching . . . ? Leary, I think."

"Carmen's going too."

"Oh no!" exclaimed Gómez. "Have you notified the LAPD?"

They both laughed. I waited for them to settle down. "We have an extra ticket."

Gómez's eyes widened. He looked like he was going to say something witty, but changed his mind. "Alex, it is a dream come true."

*****

On Thursday night we were watching Valenzuela pitch against the Expos when the screen door flew open and Carmen sailed into Gómez's kitchen. She was wearing a bright yellow blouse tucked into blue jeans. No one filled up a pair of jeans like my tía.

"Hello boys. So, this is what you do night after night? Sit in front of this little TV and watch men in tight pants run around." She pulled out a chair and straddled the seat. "Did you make the dip, Gómez?" She filled a corn chip with guacamole and tossed it in her mouth. "Hmmm, good."

Carmen ladled the next corn chip so high that large clumps of guacamole spilled back into the bowl. After swallowing it whole, she gave an exaggerated sigh and said, "Well, if I must go to a baseball game, I should know *something* about it. Let's start with the 'pitcher.' What's a 'pitcher'?"

Gómez rubbed his Hemingway. "The pitcher is the player who . . . well, better yet . . . ." The camera zoomed in and Gómez said, "There he is—the pride of Mexico, Pancho Villa in tights, Fernando Valenzuela!"

Fernando had just taken his last warm-up pitch, and while the ball was tossed around the infield he wiped his brow and pulled his cap over bushy hair.

"Oh, so that's the Fernando everyone's talking about. Doesn't look like much to me; must have a good personality."

Gómez knitted his eyebrows, as confused as I was by Carmen's comment. But, sometimes you just let things slide.

Carmen filled another corn chip with a small mountain of guacamole and said, "All right, this Fernando is a pitcher. But what does that mean?"

Gómez scooped up some guacamole and said, "The pitcher is the player who throws the ball to the hitter. Watch."

Fernando threw his first pitch. "Strike one!" said Gómez.

Carmen frowned. "Splain."

"A strike is a pitch that goes over the plate—in front of the batter is a small thing, made out of . . . well, I've no idea, shaped like a . . . well it's hard to describe . . . ."

"Stop," commanded Carmen. "Alex, you take over—and make it easy for me; I'm a virgin."

Gómez made a gesture with his right hand, as if he was passing the job over to me, and I said, "In front of the guy holding the bat, on the ground, is a little white flat box called 'the plate.'" I pushed aside the bowl of guacamole and drew an imaginary plate on the table with my finger. "It looks like that."

"Plates are round. That's not round."

I pressed on. "If the pitcher throws the ball over the plate it's a 'strike.' If the pitcher gets three strikes on the batter then the batter has to go sit down in the dugout."

"Okay."

The next pitch was a ball. "Ball one," said Gómez.

Carmen gave Gómez a baleful look. I interceded.

"A ball is a pitch that's not a strike; it didn't go over the plate. It went to the side, or it went over the plate, but too high or too low to be a strike."

"Oh," muttered Carmen, seemingly more interested in how much guacamole she could pile on a corn chip.

The Expo batter swung at the next pitch. "Strike," said Gómez, somewhat less enthusiastically than before.

"If the batter swings the bat and misses it, then it's also a strike," I quickly noted.

Carmen devoured the avocado and the corn chip it rode in on and then said, "*Mijo*, first you tell me it's a strike when he doesn't swing, then you tell me it's a strike when he does swing. I think the poor boy looks so dejected because he's as confused as I am. This is a gringo game, no Señor Gómez?"

"Si señorita."

"The gringos, they make everything so complicated."

*****

Around nine o'clock I walked into my house and heard Carmen and my mom in the kitchen, tittering over some joke.

"Alex dear, how'd the Dodgers do tonight?"

"We're losing. It's the bottom of the seventh inning."

"Oh, well. Maybe they'll be better Saturday night. Carmen says Gómez is going to be her baseball tutor at the game."

"Si," added Carmen. And then in an exaggerated, childlike voice she said, "He's going to teach me how to stroke the bat, and how to go to first base and second base and third base and—" but she was cut off by a reproachful look from my mom before they both broke into another round of girlish laughter. I just turned around and went to bed; and I must've fallen asleep quickly, which was just as well because there was no 'Hallelujah' that night.

Saturday finally came and at five o'clock I went up to Gómez's. "Hey, I brought you Eddie's glove. Maybe we'll catch a foul ball tonight."

"Thank you, son, but I have my own!" He pointed to an old, flat glove on the kitchen table. I walked over to it and picked it up. It was a catcher's mitt, the thumb attached by a shoelace, the leather cracked. I put it on.

"Alex, meet Roy."

"Pleased to meet you," I said. I pounded it with my fist. "You take Eddie's; I'll take yours. Let's go."

My tía wasn't ready, as usual, so we waited in her living room. My mom walked in the front door having just dropped off Rosa with the Sánchez's. "So, Gómez, Alex says you've never been to a Dodger game."

"That's true, señora."

"A little less formality would be fine; 'Maria,' please. Have you ever been to *any* baseball game?"

"No major league games."

"Pity; you love it so much."

Carmen entered, stopped in the middle of the room, and twirled like a fashion model. From head to toe she was a sight. Her shoes were blue with white laces. On her blue jeans were round, white, baseball-sized patches on each back pocket—including red stitches on the ball. Her white Dodger jersey she tied in a knot around her midriff, the neckline not buttoned up nearly as far as baseball regulations required. Her hair was braided in pigtails that she tied with blue and white ribbons, and on top of her head sat a blue Dodger cap. Wow. My Tía Carmen could make an entrance.

"My, my," said Gómez in rapt wonderment. "Carmen, you're an original."

"Thank you," she curtseyed.

My mom laughed, and walking over to Carmen, gave her a big hug. "I hope all those Dodgers are happily married." Then suddenly: "Wait! A picture! We can't let this moment pass without a picture. Alex, go get our camera."

As I ran out of the house it occurred to me that we needed someone to take the shot, so I stopped at Mr. Aguilar's, who agreed to take the pictures for us.

Gómez had the idea of Carmen sliding into home plate, with my mom as a left-handed batter, me as catcher, and himself as the umpire. Carmen winked to my mom as she lowered her body onto the floor. "This is what comes after third base, right, Gómez?"

When we were all in place she turned to the camera and her breasts nearly fell out of her uniform. Poor Mr. Aguilar! Seeing him pretend he wasn't looking at Carmen's nearly-exposed boobs sent us all into a laughing fit, adding to his discomfort.

"Aguilar," said Carmen, "stop staring and start shooting, or this poor button—" she pointed to the lone button preventing her jersey from flying open—"this button is going to pop right off."

"Keep staring, Mr. Aguilar!" yelled Gómez, and we all burst into laughter again.

Game time was 7:05 and we got to the stadium at about six. We bought our program outside the front gate, passed through the turnstile, and got directions to our seats.

We found an elevator, and as the door was closing, a hand reached in to stop it. The door sprang open and there was Vin Scully! He stepped in and stood right next to me. I glanced over to Gómez—his eyes were popping out of his head!

"Hey Vin," I said. The words came out just right—not so enthusiastic I sounded dangerous, but not so cool I sounded disinterested.

"Hello, son," he answered, just like Vin Scully. "How are you?"

"Doing good," I answered. "Me and my friend Gómez used to listen to you every night."

"Used to?" queried Vin, eyebrows arched over gleaming eyes.

"Well, we still listen to you, but sometimes we call the game ourselves. Gómez—" and I motioned behind me, "he's been a Dodger fan since the 1941 Dodgers-Yankees World Series. He was in a bar with his dad, and two guys thought he was good luck so they paid him fifty cents to keep still."

Vin tilted his head inquiringly.

"We think you're a great announcer, the best, but we like to give the game a little more spice, make jokes and stuff. We're home boys, I guess."

"Gómez," mused Vin. Then he turned directly to Gómez and said, "Gómez—*the god*?"

Now all of us turned to Gómez, who lowered his eyes and dropped his head as if he wanted to disappear. He muttered something unintelligible while he fumbled with Eddie's baseball mitt. Carmen said, "Gómez, what, you couldn't be Gómez the king, or Gómez the saint? You have to be Gómez *the god*?"

Vin said, "Well, how about that—we finally meet. I really did enjoy your letters, Gómez, even though I never responded. Dodger policy; I hope you understand." He stepped over towards Gómez and patted his left arm. "But, I really did enjoy them. How long have you been in town?"

"A little while."

The elevator door opened and Vin said, "This is where I get out." He extended his right hand and shook Gómez's. "It's been a real pleasure to meet you in person. I hope everything goes well for you in Los Angeles. You can still write—and now I can write back!"

The door closed and we just stood there on mute. Finally, Carmen whistled and said, "Geez Gómez, that man thinks he knows you."

"Something like that happened to me once," added my mom. "I was at a movie theater and this person swore I was the sister of a friend of hers. I kept telling her I wasn't, but she wouldn't believe me. Strange."

Gómez said nothing. As he shuffled out of the elevator his face looked as gray as his eyes. But then the field appeared before us, brilliant green in the floodlights, and he stopped. His eyes moved slowly, left to right, then up and down, as if he were framing a picture. Finally he spoke—not to us, but to himself. "It's beautiful."

I whispered, "Wow. Have you ever seen anything like it in your whole life?"

"Not while I was awake."

I looked at my mom and my tía, and they seemed moved too. The outfield was so amazingly green. Perhaps it was the stadium lights that gave the grass a luminescent glow, or maybe it was the Dodgers' breathless white uniforms, or maybe it was the spell cast on everything by the dusk settling on the hills behind the outfield walls, but we all felt the enchantment. As usual, Carmen was the first to speak.

"Food: hot dogs and beer, peanuts and popcorn—what are we waiting for?"

"Let's find our seats first," answered my mom, "then come back and get our hot dogs."

"I didn't come here to sit," replied Carmen. "I came to show off and eat, and if I have time maybe I'll watch some of the baseball game."

My mom and Carmen went for the food while Gómez and I found our seats. Once found, I went back up to help them. My mom was talking to Carmen as my tía was dressing a hot dog.

"Not now," Carmen said to my mom, abruptly. Then turning to me: "*Mijo*, your tía's gonna show you the right way to make a hot dog. Mustard and ketchup is okay, for a start"—she squeezed both onto the dog—"but if you stop there, well, that's what gringos do." She paused, as if that was argument enough. "So," she continued as she nestled my chin in her right hand and brought our faces together, "since—you—aren't—a—gringo," tapping my forehead after each word for emphasis, "I'll show you how a Mexican makes a hot dog."

Carmen placed my dog under the onion dispenser: "Onions, lots and lots of onions." Then under the relish dispenser: "Just a little relish: the gringos have to make everything sweet." Then she went to the tub of jalapeños and said, "This is where the true Mexican distinguishes himself. Chilies, *mijo*, lots of chilies. Ta-da! A Mexican hot dog!"

When we got back to our seats, Gómez still had that misty-eyed, enchanted look on his face. We sat down—Carmen next to the aisle, then my mom, me and Gómez—and dug into our food. Every time Gómez bit into that Dodger Dog he made a soft purring sound, apparently loud enough for Carmen to hear.

"Gómez," she said, "what, you've never had a hot dog before?"

He held up his hand to indicate that he'd speak upon finishing his mouthful of bliss. After a hasty gulp, he said, "Carmen, this isn't a hot dog; it's a 'Dodger Dog.' Just like you aren't a sight, you're a revelation."

"You're good, Gómez," replied Carmen, emphasizing her point with the hot dog in her right hand, "and I know good. I also know dull and ugly, and those uniforms," she pointed at the Expos dugout, "are both. Gray? Why are they wearing gray?"

"The visiting team always wears gray; the home team wears white."

"They wear beautiful uniforms when they're at home?"

"That's right."

"And ugly gray uniforms when they go visiting other teams? That makes no sense at all."

"Maybe not; but it's tradition. Baseball is all about tradition."

My mom and Carmen looked at each other and shook their heads.

"What?" asked Gómez, indignantly.

"That's the most pathetic excuse I've ever heard," answered my mom.

"It's not an excuse." He leaned towards my mom. "Tradition isn't an excuse. An excuse is something . . . like . . . like when you don't do something because you forgot, or are too lazy, and instead of just admitting it, you give a reason, but that reason isn't the real reason, it's just something you hope the other person will believe so they'll get off your back and not make you tell them the real reason, which would be embarrassing."

Carmen and my mom looked at Gómez with unblinking eyes, neither of them offering any acknowledgement at all; not even a dismissive "hrmmph." Instead, they let the silence stretch out like a rubber band, and just when it was about to snap, my mom said to Carmen, "Are men the dumbest creatures in all creation?"

"None dumber," answered Carmen. "The dumbest dog looks like a genius compared to any man. On just plain IQ, I'd pick Lassie over Einstein any time. What I don't understand is *how* they got so stupid."

"I think I know," answered my mom. "We've coddled them too long. They haven't had to use their brains in, you know, a few thousand years, and they went soft."

"I think you've got it, sister."

Gómez looked befuddled. He tried to speak—I saw his lips moving—but nothing came out.

The girls nodded to each other and continued to eat their Dodger Dogs. Point made.

Gómez kind of shuddered, and in an overly calm, stiffly measured tone, said, "Ladies, what are you talking about? Weren't we talking about baseball uniforms?"

"We were," answered my mom pleasantly.

My mom's friendly air bolstered Gómez's confidence. "And I was explaining to you why the road uniforms are gray," he continued, as if he was bringing a rebellious class back to order.

"You silly man," replied my mom, glancing at Carmen and giggling. Carmen began giggling too, and in a moment they were both bent over in laughter. "Stop it Gómez!" pleaded Carmen. "You're killing us! I'm going to choke on this damn hot dog if you don't stop it!"

Gómez began to chuckle. "Alex, do you have any idea what they're laughing about?"

I didn't, but now I was laughing too. Meanwhile, Carmen and my mom were bent over in hysterical convulsions, their heads in their hands. We quickly joined them, although neither one of us had any idea what we were laughing about, which made it even funnier.

Finally, almost as one body, we all took a large gulp of air and sighed.

"Whew," my mom said, "that was funny. I haven't laughed that hard since—well, since never." There was one last little burst and then we were all composed again, though exhausted.

"Now Carmen," said Gómez in a contrite voice, "please tell me what I have been laughing about for the last five minutes; if it's not too much to ask!"

"Of course, señor," answered Carmen. "*Manita*, would you like to explain baseball tradition to Gómez?"

"My pleasure," replied my mom, sweetly. "Gómez, dear," she began, as if she were speaking to a child who had just heard Santa Claus wasn't real, "the reason the road uniforms are gray is because they didn't wash them."

We all looked at Gómez, but the blank look on his face said it all.

My mom continued: "When the players went on the road—years ago when they probably rode on trains and were gone for weeks at a time—they didn't wash their uniforms. They got dirty and stayed dirty; so dirty they turned gray. When they were home their uniforms were washed, and so they stayed white. One day someone probably had the idea of just making road uniforms gray so the dirt wouldn't show. That's what's behind your 'tradition' of gray uniforms."

"Wow. How did you know that?"

My mom turned to Carmen. "You clean and wash and iron for thirty years and suddenly you just know things!"

Carmen smiled. "*Manita*, you make me laugh." Then turning to Gómez, she said, "But really Gómez, isn't it time to let those gray uniforms go?"

"Carmen, you win. So, what do you suggest?"

"Color!" exclaimed Carmen. "For starters, just get some color into it. Keep the home uniforms white, that's fine, and make the road uniforms *color*. Since the Expos have blue and red, make the road uniforms pale blue with black letters framed in red, or red letters framed in black. Or make the uniforms red with black socks and blue letters."

"Okay, okay!" Gómez smiled. "I'll see to it right away!"

The P.A. announcer said, "Ladies and Gentlemen, please rise for the National Anthem." We all placed our hands over our hearts and sang, led by a young man from a local high school.

When it was over Gómez said, "And while I'm at it, I'm going to get rid of the 'The Star Spangled Banner.' It's just not that good of a song, especially compared to 'America the Beautiful,' the way Ray Charles does it. Whew! *That* would be a national anthem."

"You're right, Gómez," said Carmen. "But if you really want something that gets the folks fired up, play 'La Bamba.'"

"Well, when California declares its independence, 'La Bamba' it'll be," replied Gómez. "Now, let's talk baseball. Here's what's happening tonight: the Dodger pitcher is Tim Leary. He's a good pitcher—not great, but good; solid number three behind Valenzuela and Hershiser. Montreal's pitcher is Dennis Martinez: a smart veteran; always been tough on the Dodgers."

The game began, and before the first inning was over it was obvious Carmen was bored. The exaggerated sighs and fidgeting could be ignored, but when she started throwing peanut shells it was time to take action. Gómez stepped to the plate.

"Carmen," began Gómez conversationally, "one of the nice things about baseball is the pace. There's no clock, so it isn't rushed like football, or frenetic like basketball. It mirrors life. Most of the time it seems like nothing is happening and then wham! Opportunity—or disaster—is pounding at the door."

"It may mirror your life, Gómez dear, but not mine. Let's play a word game. I'll say a word, and you guess what word it rhymes with that describes baseball. Soaring . . . Snoring . . . whoring—oops, soaring . . . ."

"You see Carmen, that's one of the charms of baseball. At football games no one talks, they just watch and yell; basketball, it's the same thing—constant action. But at baseball games people can relax a little bit. It could be boring—yes, Carmen, I understood you—it could be boring if we didn't talk about stuff like gray baseball uniforms, or national anthems, or the players, or the fans, or what's happening on the field; you can even talk about work or home or school. See, baseball requires a little effort, a little bit of creation from us, just like life. And as I always say, baseball is life, right Alex?"

"Ohh . . . kay!" said Carmen, rolling her eyes in the "whatever . . ." look, and then she said, "Sister, let's go shopping."

"Good idea!" agreed my mom.

It was only the second inning and my mom and Carmen had had enough. Oh well. Now Gómez and I could relax and enjoy the ballgame without worrying about the girls. Thank goodness for shopping.

In the fourth inning, Gibson led off with a single to right field. With Guerrero at the plate, Gibson took off for second base on the first pitch, easily beating the throw.

"I love this guy," said Gómez. "He's a warrior; a true warrior."

"Like Jackie."

Gómez looked at me and grabbed a handful of peanuts. "Yep, like Jackie."

Gibson then took a big lead off second base, unnerving Martinez, who threw the ball into center field trying to pick him off. Gibson trotted into third, slapping his hands together and exhorting his dugout. A Guerrero fly ball brought Gibson home, and the Dodgers took the lead, 1-0.

Mike Marshall was the next hitter. He took the first pitch for a strike and then hit the next pitch over the left field fence. As Marshall rounded the bases, Gibson came out of the dugout and pumped his fist. The crowd stood and applauded, and we joined them.

"Two runs," said Gómez, "and probably neither of them would've happened but for Gibson. Lots of players can steal a base, but seldom do you see it on the first pitch. It's like he's saying, 'Hey pitcher! I'm coming after you!'"

Meanwhile, Leary was pitching great. By the end of five innings, he had struck out six Expos and given up only four hits.

My mom and Carmen returned. Carmen had a little baseball bat with "Dodgers" written in script across it. She rapped it against her palm. "A girl needs to be able to defend herself."

My mom reached into a Dodger shopping bag and pulled out a hat. "Alex, this is for you."

"Gee, thanks mom."

Gómez turned my head from side to side. "Nice."

"And for you, Gómez," continued my mom, "your very own Dodger coffee cup."

Gómez held it up to catch the light. "My, my, Maria, thank you. Now I don't have to drink coffee out of my cupped hands." My tía and mom laughed, and encouraged, Gómez added, "It's almost impossible to add cream and sugar."

My mom reached into her bag again and said, "And for Rosa, a Dodger T-shirt. For Eddie—I don't know what. They didn't have any Dodger ashtrays."

"Nothing for you?" asked Gómez.

"I got a mug, too."

My tía, whose eyes had been roaming the stadium since she sat down, yelled "Look at the scoreboard!"

"The Los Angeles Dodgers Welcome Longtime Dodger Fan—Gómez!"

"Wow, Gómez," I said, "Vin Scully did that!"

Gómez glowed. "I can't believe it." He looked around us. "Do you suppose there's another Gómez?"

"Trust me on this one," answered Carmen, "there's only one."

Then coming across dozens of transistor radios we heard Vin Scully say, "On behalf of the Los Angeles Dodgers, I'd like to extend a warm greeting to one of our greatest fans. Gómez, welcome to Dodger Stadium!"

Carmen crossed her arms and put a pouty look on her face. "Geez, I dress up like a Dodger call girl and what do I get? You bump into Vin Scully in the elevator, try to hide in your shoes and you get all this. I'm telling you, God will not be pleased. Someone had better straighten this out quick or there'll be hell to pay."

It didn't take long for God to set things straight. During the seventh-inning-stretch, as Elton John's "Crocodile Rock" boomed from loud speakers, cameras scanned the crowd, stopping here and there to give fans the thrill of seeing themselves on the big screen. A camera lit upon Carmen dancing, and though it tried to move on to some other deserving fan, it kept coming back to Carmen. She rolled her shoulders suggestively and waved her arms—and that one desperate button doggedly held on, heroically keeping Carmen's jersey from flying open and spilling forth. Probably never has a single button held the undivided attention of so many men.

Again the camera tried to pull away, but a collective groan compelled it to return as Carmen, standing on her chair with her backside to the camera, showed the gringos some Latina rhythm. When the song ended and Carmen's churning hips finally stopped, an exhale of applause rolled through the stadium. Carmen bowed and waved and blew kisses and put her hands on her heart and sighed in modest appreciation. Finally, the public address announcer said, "Well, well . . . let's play ball!" and off went the camera.

Carmen collapsed in her chair and fanned herself with the Dodger program.

"Carmen, you're a star!" yelled Gómez.

My mom leaned over and gave her a long, sisterly hug. "You were wonderful!" Suddenly she pulled back: "A picture!" Out came the camera and she snapped off several pictures of Carmen from different angles, then took pictures of Gómez and I, then grabbed a fan to take pictures of all four of us.

Meanwhile, Leary pitched a masterpiece and the Dodgers made those early runs count, winning 2-0. "Alex," said Gómez when the final pitch had been thrown, "I bet Leary hasn't thrown a better game in his entire career."

"But the star of the night was Gibson."

My mom trumped us. "You're both wrong. *Carmen* was the star of the evening."

Gómez and I immediately nodded our heads. "No argument here," said Gómez.

"You're the winner, tía," I agreed.

We got home around eleven and Gómez walked us to our door. "Thank you, Maria. This was a special night." He bent and kissed her lightly on the cheek. "I'll never forget it."

As I lay in bed I thought, "Yes, it was a special night—the lights, the green field, Vin Scully, Carmen, Gómez." Then I heard the opening strains of "Hallelujah." Oh yes, and the Dodgers won.

*****

With only three weeks until The Party, The Garden was right on schedule—except for the chilies, which, despite constant attention from Mr. Sánchez, were slow to blossom. They all *looked* in prime condition, but there were no baby chilies—not a single bud. Probably it was concern over this that caused Mr. Sánchez to begin speaking to the chilies, which I first noticed early one Saturday morning as I entered Gómez's yard.

"Si, it is a bit chilly this morning."

I paused; it sounded like Mr. Sánchez was answering a question. I turned and looked at him—he was tending one of the yellows and had his back to me—and in case he was talking to me, I waited for him to speak again. But he didn't—at least not to me—though he did continue talking to the chilies.

She blames me, you know.

Fifth Jalapeño: No reply.

She doesn't say anything. She's never said anything. But I know. I can see it when she looks at the children.

Fifth Jalapeño: No reply.

Where did I go wrong, señor? What was I supposed to do?

Mr. Sánchez stands, not waiting for an answer. He turns around, his back now to the fifth jalapeño as he looks down at the fourth serrano.

Señor, do you know?

He walks down the row between the serranos and the jalapeños and stops in front of the second jalapeño.

Señor, and you?

Bending down in front of the second jalapeño, he strokes its leaves between his fingers.

No, you do not. How could you know, eh señors? You live your entire lives in the same place where you were born. Ah, had I done the same!

It was painful to hear this monologue—Sánchez's "Soliloquy to the Plants." When he stood up, noticing me for the first time, I pretended I just arrived. "Gee, Mr. Sánchez, why do you suppose these chilies aren't blooming? If these plants get any bigger they'll be trees."

He knelt in front of the first serrano. "Plants have problems just like people."

All day Gómez had me switching from one album to the next. In the middle of Bach he'd say, "Put on Mendelssohn." Or he'd ask for one song, only; from Mozart, for example. By the late afternoon, I'd played at least one song from almost every album. We'd just heard Wagner's "Ride of the Valkyries" when Gómez stood up and said, "Enough." He dusted off his overalls. "Amigos, we need to talk." He motioned for Mr. Sánchez and me to join him.

"It's the chilies," he said with gravity. "We've got to start getting some fruit, and soon! I've done everything I can think of. I've tried Bach's 'Air on the G string,' nothing; Mendelssohn's 'Spring Song,' nothing; Vivaldi, Debussy, even Wagner—nothing, Nothing, NOTHING!"

I had a thought. "Maybe the classical music is—wrong."

Gómez's head jerked back like he'd been struck. He looked at me in shock.

"Yes," murmured Mr. Sánchez.

Gómez turned on him. "What, are you mad? Was not this Garden conceived in the very womb of 'Bolero'? Were not these plants—and I mean every one of these plants!—were not they suckled on the teats of Bach and Beethoven, Mozart and Pachelbel?"

"Yes," I answered. "But maybe chilies are different."

The wolf-eyes narrowed. "They—are—not—different."

"Well," I continued, "maybe they're going through a phase. Maybe they're teenage chilies."

"Si," said Mr. Sánchez, barely audible.

"Señor?" Gómez swung his head to Mr. Sánchez, who held his gaze but briefly.

"Si, señor," he repeated softly.

Gómez's eyes bored into Mr. Sánchez; then his expression softened slightly. Doubt had entered his mind, driving a small wedge into his line of defense. Into the breach Mr. Sánchez stepped cautiously. "Alex is right. How could I miss it? These chilies, they're from a different place. Sure, they've been here for generations, but that hasn't changed what they are, or *who* they are. They're from the South, señor. They are hot-blooded, and fire flows through their veins. They are young, they are healthy, but they are homesick."

Gómez looked Mr. Sánchez dead in the eye. "Is this true? What you are saying—is it true?"

"Si, my friend," answered Mr. Sánchez. "They are out of place here. They are surviving because they are strong, but this is not their home and they feel like strangers. There is sadness here," he said, motioning to the plants, "and I feel it. All the time I feel it."

"I see." Gómez rubbed his Hemingway and took a few steps down the walkway. He turned. "Well, what can we do?" He shifted his eyes from Mr. Sánchez, to me, and back again.

Mr. Sánchez shrugged and dropped his eyes.

"Well, we can't exactly send them home, now can we?" stated Gómez, annoyance in his tone.

"Latin music," I answered.

Mr. Sánchez lifted his eyes and latched onto mine like suction cups. For the first time, Mr. Sánchez and I connected. In the "World of Sánchez," a new person had been admitted, one Alex Morales, formerly a nonentity, a kid. It felt good, too.

"Latin music?" said Gómez.

"Si," answered Mr. Sánchez, "That's what's missing, that's what my young chilies need!"

Gómez raised his arms in mock resignation. "Well then, let's do it!"

Once again it was the resourceful Mr. Aguilar who came to the rescue, supplying several old albums.

Gómez began with a mambo by Lalo Guerrero. He put the record on; then he and Mr. Sánchez stood on the walkway, waiting for something to happen. The plants didn't show an immediate appreciation—they didn't begin to rub their leaves or sway—but Gómez and Mr. Sánchez did!

It started with subtle, synchronized muscle twitches here and there, then Mr. Sánchez's right foot began to tap the cement and Gómez's shoulders began to bob. Soon Gómez was strutting along the pathway, with Mr. Sánchez joining him for a duet that was the funniest thing I'd ever seen. Even now I smile, recalling those two old men capering through The Garden, silhouetted by the evening sun. That night, long after the music was put away, I lie in bed, listening to the sound of chilies giggling in the dark.

The next morning the chilies had already begun to bud, and in the following weeks they blossomed and bore fruit at biblical speed. And it wasn't just the chilies working over-time; with school out for the summer I was now spending *days* in The Garden, too.

One afternoon I excused myself to use the restroom at my house, and as I pulled back the screen door I heard my mom and my tía laughing. When I entered the kitchen both of them instantly covered their mouths. My mom had tears streaming down her cheeks and my tía had one hand covering her eyes. She spread her fingers to see if I was still there, and then burst into hysterics. My mother joined her. I wasn't amused.

"What are you laughing about?"

"Nothing, *mijo,*" answered Carmen.

I looked at my mom. "Mom?"

"Well *mijo,*" Carmen began. "We were just talking about The Party."

"Yes . . . ?"

"You're doing a wonderful job on it—you and the boys, a wonderful job."

"And," continued my mom, "I—we—both of us are very proud of the work you've done."

"But?"

My mom smiled. What a smile. "Alex, come here, next to me."

I did and folded my arms across my chest. "But?"

"But—who's coming, *mijo*?" asked Carmen.

"A lot of people; Gómez wants to invite the whole neighborhood."

My mom pulled my arms apart and held my hands. "Exactly," she said softly. "But what are you going to serve all these people besides *The World's Greatest Salsa*?"

Both my mom and Carmen were looking at me, waiting. Hmmm. She had a point.

"Just as we thought," said Carmen.

"Yep," replied my mom. "Alex dear, take us to Gómez."

*****

"Gómez," my mom said, "we have come to save you from yourselves."

"Señora?"

Carmen stepped forward: "To save you from making a disaster out of this party of yours and embarrassing me and Maria in the process."

"Señor," said my mom, "a party requires planning. What are you serving with your salsa? Who's buying it? Who's cooking it? Who's serving it? On what? What time? Is everyone expected to sit cross-legged in the grass? Wait a second—you don't have any grass!"

"I see your point, señora," said Gómez thoughtfully, rubbing his Hemingway.

"There's more," added my mom. "Lights: what happens when the sun goes down? You can either tell everyone to go home or you're going to need lights." She turned to Carmen. "I was thinking of stringing lights on the trees and bushes, maybe even on the porches."

"Those small, white lights like you see at Disneyland," said Carmen.

"Yes; and Japanese lanterns on the stairs and walkways."

"Perfect, *mi hermana*."

My mom and Carmen continued as if we weren't there. "Oh, and dancing!" said my tía. "I haven't danced since . . . hmmm . . . Maria, what was that man's name? You know—the one who wanted to take me to Vegas and make me a headliner?"

"Alberto: the married credit union manager who claimed to know Steve Wynn."

"Ugghhh," shivered Carmen. "No wonder I haven't danced since forever. Oh well, it's time to get over it!"

My mom and Carmen were walking away, chattering like two schoolgirls, when my mom turned and said, "Oh, by the way Gómez, would you mind putting together some music? Whatever you want."

"Si, señora," smiled Gómez.

When I came back later that evening, Gómez was gliding around the kitchen table and whistling as he laid out the guacamole. "Amigo!"

"What are you so happy about? Are the Dodgers already winning?"

"Eh, what's that?" He paused briefly from his capering. "No, the game isn't on yet."

"You got some great news?"

"So I did, son. So I did!"

"What was it?"

"Well, I had this idea for a party: a Midsummer's Eve Feast. But, I've never thrown a party; ever. And then today, unexpected but not un-hoped for, your mom and your tía volunteer—insist—demand!—to manage the entire affair!"

*****

As the days lengthened, we spent more of the evenings outside, though usually we managed to wrap things up and get inside by 7:05 to watch the Dodgers. Recently our audience had grown, so that we had to move the TV to the living room. My sister Rosa was now *The World's Youngest Dodger Fan*, and Mr. Aguilar was a regular visitor, too. He never did seem to figure out baseball, but he knew that scoring runs was good and giving up runs was bad, and his ranting and raving was always the equal to ours, if a little delayed.

Even Mrs. Cortez attended some of the games, in a manner of speaking. She was in the corner of the room, in her own rocking chair that Gómez had brought from her house, knitting. Near as I could tell she was knitting either the world's longest scarf or a blanket for a twenty-foot snake. The funny thing was, in a room full of Dodger fans she was the *anti*-Dodger fan. During the game I'd hear her mutter things under her breath, such as "loser" when one of the Dodgers had failed, or "he'll strike out" when one of our boys was up to bat in a critical situation, or "here they come" when the opposition mounted even the smallest scoring threat, such as a walk. Her carping soon became background noise to all of us, but sometimes I'd become aware of her all over again and it would tick me off.

One day I told Gómez I was tired of her *nit-nit-nit* all the time, and I was expecting his wholehearted agreement; but I didn't get it.

"Mrs. Cortez, she's got some spunk."

"What? It doesn't bother you? I mean, she's in a roomful of Dodger fans and she doesn't have one nice thing to say about them; she just criticizes."

"Yes, she does."

"Doesn't that make you mad?"

"Not really."

I just didn't get it.

"Look," said Gómez, "I know she's a disagreeable old lady, but what do we know about her, really?" I had to give him that. She'd been my neighbor my whole life and I didn't even know her first name.

That Mrs. Cortez was watching the games was remarkable, but that my mom was watching them was, well, a miracle. At first, when she came to gather up Rosa she'd courteously wait until the inning was over. But recently she had settled in quite nicely, sitting down on the floor with the rest of us as she caught up on the game, and often staying to the end.

Mr. Sánchez seldom came in to watch the Dodgers, but he did listen to the games on the radio as he tended The Garden. I could tell he was listening because if something important was happening—like the bases were loaded—he'd take a brief break from his constant chatter to the plants. At such times we all usually stopped what we were doing, convinced that we had something to do with the outcome.

Mrs. Sánchez never came over to watch a Dodger game except once, in October, but my Tía Carmen did—not often, but sometimes, and always because she was looking for someone. One night we were announcing the game and Gómez—I mean Vin Scully—saw Carmen enter "the park" and brought her over for an interview.

Fans, I have a special treat for you tonight. Carmen Salazar has stopped by. Carmen, nice to see you again!

My pleasure; what's your name?

Vin, ma'am; Vin Scully.

Ah, yes, I saw you at Dodger Stadium. You look different. Say, where's the camera?

There's no camera on us, Carmen. The camera's on the game.

Yes, I'm sure, but don't you think your fans would rather see me, Vinnie dear?

Uhhh, yes Carmen. Ross, tell Bob to put the camera on Carmen, would you please?

Mr. Aguilar assumes the position of the cameraman. Carmen wraps her arms around Vin and puts her lips to his ear.

Vinnie, she says, twirling her forefinger in his hair, *is béisbol the only thing you think about?*

Strike one on Sax—no Carmen. In fact, just now I was thinking about my wife.

Yes dear, and what else are you thinking about? Her finger moves its way down his cheek to his chin.

My children, Carmen—strike two on Saxie.

Si señor, your children. She continues to trace a line down his neck and towards his heart. She whispers breathlessly in his ear. *Anything else?*

Uhhh, did I mention my wife?

Yes, you did, Vinnie dear. She gives him a kiss on the cheek. *You're a good boy, Vincent.* Turning to Ross, *Señor, are you a good boy, too?*

Yes ma'am, says Ross emphatically.

Good boy, says Carmen. She stands up and waves to her fans in TV land, then leaves.

Well, Ross, I'm thinking about going to church tomorrow.

I'll see you there, Vin. Save a seat for me in the front pew.

*****

A week before The Party I was sitting in our kitchen with my mom, my tía and Gómez. It was about four o'clock in the afternoon and they were drinking coffee while going over the shopping list. The question was always "How much?" Not how much *money*, but how much *food*. We expected for sure fifty people, but these were family and friends. How many other people might show up once the smell of *carne asada* filled the air, well, we could only guess. Also, we had placed advertisements on both sides of our street.

Street Party
Midsummer's Eve Festival
Homemade Salsa

June 23, 7 p.m.

"But Gómez dear, how will they know where The Party is?" asked Carmen.

"By following their noses, Carmen," Gómez answered. "Don't worry; we'll have more people than we can handle. And let's plan for more, lots more, so everyone who comes gets to try our salsa. Let's say fifty pounds of *carne*, fifty pounds of *frijoles* and rice, and a hundred bottles of beer."

The door bell rang and Carmen went to answer it, saying as she walked out, "I don't know how much beer *your* friends drink, but the parties I've been to, a hundred bottles of beer wouldn't last half the night."

When Carmen returned she had a man in tow—small and scruffy-looking, maybe in his late fifties or early sixties. He had a baseball cap in his hands, old and very faded, but I could make out the letter B—for *Brooklyn*—on the front. Gómez's back was to the entryway and he didn't see them enter.

"I see your point, Carmen," Gómez said. "Maybe we should have two hundred bottles of beer and serve it from behind a counter so no one has four or five."

"Gómez," said Carmen. "A friend of yours is here."

Gómez thought Carmen was playing a game—sometimes Rosa dressed in a costume to amuse us all—and he turned to face Carmen with eager anticipation. But the smile on Gómez's face froze into a grotesque parody. Someone had just stepped out of his past and into our kitchen. Oh no.

"Hello, Gómez the god!" said the little man.

Gómez didn't answer: the shock had frozen his wits. None of us said anything. The little man's eyes jumped from Gómez to Carmen to Mom to me and back to Gómez. Perspiration glistened on his face. "Gómez? It's O.C.; from Folsom."

In Gómez's pale gray eyes, dismay dissolved into resignation: the apparition was not going away. "Hello, O.C.," he said, wearily. The little man sagged. None of us spoke, and only the kitchen clock moved, the second hand marching doggedly forward.

All eyes were on Gómez. With a grim smile, he raised himself and walked over to the little man. "O.C. It is great to see you again." He turned to face us. "I'd like to introduce an old friend of mine, O.C. Martin."

My mom invited O.C. to sit down. Gómez guided him into a chair and sat next to him.

"Mr. Martin," my mom said, "would you like a cup of coffee?"

"No ma'am." His voice was high-pitched and twangy. When no one said anything, he continued: "I wouldn't wanna bother no one." The poor man was a wreck. His voice shook with every word. It was painful to watch.

"It's no bother at all. I already have a pot made. What would you like in it, Mr. Martin?"

"Sugar, ma'am. Two scoops if ya don't mind."

"Milk with that, Mr. Martin?"

"Yes ma'am." In an eerie way it seemed like my mom, Gómez and O.C. Martin were the only people in the room; as if the stage lights had faded, leaving Carmen and me in shadow.

"So, Gómez," my mom said casually, "where did you and Mr. Martin meet? Folsom, was it?"

Gómez's eyes had regained that detached, wolfish look, as if he knew where this was going, and whichever way it went, and no matter how bad it got, it was fine with him. "Folsom Prison," he answered evenly. "O.C. and I spent ten years together there." He looked over to O.C. "But we liked to think of it as Folsom University, right O.C.?"

For the first time, O.C. smiled, revealing missing front teeth.

"That's right, Gómez, 'Folsom U.' That's whatcha always called it."

Carmen moved from the doorway over to the sink so she could see Gómez's face. O.C. watched her; when she settled into her new position, he said, "Ma'am." Carmen nodded.

O.C. began to lift his coffee cup with his right hand but his hand shook, so he wrapped both hands around it and put it back on the table. Looking again at my mom, he continued: "He was always givin' new names ta stuff. Like our rooms was 'suites,' 'n the mess was 'Clifton's Cafeteria.'"

My mom put a smile on her face. "That Gómez, he's something else."

"Yep, he sure is," agreed O.C. "I could tell ya all sorts a stuff." And we sensed he not only could, but would. Here was a man who could hold up his end of a conversation, nervous or not. My mom said sweetly, "Please do, Mr. Martin. We love to hear Gómez stories! Tell me about when you met."

"Well, lemme think, ma'am. That'd be 1977, I reckon. I just transferred ta Folsom; Gómez'd already been there awhile. He was always greetin' new prisoners, goin' outta his way ta welcome 'em to 'the hotel,' as he'd say. We was friends right away."

He looked at Gómez, who smiled and said, "I remember that day very well, O.C."

"I'll never forget it!"

"Why is that, Mr. Martin?" my mom asked.

"Well, ma'am," answered O.C., lowering his mouth to his coffee cup and taking a quick sip. "The first week or so can be kind a hard in a place like Folsom. Some guys wanna test ya—wanna test ya right away. After I stowed m'gear I went out ta the yard 'n sat down 'n these two fellas come up to me 'n ask me if I have a smoke. Of course I do, but I says 'no' cuz I knowed if I'd a said 'yes' they'd take 'em. Yessir. Well, one of 'em is on m'right, 'n the other is on m'left, 'n I know trouble ain't far away."

O.C. looked over at Gómez and smiled.

"Yessir, trouble warn't far away at all. In two seconds them boys was gonna turn me upside down just ta see what falls out." O.C. demonstrated with his hands something being turned over and shook. "Next thing I know, 'Gómez the god' shows up, just appears outta nowhere like he does, 'n he says, 'Boys, like ta intraduce y'all ta m'new friend.' He looks at me and says, 'No need ta be shy; go 'head, intraduce yersef. We're all friends here.'"

O.C. laughed softly to himself and looked at Gómez like a little boy looking up to his big brother.

"Slade, he was one of 'em, he tells Gómez ta fu—, 'scuze me ma'am—ta get lost, 'n the next thing I know, Slade's laid out on the ground. Out cold like a fu—, 'scuze me ma'am—like a fish; out cold like a fish. Wilson, he's the other guy, he says, 'What the—,' 'n Gómez lays him out, too. It was like he hit 'em with a lightning bolt. One second Wilson is standin', the next he ain't."

Carmen stepped towards the table and placed a hand on Gómez's shoulder. "Gómez dear, would you like me to warm up that coffee for you?"

O.C. took the opportunity to lift his coffee cup to his mouth with both hands and suck up some hurried sips. Once Gómez's cup was filled, O.C. continued. "Saved m'butt, he did. Those boys—if they got ya down, ya never get up again. Nossir, never get up again. But anyway, they left me alone—that day 'n ever after. Thanks ta 'Gómez the god.'"

I looked at Gómez. The wolf-eyes revealed nothing: not a flinch, not even a blink. It was about to get rough. I was on his side, and I think Carmen was too, but my mom had different plans.

"Mr. Martin, why did you call Gómez, 'Gómez the god'?"

"Oh, it warn't just me, ma'am. Alla us did; even the guards."

"But why?"

O.C. picked up his baseball cap and rubbed the faded B with his thumb. "Well, ma'am, he just has a way." He turned to Gómez and said, "Tell 'em 'bout when the guards first started callin' ya 'Gómez the god,' that time in Solitary, when you popped outta yer body and was watching 'em—"

"Mr. Martin!" my tía jumped in. She stepped around Gómez and topped off O.C.'s cup. "So, did you just get out of Folsom?"

"Yes ma'am, coupla weeks ago. Livin' with m'sister in Sacramento; just took the bus down ta see Gómez."

"When are you going back?"

"Goin' back tomorrow."

"Where are you staying tonight?" asked Gómez.

"I was goin' ta ask ya if there was any hotels 'round here." O.C. smiled at the joke and Gómez winked in acknowledgment.

"You're not staying at a hotel, my friend, you're staying with me."

"Well, I kinda hoped ya'd say that."

"Come, I'll show you my place." Gómez and O.C. stood up. My mom stood up too and said, "Mr. Martin, it's been a pleasure to meet you. I've learned so much about Gómez!"

"Thankee, ma'am. It's been a pleasure ta meet y'all."

Gómez and O.C. left the room and I heard the screen door swing closed. Carmen remained where she was, leaning against the counter, but with her arms now folded. My mom gathered up the cups and put them in the sink. Still looking down she said, "Didn't I tell you, Carmen? Just a con man; just another damn con man."

"Sister, he was in prison. We don't know why."

"I don't care why."

I heard the screen slam shut again. Eddie sauntered in. "Hey, you guys meet O.C.?"

"Yes," answered my mom, surprised. "Did you?"

"Yeah. An hour or so ago, down the street. Asked if I knew Gómez. Said they did time together." Eddie was smiling. "Say, we got any Coke? I'm thirsty."

None of us answered.

"Yep, Gómez in prison. Ain't that the funniest thing you ever heard? Murder."

"What?" my mom screeched.

"Eddie," Carmen interjected, "did he say Gómez was in prison for murder?"

"What else? You think he was in Folsom for stealin' candy?"

"Eddie!" My mom's command stopped him from foraging through the fridge. She spoke slowly, carefully enunciating each word. "Did—Mr.—Martin—say—Gómez—in—prison—for—murder?"

"No, he didn't say it. I just know."

"How do you know?"

"It's obvious."

"Eddie, shut up." She wiped her hands, threw the dishtowel on the counter, and walked out. Carmen followed her.

"Fuck a duck," said Eddie, resuming his foraging, "Gómez a con. Alex, ain't that the funniest thing you ever heard?"

"Go to hell, Eddie."

That night I stayed home. Eddie was out. Rosa and my mom were at Carmen's. I turned on the TV, sat down in my father's chair, and watched the news. War, murder, crime: the whole world was losing, including the Dodgers, 7-3.

*****

On Thursday morning Gómez, Mr. Sánchez and I stood in front of the chilies. O.C. sat on Gómez's porch. He hadn't gone back to his sister's, of course. Gómez wouldn't have permitted it; not with The Party only a couple of days away. O.C. had an unlit cigarette dangling from his mouth, and his hands were moving from one pocket to the next, looking for matches.

"Gómez, ya gotta match?"

"No," answered Gómez.

"They in the house? Where, 'n I'll get 'em."

"None in the house, either."

O.C.'s eyes pinched together. "Ya quit?"

"Yep."

"Ya don't smoke cigarettes no more? Since when?"

"Hell O.C., for awhile. Maybe you should too."

O.C. shrugged and began to go through all his pockets again.

Gómez stepped onto the other side of the furrow so he was facing us. "Gentlemen," he said, "it is time."

"Time for what?" I asked.

"Time to make the salsa. You'd think we'd wait until Saturday, but with salsa you don't want to do that; salsa is better when it ages a little. The chilies work out their differences, the *tomatillos* come to an agreement with the garlic; it's quite a shock for all of these vegetables to be cut up and thrown willy-nilly into a bowl. It takes a little time for everyone to settle down and work together. Si, Mr. Sánchez?"

"Si."

"Well, before we begin we need to choose some—"

"Your flute," I said.

Mr. Sánchez snorted in approval.

"No," answered Gómez firmly, "the flute isn't appropriate; not at all. This is a big occasion. This is the harvest reaping. We need—"

"Get your flute," said Mr. Sánchez.

Gómez began to protest, but quickly realized the futility of going up against Mr. Sánchez. He shuffled into his house and returned with his flute and a pack of matches that he tossed to O.C. "What do you want to hear?" he said to no one in particular.

"You play more than one song?" I asked innocently.

O.C. laughed out loud. "Ya noticed, huh? I swear. All the years I heard 'im on that flute, damn if he ever played more than one song."

"Very funny," said Gómez. "Did it ever cross your silly, small minds that maybe one song is enough? Haven't you ever heard about the old Indians singing their Life Song? Well, this is my Life Song: one song, many verses."

"'N they all sound the same!" laughed O.C.

"Of course they do, O.C. Things don't change much in prison, now do they?"

O.C. rolled his eyes. "That's one way ta explain it." He took off his baseball cap and tossed it in the air, catching it on his head.

Gómez smiled smugly. "And furthermore, this flute has a name, and it isn't 'that flute.' How would you like it if people just called you 'dirt farmer'? A name means you are special. From now on, please call this instrument by his name: 'Angelo.'"

Gómez moistened his lips, and as he raised Angelo to his mouth, Mr. Sánchez said, "Before you play, Gómez, a benediction."

Gómez looked at me and winked. "Mr. Sánchez, if you please."

"My friends, we are met here today to conclude one of the cycles of life, a first harvest." He addressed each of the chilies in turn: "Jalapeños!—you are commended! Serranos!—you are commended! Yellows!—you are commended!" He looked down on the onions in the fourth and fifth rows: "My friends! Soon we'll be harvesting your bounty. We salute you with high praise!" He turned around to face East Garden. "My children," he said, looking at the *tomatillos* and cilantro, "We commend you!"

Gómez put his arm around Mr. Sánchez, and beckoning me over, put his arm around me too. "Men, we've done well."

He sat down and commenced to play his Life Song. I was working the end of the first row when—I don't know how much later—Gómez crouched next to me, tugging on a *tomatillo.* We looked at each other, mirroring the contentment felt by people have who have labored long and well.

When we completed the harvesting, we went into Gómez's house to rinse the vegetables and prepare the salsa. The Dodgers, playing a day game in San Diego, were just taking the field.

Mr. Sánchez fastidiously washed each of the chilies: first the jalapeños, then the serranos, and finally the yellows. O.C. had the job of stripping the store-bought garlic bulbs and peeling the skin off each clove, which to my mind was the most unpleasant of the assigned tasks; it was monotony times ten. O.C. didn't seem to mind at all, though, and years later, when I had seen and experienced more of the variety of life, I realized that O.C. was one of those uncommon personalities who could work at a task hour after hour without break, chipping away at a mountain of work until at last it was all gone. I wasn't like that, and Gómez wasn't either. He had a bag of yellow onions, some from The Garden and some store-bought, and his job was to cut them into quarters. He was done in about ten minutes.

From my bag of *tomatillos,* I systematically took out each one and removed its papery sheath. *Tomatillos* are unique in that each one is wrapped in a thin, brittle cover. Gómez was poking O.C. and pointing to me with a knowing smile on his face. I let it go, refusing to ask what was so funny, but Gómez couldn't hold back and said, "Say, O.C., look at Dr. Morales over there, circumcising the *tomatillos.*" O.C. chuckled and Gómez laughed himself into a coughing fit. I didn't think it was funny at all. Frankly, I had no idea what he was talking about and didn't *want* to know either. Mr. Sánchez, the standup comedian's nightmare, was equally unimpressed.

When I finished circumcising the *tomatillos* I put them on the counter next to the sink, assuming that Mr. Sánchez would want to wash them himself, individually, with painstaking care, and I joined Gómez in front of the TV.

"Alex, while we wait for Mr. Sánchez, how about we give Vin and Ross a hand?"

"Ho-ho!" said O.C. "Ya still doin' that?"

"And why not? The Boys still need my help, same as before." Gómez plopped onto the floor. "Let's see what we have here . . . . *Ross, who's first up for the Dodgers?"*

Mike Scoscia, Vin.

Okay, let's see if Mike can get something started. Ross, how's he done against Whitson in the past?

Vin, Mike has faced Whitson seventeen times, and has one hit and six strikeouts.

Yikes, Ross. Mike's going to need some help.

Do you mean . . . .

Yes, the Vulcan Mind Meld.

Vin, isn't it a little early—strike one.

Yes it is Ross, but even now, as I touch the fringes of his mind, I can feel Mike's despair.

Me too. But Vin, you sure it's okay to take over someone's mind like that?

Ross, I'm not at all sure. A man's free will is, well, it's what makes him free. But the poor lad! I'll tell you what, I won't completely take over his mind; I'll just quietly enter and give him some confidence. You okay with that, Ross?

Well Vin, I'm not sure—strike two. On the other hand, it's really no different than giving him a pep-talk, when you think about it. Better get in there quick though!

I made a high-pitched whining sound, signifying that Vin was preparing to enter Scoscia's body. O.C. howled. "That's a new one!"

While I whined faster and faster, Gómez laid on his back and made a sputtering sound, sort of like a car engine that won't turn over, and then he suddenly exclaimed, "*I'm in!*"

Ball one—what do you see, Vin?"

It's bad, Ross, Gómez whispered, as if he were far away. *It's worse than I thought. The poor boy! His confidence is shattered! Doubt. Worry. Humiliation. Say, what's this? A piñata?*

A piñata? I whispered. *What're you talking about Vin?* Then in a normal voice—*Scoscia steps out of the batter's box. He takes off his helmet and taps his shoes with his bat.*

Give me a second here, Gómez said softly, as if he were in the middle of something. *Hmmm . . . no, don't do that; that's not right. You shouldn't do that!*

Do what, Gó—Vin? Don't do what? I whispered earnestly, and then in a normal voice—*Mike puts his left foot back into the box. He shakes his head. Now he's banging his head with his right hand. Okay, Mike's all right. He puts his right foot in. He swings the bat back and forth, back and forth; he's ready. Whitson winds and here comes the pitch: ball two.* And then in a whisper—*Vin, you still in there?*

Shhh, not now, Ross.

I whispered, *Okay, Vinnie—folks, we're in a pickle here. Wait a second! Mike steps out of the box again. He's called time out. Here comes the trainer. Mike's shaking his head again. Poor kid; he's in a Vulcan Mind Meld and he doesn't know it! Hang in there, Mike! It'll be okay! Then, in a whisper: Vin?*

Shhh.

Hurry up! I croaked.

Done, said Vin, like a brain surgeon who has just completed the most difficult part of the procedure.

Is Mike okay?

What? said Vin in a slightly perplexed tone. *Oh, yeah, sure, he's fine. I took care of that in no time at all. It was the extraction that was so sensitive. There can't be any trace of a foreign presence or his confidence could be undermined—forever!* Even I was unnerved by the foreboding in Vin's voice.

Now Tommy Lasorda is coming out to have a look at Mike—so Vin, what was the problem, the problem with the piñata?

Oh, that. Well Ross, I don't know if I should tell you. It's personal, you know.

I understand, Vin; really. And it'll be personal when I wrap my fingers around your neck and choke the last breath out of you. Comprende, Vincento?

Comprendo, Señor Ross. So, it turns out that Mike was at a birthday party when he was seven years old. There was a piñata; all the kids were blindfolded and . . . .

Hold on a sec, Vin—Tommy's going back to the dugout with the trainer. Looks like Mike is fine now—go on, Vin.

I could have told you Mike was okay. Anyway, at the party there was a piñata and all the kids took swings at it, blindfolded. Well, the birthday boy didn't want Mike to break the piñata, so he kept raising it so Mike couldn't hit it. All the kids were laughing, at him is what Mike thought, and he just got more and more frustrated swinging at that damn piñata, tears running down his cheeks. Finally, he just quit.

Mike's back in the box now. He takes a couple of practice strokes, and here comes the pitch . . . . Whoa! Mike hits a wicked foul ball down the left field line. Geez, that ball was smoked!—so, Vin, what did you do about it?

Nothing, really; well, nothing major. Mike's eyes were blindfolded, remember, so he couldn't see what the boy was doing. I just showed him what really happened. He wasn't too happy about it, either, not too happy at all. Oh, by the way, the kid was thin, with wide-set eyes and brown hair, like Whitson.

Gotcha, Vin—and here's Whitson's next pitch to Mike. Thwack! A line drive to center . . . it's a hit! Wow! He hit that ball so hard he dented it. I think Mike's okay now, Vinnie

Ahh, he's a good kid. Say, Ross, guess who his favorite announcer is.

You're funny, Vin.

After five innings the Dodgers led 1-0, but in the top of the sixth the Padres scored five runs. This was a good Padres team, and someday Padres fans would look back wistfully on a club that included Tony Gwynn, Roberto Alomar, Benito Santiago, Garry Templeton and John Kruk.

Mr. Sánchez came out of the kitchen and said, "Ready." He was not a man to waste words. On the stove were two large pots filled with water, a high flame under each. He put serranos in the first pot, while Gómez loaded yellows in the second. Into each were added yellow onions. "Ten minutes," said Mr. Sánchez.

"What about the jalapeños?" I asked.

"We're going to grill them for the salsa," answered Gómez. "We put them in the broiler for a few minutes until they're partially blackened. It gives the salsa a smoky flavor; very yum, courtesy of Mr. Sánchez." I glanced at Mr. Sánchez; he was laying out a rack of jalapeños on the broiling pan and couldn't be bothered with accolades.

When the serranos and yellows were done, Mr. Sánchez removed them, but left the yellow onions to cook, adding the *tomatillos*. "Don't overcook *tomatillos*," he said, "they turn to mush."

"As you say," replied Gómez.

Soon the *tomatillos* turned from bright green to pale greenish-brown and Mr. Sánchez quickly scooped them out with a straining spoon. Another ten minutes and the yellow onions were done too. "We're ready," proclaimed Mr. Sánchez.

Gómez rubbed his hands together in anticipation. "At last, the great moment has arrived." He stood up and placed his hand on Mr. Sánchez's shoulder. "So, what's next?"

"We prepare them in the traditional way. I cut each chili by hand, finely. The *tomatillos* are peeled and then smashed in a *molcajete*." He reached into a paper shopping bag on the floor and pulled out a *molcajete*. "The peels are given to the pigs."

"We don't have pigs," I said.

Mr. Sánchez gave me a reproachful look and continued: "The yellow onions are diced, finely, as is the garlic. Everything—the chilies, the *tomatillos*, the onions and the garlic are mixed and set to cool."

"For how long?" I asked.

"Until they stop talking," answered Mr. Sánchez curtly.

I had an urge to say something impolite when Gómez jumped in. "Alex, Mr. Sánchez is right, but there is more. This is one of the things that separates true Mexican salsa from what the gringos make. The salsa has to be cooled down—both literally and figuratively! They've been yanked on and pulled and cut and scalded and diced and then thrown into a pot with total strangers—whoa! That's too much for *anyone* to take without some hard feelings. So, before we add the green onion and cilantro—my, my, how I am looking forward to the taste of fresh cilantro—the whole pot has to cool down to room temperature. Do I have it right, Mr. Sánchez?"

From Mr. Sánchez there was a loud no-reply.

Back in the living room, Tony Gwynn had put the Padres up 7-2, hitting a triple down the right field line and driving home Roberto Alomar. It was looking bad for our boys. In the eighth inning we got one run back and in the ninth we got another, but it was too little, too late. We lost, 7-4.

"Not good," said Gómez, "but no problem! We'll win tonight!"

"Tonight? Is it a double-header?"

"Yep. Sutton vs. Dennis Rasmussen."

"Rasmussen . . . don't know him."

"Big lefthander: good fastball; good curve. Typical pitcher who thinks that talent is all it takes, which is one of the great fallacies of sport. Everywhere teams look for exceptional talent and almost always they're disappointed, because it isn't talent, but brains, that separates players. Of course it takes a certain amount of talent to play the game, but far more important is smarts, and what do the smart guys know? That it takes practice to perfect an art form—any art form, of which baseball is the highest form yet discovered by man."

O.C., who I thought had been napping, burst out laughing. So did I. Mr. Sánchez came out of the kitchen to see what the ruckus was about.

"What?" protested Gómez, palms upturned.

"Ya had me goin' there fer a minute," answered O.C. "The highest art form?" He took off his dirty cap, inspected it briefly, and then pointed to the faded "B." "Baseball?"

Gómez challenged him instantly. "Oh, and have you ever seen DiMaggio glide under a deep fly in the gap? Or Jackie slide into home plate beneath the catcher's tag? That's not art? Are you telling me that Koufax, left arm extended behind his back, right leg suspended in midair, are you saying that isn't beautiful? Did you ever see Marichal pitch? Did you?"

O.C. wasn't intimidated at all. In fact, he was smiling. There was something playful in their posturing, and I suspected that this scene, or one similar, had been acted out many times.

Gómez continued to press the point. "Dance—take dance for instance. Everyone acknowledges dance as an art form, even an illiterate, backwoods dirt farmer like you. But tell me, how is that different from Clemente throwing a perfect strike to home plate? Or Mays catching a fly ball off his rib without even watching the ball go into his mitt? Or Mantle laying down a drag bunt and thundering to first in the most perfect balance of power and speed that has ever graced this planet? I'll tell you how it's different: baseball is *spontaneous art*, that's how. It isn't scripted; there aren't any rehearsals. And that's why I call it the *highest* art form—because it is Man responding to adversity, in the moment, with a grace and beauty that takes our breath away. O.C.! Are you listening to me?"

O.C. had dropped his head, pretending he went back to sleep. At Gómez's question he lifted his head slightly and winked at me beneath the bill of his cap.

"I saw that, dirt farmer."

*****

I went home to check in. My mom and Rosa were gone, but Eddie was in the kitchen rummaging through the fridge. I said hello and he grunted, "Jesus, nothing."

"Let me look. I think there's still some tamales tía brought over." I stepped around Eddie to look inside the refrigerator, but the stench of alcohol repelled me like a force field.

"Jesus, Eddie; you stink."

"Fuck off."

"No, really, you stink bad."

Eddie grabbed me by the shirt. "Somethin' about 'fuck off' you don't understand?"

His eyes were bloodshot, his breath reeked, but what grabbed my attention most were the bruises on his face.

"Eddie—your face!"

He let go of his grip and turned back to the fridge. "You should see the other guy."

I backed up a couple of steps to remove myself from the stench zone. "You okay, Eddie?"

"I'm fine," he answered conversationally. "How are you?"

"Knock if off, Eddie."

He didn't answer, but when he found the tamales he shoved one into his mouth and then grinned at me, chunks of tamale smeared over his front teeth.

"You're disgusting, Eddie."

"Happy to oblige, little brother." He bent over to look inside the fridge again. "Fuck. A million beer-drinking Mexicans in L.A. and what do I get?" He pulled out a bottle of club soda. "Fucking fizzy water."

"So what happened?"

"Initiation." He turned and showed me his right arm. There was a fresh tattoo, the skin swollen and inflamed: the head of a bull, horns curling above the face, flared nostrils pierced with a ring, eyes crazy with battle lust—the tattoo for Los Toros, our local gang. "I'm in. Last night I beat the crap out of some pussy from the Caballeros."

"Hard to tell you won the fight."

Crack! In a flash he slapped me with the back of his hand.

"I don't think I'm gonna be takin' any more crap, Alex; not from you, not from mom, not from anyone. *Comprende?"* Eddie's eyes had the battle lust in them, like the bull tattoo.

"Goddamn it! That hurt!"

"Well, life hurts; there's your first lesson. Class over." He turned and walked out of the kitchen, leaving the refrigerator door wide open.

*****

It was dark when I went back to Gómez's. The TV was on but the sound was off. O.C. was lying in front of it, asleep again. Gómez was in the kitchen; I could hear him speaking to Mr. Sánchez. I sat down.

"The base is extraordinary, Mr. Sánchez."

"It's the garlic. All the ingredients are in perfect measure, but it's the garlic that binds them. Too little garlic—the base is weak. Too much—the other flavors are overwhelmed."

"Well, you've got it just right. Let's add the cilantro and green onion."

"No," answered Mr. Sánchez in that unequivocal tone of his. Usually that tone annoyed me, but not tonight; tonight it felt right. And now as I look back over the years, leafing through the hundreds of people I've known since the days in our little villa, the quality of stating a fact as a fact, without elaboration, without qualification, stands out as my favorite Sánchezism. He wasn't asking for approval and wouldn't have cared if he got it.

"No?" queried Gómez. "But The Party is Saturday!"

Mr. Sánchez didn't reply, probably to give Gómez time to realize how unnecessary it was to state such an obvious fact.

Gómez continued: "Wouldn't it be better to add the cilantro and green onion today?"

"No."

"I see," answered Gómez. There was a pause. "Okay then," followed by another pause. "Well, I'll go check on the ballgame." He turned the corner and saw me. "Alex! What happened?"

I don't know why it is guys are compelled to answer a question like that with "nothin'." Head down, shoulders slumped; if we saw ourselves, we'd realize how stupid we look.

"Nothin'."

Gómez sat down against the opposite wall, legs bent and arms resting on his knees. He didn't speak.

"Eddie," I said.

"Uh-huh," replied Gómez in a way that said *continue.*

"He got pissed off at me."

"Uh-huh."

"I told him he stank so he slapped me in the face."

Gómez didn't reply for a few moments, and then said, "Is there anything more?"

"Yes!" I answered hotly, "Eddie is a fucking prick. He's always been a prick, but now that he's 'Los Toros,' he's a *fucking* prick."

"'Los Toros?'"

"That's the gang he belongs to. He got his initiation last night."

"I see."

Gómez scratched his Hemingway. "Well, the game is going to be starting in a few minutes. Would you turn it on, Alex?"

I turned it on. The Dodgers were taking the field, but Gómez wasn't watching; his eyes were inward and his fingers absently made circles in his beard. There was a commercial break, and when the game returned so did Gómez.

"Well, there's more work to be done." He stood up. "Shall we check on the salsa?"

Mr. Sánchez was rinsing the cilantro. Gómez took a handful and pressed his face into it. "My, how I've missed you." Mr. Sánchez snatched it out of his hands, rinsed it again, patted it dry with a paper towel, and put it in a large baggy. As he did this, he answered Gómez's question from a few minutes before: "The reason is contrast; properly prepared food has contrasts: contrasts in color, contrasts in texture, contrasts in taste. In good salsa, on one side we have the base, which ideally has sat for a couple of days, and on the other side we have the green onion and cilantro—which should be fresh, added just before serving."

"I didn't know that, Mr. Sánchez."

"I know," replied Mr. Sánchez, as he bent down to put the bags of green onion and cilantro into Gómez's refrigerator. "I'll dice everything tomorrow."

"Say Alex, you haven't heard the latest. Carmen knows a guy who'll make the tortillas tomorrow. Can you believe that?" Gómez looked over to O.C. who was still lying on the floor. "Hey O.C.! Can you believe it? Fresh homemade tortillas for our *carne asada*?"

O.C. lazily opened one eye, smiled dreamily, and then let it drop shut.

"Sweet dreams, O.C." Then turning to me: "Alex, Mr. Sánchez's homemade salsa verde, carne asada, fresh tortillas, music, friends . . . ."

"Sounds good," I answered flatly.

Gómez's eyes betrayed his concern about me, but his voice said, "Let's see how our boys are doing."

Leading off the fourth inning was Rick Dempsey, who on the first pitch hit a home run over the right-center field wall. Score tied, 2-2.

"We show up, they score," I said.

"Yep," answered Gómez. "That's because we're lucky. And because we know that luck has to be continually created. The next step—sit on our heads." He placed the back of his head against the wall and threw his legs up. They bounced against the wall and he fell over in a tumble of arms and legs.

Davis hit a soft line-drive to right, which Gwynn caught easily.

"Hrmmph," grunted Gómez. "All right, then watch this: another headstand—" up went the legs, and this time they hit the wall, wobbled for a moment, then settled back down against the wall "—followed by a roly-poly."

Anderson struck out on three pitches. "What the . . . ? Alex, what did he do his first time up?"

"He doubled."

"Well, that explains why the magic didn't work. Anderson already had his quota for the month."

"No excuses, Gómez. You're a fake; a phony; a two-bit carnie hustler, like my mom says."

Gómez raised one eyebrow, but before he could comment O.C. said, "Found ya out already, eh Gómez?"

"Shut up, dirt farmer."

O.C. chuckled to himself. "Alex, yer the winner. It took me a year ta realize Gómez was six pounds a bullshit in a five-pound bag. Ya did it 'n just a coupla months."

"And my mom did it in five minutes."

Gómez arched his eyebrow again and raised a challenging finger towards me, but smiled and let it drop. "That was quite an interrogation she did on O.C. and me; masterfully done. She carved us up into little pieces and never stopped smiling. She would've made an excellent lawyer. So, she's still upset?"

"I think so. She's had that serious look on her face."

"Yes, I remember that face from the first time we met. It's an excellent Serious Face. Few better. O.C., have you seen a better Serious Face?"

O.C. shook his head slowly and gave Gómez a disapproving look. "Señor, do not go where angels fear ta tread."

"Wisely put, O.C. But seriously, a Serious Face, when created with such care and performed to such a high standard, should be appreciated. It is hard to do!"

O.C. and I chuckled softly.

"You laugh? All right then, let's see you do it." He looked at me, then O.C. "Either one of you—come on, let's see a Serious Face!"

We both laughed again and Gómez said, "Just as I thought—you can't! Well then, I'll have to set the example. Here goes . . . ."

He slowly brought his right hand down across his face, and as it passed there appeared a rigid, solid, stony look. He held it for a moment and then raised one eyebrow. That was good, but when he slowly turned his head as if to ignore us, we both burst out laughing. It wasn't exactly my mom, but it was close.

"Still laughing? Okay, O.C., let's see you do better!"

O.C. looked at him impassively, licked his lips slowly, and as he crossed his legs he turned his face from us, sighing "How drrrr-ollll."

Gómez roared. "You don't even know what 'droll' means, dirt farmer!" He threw a floor pillow at him and added, "But that was good, O.C., *very good.*"

"Thankee," answered O.C., tipping his cap. "Now Alex, let's see whatcha got!"

Ignoring them both, I stood up and headed towards the kitchen. As I walked I moved my head slowly from right to left and back, trying to portray my mom's effortless way of showing, well, not disdain exactly—more like disappointment—as if she had dared to hope for more, only to have been let down once again. It was an attitude that easily fit my mood.

Gómez said, "Alex, that was very good! You didn't come in first—I did, and you didn't come in second—O.C. did, but yours was a very strong third!"

"I'll get better."

"Yes, if you study and work it at you might be, well, as good as O.C. one day."

"Ya set the boy's sights too high, Gómez."

*****

I awoke on Friday morning around nine and went to the kitchen for breakfast. Gómez was already there, sitting at the table with Rosa in his lap.

Tía Carmen was next to Gómez, and my mom stood against the counter, her hair in a tight bun, her face expressionless. Her Serious Face was #1 and no one else was even close.

"So," said Gómez, "let's go over this again."

My tía rolled her eyes and said, "*Manita*, I told you we shouldn't bother explaining it to *un hombre estúpido*. It just goes in one ear, rattles around a couple of times, and comes out the other side."

My mom ignored the jest. "Focus, Gómez. Tomorrow around eleven, Peter Piper's Party Palace will be delivering the tables . . . ."

Gómez bent down to Rosa and in an exaggerated manner silently mouthed P-e-t-e-r P-i-p-e-r'-s P-a-r-t-y P-a-l-a-c-e, which Rosa mimicked as she followed Gómez's lips with her saucer eyes, her mouth opening and closing in the same exaggerated manner.

Barely tolerating it, my mom waited until they finished. "There are ten tables and eighty chairs; you need to set them up: two in my yard, four in Mrs. Cortez's, four in Carmen's." She was speaking in a brief, emotionless, business-like way. It reminded me of how she used to speak to my father after they had an argument: saying enough to answer the question, but not so much as to imply all was forgotten.

My mom continued: "Then, string these lights on each patio." She reached into a bag and pulled out a box of white Christmas lights. "Six boxes—one for each house."

Gómez whistled. "Maria, this will look great! Now it really is a Midsummer's Eve party."

My mom said nothing.

"And don't forget the lanterns," added Carmen. "I think about five lanterns on the sidewalk in front of each house—five on each side of the sidewalk, that is, and one on each stair, also on both sides."

"Beautiful," said Gómez. "Is it just one candle in each? Couldn't the wind knock it over?"

"See for yourself," answered my mom, flatly. She went into the living room and reappeared with a shopping bag of small, squat candles. Gómez looked one of them over and juggled it in his hand. "Well, I'll check it out. I could always put in a weight of some kind if there is a problem."

"I'm sure you'll think of something," my mom answered. "Someone as clever as you; after all, you're 'Gómez the god.'"

The icy bitterness in my mom's words stopped all of us and I thought, "Here it comes." Since the day O.C. showed up and disclosed Gómez's past, my mom had been angry, hostile, bitter, resentful and every other synonym for pissed off. With Gómez present, she had hidden her emotions behind a façade of brusque efficiency. That façade was showing its first crack. No one spoke. We watched her, waiting for the crack to widen. She fooled us all.

"But," she continued, "before that you need to set up the dance floor."

"What?" Gómez said, startled. He too had been expecting my mom to cut out his heart as she engaged him in pleasant conversation. It took a couple of seconds for the words to sink in. "We have a dance floor?"

A smile made a brief appearance on my mom's lips, but my tía was grinning ear to ear. "Si señor! We have a dance floor—if you and Mr. Aguilar can go pick it up."

"You bet!" Gómez shifted his eyes around the room. "But where are we going to put it?"

"Sánchez's," answered Carmen.

My mom tilted her head questioningly. "Okay, but where does the *mariachi* band go?"

"*Mariachi* band?!" shot Gómez. "We have a *mariachi* band?"

Finally, my mom's Serious Face softened, if only for a moment. The anticipated effect on Gómez—conceived before O.C. arrived—was exactly as they had hoped. "A *mariachi* band!" he exclaimed again. "I haven't seen one since I was a kid!" He waggled a finger at my mom and said, "Maria, you aren't kidding me now, are you?"

"No. A friend of mine has a brother who—never mind. It's free; can't beat that."

"Wow. Incredible. Nice going, girls!"

"All right, so you'll set up the dance floor," said Carmen, putting the conversation back on track.

"Done!"

The burst of enthusiasm was short-lived, thanks to my mom. This was her show. "Enough chit-chat," she said abruptly to Carmen. "We need to organize." She turned to rinse out her cup. It was our cue to leave.

As I stood, I looked at Carmen. She grabbed me with her eyes and nodded as if to say, "It'll be okay, *mijo*. I'll take care of it."

A Party

At 7 a.m. I awoke to "Sunrise" and jumped out of bed, ready to go. Eddie wasn't home, so let the music play!

On my way through the living room I heard the rattling of pots and pans in the kitchen. I peeked in and there she was: my mom. She had on the old white smock I'd seen her wear a thousand times, a short braid of loose threads hanging off the back hem. On her feet, the slippers with the beaded roses stitched into the tops, about a third of the red and white beads missing.

"Good morning, dear. I thought you'd be up—once I heard that infernal music."

She stepped onto a footstool and, standing on her tiptoes, reached way back into a cabinet, dipping her left shoulder to extend her reach. A strand of black hair came loose. She smiled helplessly.

At that moment she was as beautiful as anyone I'd ever seen, before or since. This was my mom as she really was, the kind of woman that a man would throw himself in front of a speeding car to protect, and be thankful for the honor. I must have been smiling because she blew the hair out of her eyes and said, "*Mijo,* don't laugh at me. I'm stuck!"

I realized then what had happened—she had lifted herself up to get into the cabinet and now her feet were dangling above the stool. I took her by the waist and lowered her to the floor. She pulled me to her chest and hugged me. I began to pull away, but she held the embrace. I felt hot tears on my cheek.

How stupid I'd been. Since my father died I hadn't given one thought to how my mom was doing. Yes, it'd been rough before, but at least it wasn't all on her. Now every bit of it was on her. I felt my throat clench; a surge of emotion nearly burst out before I could push it back.

She squeezed me tight. "I need you, Alex. More than ever I need you."

She squeezed me again, then pulled away and quickly wiped her eyes. She kissed me on the forehead and straightened out her smock. "Can you reach back in there? There's a plastic container in the back—you'll see it. I need it for the beans."

I got it of course; I would've climbed Mount Everest to retrieve it.

*****

When I walked into Gómez's he was dancing to a jazz guitar on his record player. "Alex! Can you believe this guy? Is he the greatest?" He spun away from me with all the grace of an old, blind bil*l*y goat—with arthritis, and club feet.

"Who is it?"

"Yesterday Mr. Sánchez and I were talking about music. He said there was a guitarist he heard when he was a child; he still had the record. All he knew was that the guitarist was a gypsy—not some gypsy-wannabe, but a real gypsy, from France. Just think of it, a gypsy guitarist from France has a record that ends up in a small village in Mexico. And now it finds its way here, on the day of The Party. Incredible! *Django Reinhardt*—you genius son-of-a-gun!"

Mr. Sánchez arrived a little while later, and with Django's jazz guitar still playing, Gómez went right up and wrapped his arms around him.

Mr. Sánchez simply said, "I understand."

Gómez wagged his shaggy head and pointed a finger at Mr. Sánchez. "You, my friend, are like a great book that chapter after chapter continues to surprise. Thank you, señor. Thank you for sharing this priceless music with me."

Mr. Sánchez placed a strong hand on each of Gómez's shoulders and squeezed. "Now, let us begin!"

All morning we heard nothing but Django Reinhardt. Gómez was right; it was music like no other I'd ever heard, and a perfect compliment to our soaring mood. Gómez skated in and out of the house, Mr. Sánchez tapped an inconspicuous foot, and when my mom walked in she realized in a glance that we had all lost our minds. She handed me a stack of pink party advertisements. "Go get Rosa and pass these out in the neighborhood. My only worry is that we won't have enough people come."

An hour later, as we walked back up the stairs, the reality of The Party sank in. Tables covered in white paper cloths were scattered among the various yards, eight chairs neatly tucked into each one; the Christmas lights were up, although unlit; the dance floor was being cleaned by Mrs. Sánchez; and Mr. Aguilar's oil drum barbecue was on our patio, just as it had been for my father's Memorial so long ago. The villa was quite a sight. Gómez saw me and hollered to come up.

"Can you believe it, a doubleheader on our Party day? And not just a doubleheader: Hershiser and Valenzuela!"

"Geez!" I answered. "Who's pitching first?"

"Hershiser, but unfortunately we won't have much time to watch it. At least—" he winked, "we don't want to be *caught* watching it; not with the girls running around!"

"Well, I'll just drop in now and then to see how it's going. How's the salsa coming along?"

"I wish I knew," answered Gómez, forlornly. "Mr. Sánchez has vowed to do terrible things to me if I come into the kitchen again."

I was sweeping the walkway on the middle landing when Carmen passed me carrying two large grocery bags. "Move over for the tortilla lady!" I stepped aside and she passed into my house without another word.

Suddenly I heard a whoop from Gómez's house, followed by "Alex!" I ran up and there was Gómez standing in front of the TV with his hands against his lower back, palms in as always. Stubbs was in the dugout getting High-Fives from his teammates. "He just hit a two-run homer! Now Kirk's up."

On the second pitch, Gibson hit a line drive that went right into the Padre bullpen—another home run. "Damn, that was faster than a speeding bullet! Son, I think we should sit down; the Boys may not be done yet!" Mike Marshall was next up and he hit one into the left-center gap for a triple. Then Shelby hit a line drive to left—another hit and another run. The next batter was Hamilton, who hit a bullet right to Flannery at third for the final out.

With the inning over, I went to check on the girls and it was like going from zero to sixty in a second. The stove was full of steaming pots, and sweat beaded my mom's face as she moved from one to another, stirring the contents. My tía was wrapping plastic forks and knives in paper napkins while she earnestly made a point with my mom. Not pausing for a moment, my mom turned and wiped a strand of lank hair from her eyes with the back of her hand and said, "I'll admit he's the nicest convict I've ever met; he's also the *only* convict I've ever met."

Carmen was about to reply when she saw me in the doorway. "*Mijo!* Come here! It's time for your tía to show you something every man needs to know."

I backed slowly out of the kitchen and just as I began my dash for the door, my tía raced up and tackled me on the carpet. I flailed my arms and legs as we rolled. Carmen laughed, "No you don't! What's this—running away from your tía?!"

She rolled me on my back and pinned my arms with her knees. I was looking right up at her heaving breasts when a sudden warm feeling swept over me. I got a narrow look from my tía. Damn! It was as though she could see the thoughts parade across my forehead.

"You're too young to be thinking that, *mijo.* But you aren't too young to save your tía from the most boring job of her life!" She pulled me to my feet. "Now march into that kitchen and I may just forget what was going on in that little man's head of yours."

Carmen might forget, but I never would. I followed her into the kitchen and took her place at the table. I may have prepared ten of those little utensils packets, or I may have prepared two hundred. Time passes fast when your mind is focused on large, heaving breasts. When I finished I climbed out of my thoughts and looked up. Carmen and my mom were leaning against the counter, arms folded, looking at me with amused looks on their faces.

"Not funny, tía." I stood up to leave.

"*I* think it's funny, *mijo,*" answered Carmen conversationally. "Sister, do you think it's funny?"

"Not funny, *manita*—adorable. My Alex is adorable." This had gone beyond any boy's tolerance and I hastily excused myself.

When I returned to Gómez's, the Dodgers were leading the Padres 11-1. Gómez and O.C. were sprawled out in front of the TV and Gómez hailed me as I walked in. "Alex! Where were you?"

"Stuck." I sat down between them.

"Do you know what's happened since you left? The Allied Invasion of Normandy; Sherman's March to the Sea. We're pounding the Padres into brick dust! We have eleven runs, thirteen hits, four home runs and two steals. What a game! And this is only the first one!"

Mr. Sánchez walked into the living room carrying a tray. "Señors, may I present the fruits of our labor—'Salsa Gómez'!" On the tray was a bowl half-filled with salsa, another bowl full of corn chips, and a plate filled with cut-up celery stalks.

"Oh my," said Gómez as he leaned forward. "'Salsa Gómez'? No señor, 'Salsa Sánchez.'"

"Although the recipe is mine," replied Mr. Sánchez, "the inspiration was all yours."

"Gracias, señor," acknowledged Gómez. He grabbed a chip and scooped up a large helping of the salsa, lime green with dark strands of cilantro. We all watched as he ushered the chip into his mouth. He closed his eyes and worked his jaws slowly. Then he hugged himself and laid down on his back, his eyes still closed. "Ahhhhh."

O.C. and I reached for a chip and Mr. Sánchez picked up a celery stalk—I guess they were for him. I filled a chip with salsa. Crunch, crunch, crunch—"It's kind a hot."

Gómez laughed. "That's because you've been living among the gringos too long!"

O.C. was already reaching for his second chip and in a swish had it filled with salsa and plopped into his mouth. "Don't worry, Alex," he said as he munched, "once the first layer of yer tongue burns off ya won't even notice it."

As Gómez was reaching for his second helping, Mr. Sánchez hadn't even dipped yet. Instead, he watched our reactions. When Gómez had devoured his second helping and O.C. had already prepared his third, Mr. Sánchez asked, "Too hot?"

"Not on your life!" answered Gómez. "It's perfect. Damn, that's good salsa. My taste buds are in a frenzy!" Mr. Sánchez looked at O.C. expectantly. "Sánchez," O.C. said gravely, "it makes me wish I was Mexican."

Apparently, this was the acknowledgment Mr. Sánchez had been waiting for. He nodded gravely and dipped. "Try it with celery and taste it in its purity."

"You bet!" answered Gómez. "I'll dip a carrot if it means getting more of this salsa!"

The little plate of celery disappeared under the fast hands of Gómez and O.C., and well-pleased, Mr. Sánchez disappeared back into the kitchen. In a minute he returned with another tray full of goodies—this time his "Grilled Jalapeño Salsa," forever after known as "Salsa Sánchez," accompanied by a plate of small sausages speared with toothpicks. Gómez and O.C. rubbed their hands greedily and dug in. I tried one too and it *was* good. It was milder than the "Salsa Gómez," which suited me, though I wouldn't let the boys know.

The Dodgers finished pounding the Padres, 12-2, with Hershiser throwing a complete game, but we had little time to revel in the victory. The screen door whipped open and there was Carmen. She swept the room in one quick glance, found her targets, and opened fire. "Just as I thought! Stretched out like a bunch of drunks! If you boys think Maria and I are going to cater this party all by ourselves while you sit on your asses, guess again!"

I looked over at Gómez, who stared up at Carmen in wondrous admiration. "Carmen," started Gómez, "you are the most . . . ."

"Shove it, sailor!" shot back Carmen. "Now get off your brains and march down to Maria's. If you can't find enough work to keep you out of trouble, we'll help." She extended her right arm towards the door. "Now *march*!"

Carmen passed us on the stairs and met us in the kitchen. My mom and Carmen appeared to be laughing, but when Carmen saw us shuffle in, her face changed; the laughing face disappeared so fast I wasn't really sure it had ever been. In its place was the very picture of wrath, with piercing eyes searching us for the smallest excuse to strip the hide from our backs. My mom, however, wasn't as quick as Carmen and had to disguise her laughter by covering her still-smiling lips with her hand, although her eyes continued to giggle as Carmen began her harangue.

"Maria, what did I tell you? Have you ever seen three more guilty men in your life?"

The three of us, lined up in front of the girls like police suspects, glanced at each other. None of us spoke, but it seemed like we all shared the same thought: "Yup, we *do* look guilty."

"So Maria, what should we do with these characters?"

"Well, I'm still worried we won't have enough people come. I'd sure like to pass out more fliers."

"No mom! I did that all morning!"

Gómez put his arm out and pushed me back as if he were trying to protect me from Carmen. "Not now, son," he whispered sideways. He stepped forward and said, "Maria, that's a very good idea. On behalf of myself and the boys, let me say that it would be a pleasure to be of any help we can, and if you want fliers passed out, then that's what we'll do. Right, boys?"

O.C. looked as thrilled about it as I was.

"Good," said Carmen. She handed Gómez a stack of pink fliers. "Maria, where would you like them passed out?"

"Just around the neighborhood—and the park."

"Very well. You heard her, boys. Now scat before you make me mad. And be back here by four. That's one hour!"

As we walked out the door, I again heard laughter from the kitchen, immediately followed by Gómez's own, "Ooooh-weee! Alex, that tía of yours could skin a man with just one glance—and devour him in the next! What a beauty she is, eh, O.C.?"

But O.C. didn't look like he was quite up to laughing; not now, maybe not ever. Gómez patted him on the back. "It's okay, O.C. You're not back in prison. It just looked that way for a minute!"

We passed out a few fliers on our way to the park, but once there we found a nice shady spot beneath a large elm tree and sat down. After just a few minutes, O.C. expressed the guilt that I also was beginning to feel. "It don't seem right, us restin' in the shade but Sánchez 'n the girls workin'."

Gómez stretched his legs and put his hands behind his head. "When the hunting is over, it is only natural for the men folk to repose for a little while. That's the way it's been since time immemorial." Gómez paused to yawn, then continued: "And I see no reason to change now. Do you, Alex?"

"I guess not," I answered, twirling a blade of grass in my mouth.

"Besides," continued Gómez, "why should we be penalized for getting our work done already? Haven't we been working in The Garden every day for months?"

"Well, that's true," I answered.

"Last minute work is for people who wait to the last minute. That's what I call an irrefutable fact."

"And that," chimed in O.C., "is what I call a ten-dollar word if I ever heard one: ire . . . fyoo . . . somethin'. Damn impressive, Gómez."

"Words are drawn to the truth, O.C., like bears to honey."

"Or flies ta bullshit," answered O.C., giving me a wink.

"Bullshit?" Gómez dropped his arms and pointed an accusative finger at O.C. "Well, a dirt farmer like you *would* know a lot about bullshit, I suppose."

"Better shut yer mouth 'fore the flies start ta gather."

"You piece of cow-dung!"

"Buzzzzz . . . here they come!"

"Why you . . . !" Gómez grabbed O.C. and rolled him over and over on the ground. "You boil on a bull's ass! You obstinate Okie! Cantankerous con!" Gómez now had O.C. in a headlock and was rubbing O.C.'s head with his balled fist. "I'll rub the last bit of hair off your blighted head before I take any more sass from the likes of you!"

I was laughing so hard it hurt, and O.C., having passed beyond laughter, was slapping his hands and feet on the ground as if he were drowning. Gómez paused to gather his breath and then started a cough that lasted five minutes. O.C. crawled over to me and leaned back up against the tree while we waited for Gómez to regain his breath.

"Excuse me, boys," Gómez finally gasped as he fell onto his back. "Whew! Almost lost a lung there!"

"Yer lucky," O.C. said. "The last man who spoke ta me like that came off much worse."

Suddenly I remembered the Dodgers. "Hey, we forgot about the game! It's probably already started!"

Gómez sat up on his elbows. "Well, we better head back then; our work is done."

O.C. looked at me and shook his head. "I guess so. Whattaya think we should do with these?" Each of us still had a stack of fliers an inch thick.

"Well," said Gómez, getting onto his feet, "I think they gave us too many. To leave them here would be littering. Therefore, the right thing to do is to throw yours in the trash, O.C., and yours, Alex, and we'll pass out the rest of mine on the way back."

Gómez did manage to pass out a few fliers on the way back and had only a small handful left when he ascended the stairs of our villa. I'm sure each of us hoped to get up the stairs without being seen by my mom or Carmen—particularly Carmen—but our luck didn't even last to the first landing. Standing on our patio next to the oil drum barbecue was my formidable tía, her arms folded across her never-far-from-my-thoughts chest, a look of reproach already on her face.

She tilted her head down and lifted an eyebrow.

"I passed out most of mine, Carmen," answered Gómez in a cheerful tone. "But these two threw most of theirs into the garbage."

O.C. and I looked at Gómez dumbfounded.

"See, Carmen," Gómez said, pointing to us. "Have you ever seen two more guilty men in your life? Look at those faces!"

Carmen gave Gómez a skeptical look, who, undeterred, merrily strolled down our pathway. "Here you go. I wasn't able to pass out all of them, but I made a pretty good dent."

Carmen accepted the few remaining fliers and looked over at me. I was stunned by Gómez's actions, and Carmen saw it on my face. I looked at O.C.—his jaw was as slack as mine. My tía smiled. "Señor, you amuse Carmen. It pleases me to find a kindred spirit."

"Señorita?" Gómez asked innocently. "I'm sorry, I'm not sure I understand."

"I'm sure," replied Carmen. She put her hands around his cheeks and drew his face to hers. "You've been a good little boy Gómez, passing out all those fliers by yourself. Now you boys go clean up; it's almost party time."

As Gómez walked back to the central walkway, he stepped off our path to circumvent us, which was a smart move, because O.C. tried to kick him in the butt even though he was out of reach. Gómez reacted as if he really *had* been kicked, and then quickly scooted down the walkway like a beaten dog. "You missed, dirt farmer!" he yelled as he bounded up the stairs. O.C. followed, yelling as he ran, "I won't miss next time, Gómez the Liar!"

After they passed onto Gómez's landing I looked at my tía; she twirled her right hand in a tight circle near her right ear and mouthed the word "Loco."

After checking in with my mom, I went to Gómez's; O.C. was in his room and Gómez was in the shower. I joined Mr. Sánchez in the kitchen, which was entirely clean. The only evidence of his labors was two large plastic containers filled with "Salsa Gómez" and "Salsa Sánchez."

"You're done!" I said.

"Of course."

"And you've cleaned up, too!"

He didn't reply, it being too foolish a statement to expend any effort acknowledging. He reached into the refrigerator, and pulling out another container of salsa, said, "Alex, here is your own personal 'Salsa Gómez'; it's milder than the first batch. Please, try it and tell me if I got it right."

He put the container on the counter, poured some Wampums into a small bowl and handed the bowl to me. It was delicious, and this time my attention wasn't diverted from the wonderful taste by the raging fire in my mouth. "Mr. Sánchez, that's perfect."

He smiled. "This is your private salsa. I wrote your name on it—not that this would discourage a couple of rascals such as live in this house."

Gómez walked in, still drying his silver hair with a bath towel.

"Hello, traitor," I said.

"Did you hear that, O.C.?" Gómez yelled. "Alex says he forgives me."

"I'll forgive ya too," replied O.C. on his way to the bathroom, "after I get my revenge."

Gómez shook his head sadly. "He's still just a child." Then, turning to Mr. Sánchez, Gómez said reverently, "My, my, Mr. Sánchez, you did it."

Mr. Sánchez bowed. "Now, gentlemen, if you'll excuse me, I'd like to go home and take a short nap before The Party begins."

Gómez sat down in front of the TV and flipped on the Dodger game. The score flashed on the screen—we were already down 3-0. "Damn!"

"It's early, Gómez. We've got plenty of time."

"It's not that," answered Gómez. "I still need to put out the lanterns." He pulled himself off the floor and yelled, "O.C.!"

O.C. came ambling out of the bathroom. "Yes, master?"

"O.C., I'm glad you figured that out. Help me with the lanterns."

The three of us went down to my house to gather up our lantern supplies. The house was surprisingly quiet. We walked into the kitchen—no one there. On the table was a mountain of food containers. My mom walked in, her hair still wet from the shower. She was wearing a sleeveless summer dress, yellow with a faint white pattern in the fabric. O.C. let out a whistle, and then turned bright red.

"Sorry, ma'am." He dropped his head.

Gómez exhaled. "Hello, Maria." It was a simple statement, so unaffected that we all looked at Gómez, expecting something more. After a long pause, my mom answered in kind.

"We need to do the lanterns," Gómez said, explaining his presence.

"The lunch bags are over here." She walked around the kitchen table, bent down and picked up a bag. "And the candles are over there, in front of the pantry."

Outside, O.C. and I divided the bags and candles between us, and then starting at the bottom of the stairs we worked our way up—O.C. on the left, me on the right, Gómez trailing behind, zigzagging across the sidewalk and lighting candles almost as fast as we put them down. In no time at all we were done.

Gómez looked back down the stairs. "Well boys, it's almost party time."

*****

At around 6:30 I walked out of our house. On our patio, Mr. Aguilar had the charcoal flaming in the oil drum barbecue. The food table was filled with food, including two large bowls of salsa. To the side of the table was an old four-legged bathtub filled with ice and beer and soft drinks. "Nice touch on the drinks, eh?" said Mr. Aguilar.

"Yes. Where did it come from?"

"Mrs. Cortez. It's hers."

"Geez," I answered. "I hope someone rinsed it out first."

"You kidding? I scrubbed it with bleach—twice. That tub's *never* been this clean!"

People were already starting to arrive—relatives mostly: the same people who came to my father's Memorial. I saw my Tío Julio and Tía Estella ascend the stairs and beeline into our house to claim their chairs. Already, there were probably thirty people at The Party.

I was helping Mr. Aguilar with the tortillas, piling them into clay tortilla warmers as fast as he could pull them off the grill, when I heard someone yell, "Olé!"

I turned around and saw the *mariachi* band coming up the stairs. One of the members had a guitar, one a violin and the third a trumpet. I had seen *músicos de mariachi* before, but never so young—at the most they were in their early twenties, and as lean and graceful as bullfighters. Each wore a tapered black coat; tight embroidered pants from which hung a red sash; a white dress shirt, open at the neck; a red scarf and a black sombrero. It was easy to guess where all the young girls would be tonight.

My mom came out of the house to check on things. Wow, she looked great. She had changed into her party dress: a traditional white cotton dress with red, green and blue embroidery. Her shiny black hair was folded up and pinned in back; from her ears hung modest gold rings; on her neck was a modest gold cross; on her feet were modest black flats. In a word, she looked attractive and modest. That's my mom.

Carmen soon arrived and she was dressed very much like my mom, minus the modesty. The cotton dress was cut low, showing her endowment—just what I didn't need to see. Whereas the tapered waist looked "sharp" on my mom, on Carmen it emphasized her sexuality almost beyond endurance. From her ears hung huge gold loops, and drawing attention to the cleavage of her breasts was a gold, "Y" shaped necklace that flowed down her brown skin. Her hair cascaded over her exposed shoulders in shiny amber waves. On her arms were perhaps a dozen thin gold bracelets. I'd tell you what she had on her feet, but my eyes never made it that far down. She could've been barefoot and nobody would've noticed. Yeow.

"Well, look at that!"

I followed Mr. Aguilar's eyes up the stairs. At the top, arm in arm, Mr. and Mrs. Sánchez began their descent. They were a vision: a royal couple at the Royal Ball. Mr. Sánchez was dressed in a, well . . . you're not going to believe this—a Zoot suit! Even now, all these years later, I can see exactly what he wore, pulling from memory details as precise as a photograph; but at the time my first impression contained no details—there was only the impact of style, class, and of course, red.

That's right—red; both the jacket and the pants—red. The unbuttoned jacket had wide shoulders and wide lapels and reached to his knees. He had on a black shirt, thin white suspenders, and a tie that had long, wavy, vertical lines of red, black and white—absolutely stunning. The high-waisted baggy pants tapered narrowly at his ankles. Around his waist was a thin black belt, and dangling from a belt loop were two gold watch chains that looped down to his right calf and back up to his right pocket. His shoes were two-toned—red along the sides, white above the toes. To top it off he wore a black Zoot hat with a broad, red band, from which arched a long white feather. The overall impression was so striking that I staggered back from the impact. Then I saw Mrs. Sánchez.

Well, it must have been Mrs. Sánchez because she was walking with Mr. Sánchez, but there was little about this woman that reminded me of Mrs. Sánchez. This woman was a queen.

I'll begin with what first captured my attention: her long elegant neck and the bare skin of her shoulders. Her dress was white satin and lace, open at the top, skirting the breast line. A delicate, intricately carved silver necklace hung from her neck. Small, white, cap sleeves rested slightly off-shoulder. A red sash highlighted her tapered waist and flowed into the full skirt that extended to her mid-calf. On her feet were red satin heels. The overall effect was remarkable, summarized in one word: class.

Mr. and Mrs. Sánchez moved with such grace and elegance that I wondered who these people *really* were. Simple peasants from the mountains of Mexico no longer seemed possible. When they reached the bottom of the second landing, they continued to our pathway and turned towards my house. I looked behind me and there was my mom and my tía, standing on the patio beside Mr. Aguilar, as awed as I was.

The Sánchezes stopped in front of my mom, whereupon Mr. Sánchez bowed gracefully and said, "Mrs. Morales, may I present my wife." Mrs. Sánchez curtseyed and nodded slightly.

"Mr. and Mrs. Sánchez, it is a pleasure."

The Sánchezes then turned, took two steps, and presented themselves to Carmen. I walked behind the barbecue so I could watch. Mr. Sánchez once again bowed and said, "Señorita, may I present my wife." There was no boyish blushing in Mr. Sánchez's face. The King of Spain could not have looked more at ease. My tía nodded. Then Mrs. Sánchez curtseyed, and as she did so, even the graceful way she lowered her eyelids enthralled.

The same ceremony occurred in front of Mr. Aguilar, and then, to my utter shock they presented themselves to me!

When the Sánchezes had completed their introductions, my mom stepped forward and asked Mr. Aguilar to begin cooking. She then guided the Sánchezes to two chairs and said, "Please, won't you be seated? I'd like you to be first when dinner is served."

Mr. Aguilar tossed long strips of *carne* onto the grill, and the sizzling sound of roasting meat was like music. I was starving! Suddenly the sound of *mariachi* music began: *"Cuándo Vayas a Mi Tumba"* as I found out later, and as if on cue I saw Gómez at the top of the stairs, dressed in solid white.

Suit coat, white; trousers, white; Panama hat, white with red band; boots, white. He even had a white cane in his right hand. Everything white except the hat band, a red handkerchief in his jacket pocket, and the red scarf tied around his neck.

Behind Gómez, as if to provide comic relief, came O.C. He was dressed simply: white cowboy shirt with black piping on the pockets; clean and pressed blue jeans; a belt with a large silver buckle; black cowboy hat and black cowboy boots. The rather plain backdrop served to emphasize the most pronounced thing about O.C., his gap-toothed smile. He took off his hat and waved it to the crowd below. Cries of "*Olé!*" and "*Bravo*!" greeted the gesture. Even Gómez got into it, turning to his friend and extending his right arm up to O.C. as if he were presenting him to the crowd. The *músicos* finished their number with a rousing flourish just as O.C. took his first step down the stairs.

When Gómez and O.C. reached our house, they walked up to my mom and bowed. Then they proceeded to Carmen, who curtseyed like a schoolgirl, and then to Mr. and Mrs. Sánchez, where the introductions were performed with a solemnity matched only in the courts of Europe. Finally, they came to me. O.C. pulled out a white handkerchief and spread it on the ground in front of Gómez, who knelt down and placed his left knee on it. "My friend, my 'fortuitous friend' as I once called you, at the beginning it was you and me. Come," he said, beckoning me with open arms.

Tears welled in my eyes, and to cover it up I nearly jumped into Gómez's arms. I don't know what hit me, but it was completely unexpected. Gómez pulled me from his shoulder, looked into my eyes, and kissed me on each cheek. O.C. tousled my hair and said, "Spud." I looked at my mom; she was wiping her eyes with the back of her hand.

Gómez stood up and addressed the crowd, which had swollen to probably seventy people. "Ladies and Gentlemen, welcome to our *Midsummer's Eve Party*! On behalf of Mrs. Maria Morales, Miss Carmen Salazar, Mr. and Mrs. Humberto Sánchez, Mr. O.C. Martin, Mr. Roberto Aguilar, Mrs. Estella Cortez, Mr. Alex Morales, and myself: Eat! Drink! Dance!" Then turning to Mr. Aguilar he said, "Bring on the tacos!"

Mr. Aguilar speared several browned strips of *carne asada* and dropped them onto a large serving plate held by my sister Rosa, who in turn handed it over to my cousin Mariano, who had been drafted to slice the meat into bite-size pieces. Soon there would be a never-ending supply of *carne asada.*

Gómez, O.C., and I leaned against the retaining wall, to the left of Mr. and Mrs. Sánchez and close to Mr. Aguilar and the barbecue. We were chatting and sipping our drinks, Gómez and O.C. with their Corona's, me with a bottle of orange soda, when Rosa appeared before Mr. and Mrs. Sánchez and placed a TV tray in front of each of them. Mr. Sánchez tilted his head back at Gómez, who shrugged. A moment later Rosa presented to Mr. Sánchez a plate piled high with *carne asada* tacos.

"Wait," she said, dashing away and reappearing with a small stone bowl filled with "Salsa Gómez."

Mr. Sánchez whispered to Rosa, who ran up to Gómez's house to get my personal salsa container. In a minute she returned, and Mr. Sánchez prepared a taco for me, then ladled "Salsa Gómez" on four tacos, handing one to Mrs. Sánchez, one to Gómez, one to O.C., and keeping one for himself. Raising his taco to us he said, "Salud!" We in turn raised our tacos in a toast to health and happiness.

Each of us sighed with contentment as we savored our first bites, and for the next half-hour we found more and more ways to describe the unparalleled flavor of our salsa. Meanwhile, the *mariachis* played, the sun flickered out as day gave way to twilight, and Rosa, serving as our personal hostess, refilled our plates. When she appeared in front of Gómez, he said, "Thank you, Rosa, and I say, you look beautiful today." Rosa curtseyed and then leaned up to Gómez's ear and said rather loudly, "I know." Gómez laughed out loud.

Mr. Aguilar broke away from his duties and approached us. "My friends!" he said, wiping his forehead with his forearm, "are you contented?"

"Si! Si! Muy contento!" answered Mr. Sánchez.

Gómez beckoned Mr. Aguilar. "My dear Rosa has been catering to us like we are under her personal care."

Mr. Aguilar smiled conspiratorially. "Si señor," he said, nodding towards my house, "on orders of management."

"Comprendo," answered Gómez.

My mom burst through the doorway carrying a large pot of Spanish rice. Her cheeks were flushed and strands of wet hair were pasted against her forehead. She was a woman on a mission. There was something about my mom that inspired admiration. It wasn't that she was beautiful, though she was; and it wasn't that she was smart or witty or funny, although she was all these things, too. She had a quality that wasn't easily definable, possibly because no one quality stood out from the others. Rather, my mom was like a composition of qualities, arranged in such a harmonious and pleasing way as to declare, "This is beauty." I looked at Gómez. He too was looking at my mom, admiration in his eyes.

Dusk had settled and the lanterns on the walkway were starting to glow, as were the little white Christmas lights strung along the patio. We probably had well over one hundred guests now, and my mom had long since begun whipping up another batch of beans and rice, "just in case." My Tío Julio, against his wishes, and on condition that we reserve his chair, was dispatched to a *carnicería* to pick up more *carne* and tortillas—again, just in case. God forbid that a guest should come back for a third helping and walk away with an empty plate. "Not in my world," as Gómez would say.

Hot grilled *carne* on a warm, homemade corn tortilla and seasoned only with fresh salsa, together with helpings of Spanish rice and fresh frijoles sprinkled with *queso*—damn. Every bite was bliss.

Our guests seemed to be pleased as well. There was a constant line at the food table, next to which Mr. Aguilar flipped *carne* from the bowl to the grill to the serving plate with the speed and flourish of a symphony conductor, timing his movements to the rhythm of the *mariachis*, who were playing *"El Mariachi Loco."*

Apparently, the word had gotten out about the salsa. Many of the guests, particularly the older men, would toast us as they ladled the salsa onto their plate. *"¡Esta salsa es la mejor!"* was repeated many times, and we consumed each compliment with the same relish as our tacos.

Gómez had once mentioned that only two things concerned him about The Party: running out of beer and the police; but neither proved a problem.

Concerning beer, it turned out that many guests brought their own six packs, and by the end of the night we actually had some beer left over.

Regarding the police, well, a patrol car arrived a little before nine and two large, serious officers ascended the stairs to the second landing. The irresistible Carmen Salazar greeted them and escorted them to the food table, personally preparing their plates and chatting and laughing and dazzling them all the while. When they had finished their second helping, they too appeared in front of us to express their compliments for the finest *carne asada* they had ever eaten. As they descended the stairs, O.C. pushed his chair back and let out a howl.

We had eaten until we could eat no more, and we had almost begun to run out of superlatives to describe such a fine feast, when the *mariachis* struck a chord and Gómez yelled *"Una Aventura!"* He jumped up and exclaimed, "Señor Sánchez, it is time to dance, no?"

Mr. Sánchez nodded in his solemn way, then stood in front of Mrs. Sánchez and requested her hand. She granted it and they walked to the stairs and up to the dance floor. Until then no one had been dancing; there were only small children gyrating about. All that changed when Mr. and Mrs. Sánchez took the floor. They met in the center, arms extended, hands clasped, and then suddenly they were gliding with a speed and grace that stunned us.

Sometimes they danced arm in arm, sometimes Mr. Sánchez sent his Isabella to the other side of the floor, whereupon she would entice him to join her, coyly baiting him, first reaching then withdrawing, while he stamped his feet like a tethered bull. In his red Zoot suit he was a dancing flame, and against the dark blue sky she moved like quicksilver. The audience was enthralled and the three of us hooted and hollered and whistled and howled. It was the most evocative thing I'd ever seen, but as it turned out, the night was young!

When the dance ended they were standing back to back, arms outflung, heads arched towards each other. The crowd exploded in applause. The Sánchezes bowed, and when the *mariachi* band struck up *"Lampara Sin Luz,"* they beckoned the crowd to join them. Many couples did; but I didn't even entertain the thought, and I don't think O.C. did either. Gómez though was like a revving car engine.

Now the curtain of night was fully drawn and all that illuminated us were the paper lanterns, the Christmas lights and the bare bulbs on our porches. The Sánchezes glided in and out of the growing crowd of dancers as the *mariachis* played one favorite after the next: *"Cu Cu Ru Cu Cu Paloma," "El Sinaloense"* and *"El Ausente."* In the middle of *"El Ausente"* my tía arrived, scanned the crowd for a worthy partner, and grabbed Gómez. Without slowing down or missing a step, the Sánchezes welcomed Gómez and Carmen with a flourish of their arms.

Once Carmen began to dance there were slack jaws all around. One understanding spouse gently pushed her husband's jaw closed with her forefinger, but when she removed her finger his jaw just fell open again. It was impossible to resist the charms of my tía. There was something unabashedly sexual about Carmen that bypassed social convention and struck directly at whatever it is that makes a man a man.

And Gómez? Was he even there? For most people observing them dance—no, he was just a nondescript fellow following Carmen like a pale beam of moonlight. But O.C. and I noticed, and although Gómez wasn't a graceful dancer—he wasn't a Mr. Sánchez, for instance—what he lacked in talent he made up for in enthusiasm. He was half-way through his second dance with Carmen when the first of Carmen's admirers tapped him on the shoulder. When he came off the floor, he dropped his body into the nearest chair like a sack of potatoes. O.C. and I went over to tease him.

"Whew," he said weakly. "That Carmen, she wore me out."

"After one dance?" countered O.C. playfully.

"One dance with Carmen, O.C." Gómez paused to catch his breath: "Big difference."

"I'll give ya that," answered O.C. I pulled up two more chairs and we joined Gómez outside the ring of guests. Sometimes a gap would open and we would see a brief flash of color as a dancer glided across the floor. Carmen we saw many times, seemingly each time with a new man in tow. The

Sánchezes we also saw many times; they hadn't stopped since the dancing began.

When the *músicos* struck up *"Esclavo y Amo,"* the Sánchezes did the tango while the crowd formed a circle around them and clapped to the beat. We couldn't miss this, so we walked over to the dance floor and edged ourselves in for a look. Mr. Sánchez was a man transformed. I could see the young Humberto Sánchez "walking the pond" on late summer nights, the southern stars wheeling overhead. And Mrs. Sánchez—in her youth how the heads must have turned!

When the song concluded, the crowd cheered and whistled, and with hardly a pause, the mariachis launched into *"Viva El Mariachi."* I saw Carmen approach Mrs. Sánchez, and when Mrs. Sánchez turned towards us she had the stem of a red rose clamped in her teeth. *"Brava!"* yelled Gómez! *"Brava!"*

My mom appeared by my side, between Gómez and me. As the Sánchezes glided by, Mr. Sánchez waved to my mom with a flourish of his arm, and somehow it seemed that Mrs. Sánchez had actually stopped and curtseyed, but that might have been an illusion. In any event, my mom's face had an angelic glow to it, as if she were witnessing the most magnificent thing she'd ever seen. When it was over, she leaned against me and whispered, "It takes my breath away."

The *mariachis* quickly began the next song, *"La Negra,"* and the dance floor swelled with dancers. I saw my Tío Julio swept towards us by a wave of dancers—he had given up his chair! When he reached us, he grabbed my mom's arm and pulled her into the mass of bodies. I don't think she resisted very much. I looked at Gómez; he too was watching my mom.

When *"La Negra"* was over, the *mariachis* changed the tempo of the night, choosing for their first ballad *"Entrega Total."* Many of the dancers stepped off the stage to catch their breath, including my mom. However, Gómez suddenly stood up and intercepted her, leading her back onto the floor.

"'Bout time," I heard O.C. mutter.

They danced, at first my mom's head resting on Gómez's shoulder, then pulling back to acknowledge something Gómez said, then a smile, a word, and back to his shoulder. I saw my tía in the arms of one of her admirers, but her eyes were not on her partner, they were on my mom.

The slow dances continued one after the next. Once, during *"Amor Eterno,"* a guest tapped Gómez on the shoulder. Gómez whispered something to my mom; she lifted her head, shook it slightly—causing the hairpin to slip out and her hair to fall free—and put it back into that comfortable spot on his shoulder. Alone on the dance floor and uncertain what to do, the interloper lifted his eyebrows and looked around. Suddenly my tía took his hand and inserted herself into his arms. A broad smile appeared on the man's face. He said something to Carmen and she threw her head back, laughing.

It was probably after eleven and for the first time I began to think of The Party ending. A moment later it did—when Eddie arrived with his band of desperadoes.

In my memory, Eddie's appearance is a still photograph. I can see the *mariachis* behind my mom and Gómez, the horn player with his eyes closed and his cheeks distended, oblivious to the monster that has stepped out of the night. The other two *músicos* do see Eddie, but their eyes don't yet register the message of fear that their minds will soon convey. Gómez's back is turned to Eddie, but my mom, her head resting on Gómez's shoulder, sees him, and in her eyes there is complete recognition—of Eddie, and what his appearance portends.

Eddie's voice sliced through the night like a machete. *"Hola, caballero!"*

Gómez turned.

"Good choice," Eddie said appreciatively, pointing a bottle of Corona towards our mom.

"Eddie," Gómez acknowledged.

"But señor," Eddie said, advancing on the stage, "I don't recall giving you permission to dance with my *madre.*" He turned to his hoodlum friends. "Did I say anything to you, Esteban?" A wicked grin spread across his pal's face. "Pedrito?" he said to another *cholo*. "Y tu, Bobby? Do you recall me giving this *pícaro* permission to fuck my mother?"

"Eddie!" my mom barked.

"No, Señor Gómez, the man with no last name," continued Eddie calmly, "I don't recall giving you permission; but I do recall telling you that this is *my* kingdom, these are *my* people. Do you not remember this, *viejo?*"

"I remember very well, Eddie," answered Gómez. He was now standing beside my mom, his hat in his right hand, my mother's wrist in his left.

"Ahh, I see," said Eddie, nodding his head excessively. He lifted his beer and took a long pull, belched and laughed. "I see! So it's a matter of respect. *¿No tienes consideración por el hombre de la casa?*"

"I intended no disrespect. Your mother is an honorable woman; nothing has happened here that would compromise her reputation."

Rage twisted Eddie's face. "I've had enough of your crap. Gómez the bullshitter! That's what I'll call you!" Eddie and the *cholos* saluted each other with their Coronas and then Eddie turned and threw his bottle across Gómez's yard. It shattered against his front door.

As I swung my eyes back towards Gómez, I saw my tía standing next to O.C. She began to move towards Eddie, but O.C. grabbed her hand and pushed her back. Her eyes bored into O.C., but he didn't look at her. He just squeezed her hand a little harder and kept his eyes riveted on Gómez. It occurred to me then, that of all the people here only O.C. *really* knew Gómez. I flashed back to the story of the day they met at Folsom, then I followed O.C.'s eyes back to Gómez.

"Enough," said Gómez.

"Enough, old man? I'll tell *you* what's enough."

"You've crossed the line, Eddie."

Eddie smirked. "The line?" He turned back to his buddies. "Any of you boys seen a line around here?" They shook their heads. Eddie turned back to Gómez and drew an imaginary line with his foot. "Is this the line, señor?" He jumped over it and then back. He then did it several more times, like he was jumping rope. "Look at me! I'm crossing the line!"

"Eddie!" Gómez commanded. The wolf-eyes were hungry; Eddie stopped jumping. He was panting and his body tilted to the right side, but he stopped—and he was listening.

"You crossed the line. Now there is no turning back." Eddie began to speak, but Gómez interrupted him. "Attend!" He put the Panama hat on his head and untied the red scarf from his neck. "We must go forward now, Eddie—to a duel!" He flung the scarf at Eddie's feet.

Eddie looked at the scarf for a long time, his face a picture of utter non-comprehension.

"A duel, Eddie. Man to man. No weapons but this—" pointing to his head, "and this—" pointing to his heart, "and these—" lifting his fists.

Eddie was now starting to get the picture. He smiled. "*Comprendo,* señor. *Comprendo muy bien*. You wanna die."

"We shall see, Eddie. One week from today, on the street, an hour before the sun goes down. Be there!"

Eddie contemptuously flicked his hand towards Gómez in a dismissive gesture, signaled his three amigos, and descended the stairs into the darkness below.

The Party was over.

The Last Duel

There was no "Sunrise" when I woke up Sunday morning.

There had been quite a stir when Eddie left, though Gómez downplayed the whole event. He tried to revive the party mood and the *mariachis* tried too, but our guests were electrified by what they'd witnessed and the music was just an annoyance. After a couple of valiant efforts, the band packed up their instruments and bid us goodnight. Gómez praised them effusively and handed them a $200 tip.

My mom and Carmen went down to our house to put Rosa to bed, and over the next half-hour people trickled down the stairs until only the villa residents remained. We formed a circle of chairs on the dance floor and sat down—partly to savor again the events of the night, but mostly to hear Gómez explain what the hell had happened with Eddie. Apparently, Eddie was the last thing on Gómez's mind.

"Mr. Sánchez, Isabella, there is something I've been wondering: where in the world did you learn to dance like that?"

Mr. Sánchez removed his Zoot hat and rotated it in his hands reflectively. "Isabella, would you like to answer his question?"

Mrs. Sánchez gave Mr. Sánchez a warm smile and said, "No, Humberto. Please, go ahead."

Mr. Sánchez leaned back in his chair. "Well, we were young, fourteen or fifteen I think, and Isabella," he looked affectionately at Mrs. Sánchez, "Isabella was the most beautiful girl in our village. After the spring planting there was always a dance. Isabella was dancing with a handsome young man, Eduardo de la Montaña, the son of the mayor. She was wearing a yellow chiffon dress."

He stopped, looking intently at the mental image of the young Isabella. "Across her shoulders she wore a white shawl. In the firelight it glows pink." His chair slipped backward just a bit, pulling him out of his dream. He smiled at Mrs. Sánchez, like he was confessing to his weakness. "I couldn't take my eyes off you."

"I'm amazed you can still remember what I wore that evening. It was so long ago."

"I will never forget that night. I remember the way you held your hand just so when you danced, and how your head tilted when you turned. One time a strand of hair fell in front of your eyes; I wanted to lift it with my finger and put it back."

"And I remember you, Humberto. I remember seeing you coming across the dance floor. I knew you were coming for me. You were so bold and confident."

"Bold and confident?" His eyes scanned us quickly. "Scared to death! I was skinny, I was shy, and I couldn't dance! But more than anything I was afraid that the girl I loved would fall in love with another—so I had to act!"

Mrs. Sánchez reached out and grasped Mr. Sánchez's right hand.

"You were dancing with Eduardo. I waited, then walked out and tapped him on the shoulder. He looked at me like I was a bug! Humberto Sánchez, a poor farmer's son, cutting in on Eduardo de la Montaña? But what could he do? As we danced I saw Eduardo standing on the perimeter with his friends, pointing at me and laughing."

"Why was he laughing?" I asked Mr. Sánchez.

"Because I couldn't dance; I was awful! There is a dance we did in my village called *'El Cabrito.'* It is a wonderful dance, but difficult, with very precise foot movements, heel to toe, toe to heel, almost like tap dancing and square dancing combined, and I didn't know how to do it. I looked like a mule plodding through a muddy field!" He smiled at Mrs. Sánchez as they shared their private recollection.

"So what did you do?" I asked.

"I made it through the dance, thanked Isabella, and raced home. Dejected—but exhilarated at the same time! I had failed, but I had tried! And now I knew how to win Isabella! So for the next two or three months I practiced every day with my sisters and my *madre*, and in June there was another big dance. Again, Eduardo was dancing with Isabella. I went up to the band and asked them to play *'El Cabrito.'* I took the microphone and I called Isabella's name."

"He did, too," confirmed Mrs. Sánchez. "In front of everyone."

"I hopped off the stage and headed towards her. Eduardo had no choice but to step aside. Again he watched me through the entire dance, standing there with his buddies, but this time he wasn't smiling." But Mr. Sánchez did, and so did Mrs. Sánchez, who added, "You were magnificent, Humberto."

Mr. Sánchez squeezed her hand. "Because of you, Isabella. It was all for you."

"*Bravo*, my friend," said Gómez, clapping his hands. "*Bravo*!" Then he turned to Mr. Aguilar. "And how did you manage to feed all those people practically by yourself?"

Mr. Aguilar began to speak, but was cut off. "*Excuse me*?" rasped Carmen, bursting upon our circle, my mom in tow. "By *himself*? What, you didn't notice two crazy women running in and out of Maria's house all night long?"

Gómez raised his hands as if apprehended by the police. "I only meant to compliment Mr. Aguilar on the splendid job he did with the *carne asada*. I apologize, Carmen!" He said 'Carmen,' but he was looking at my mom. "Without you and Maria there wouldn't have been a party."

"Apology accepted," replied Carmen. "And Aguilar, you *were* splendid."

"It's all in the wrist," he said.

O.C. was anxiously waiting to get a word in. "Mam—er, Carmen, that was some fine dancin' out there."

Now Gómez jumped in. "Carmen, you were *amazing!* Oh! And what about those policemen?"

Carmen rolled her eyes. "Policemen are just men who wear their pistols on the outside." That got a laugh.

My mom raised her hand as if she needed permission to speak. "Yes?" said Gómez.

She clasped her hands together in front of her chest. "I had the most wonderful time. Thank you." She turned to go and then stopped. Carmen touched her arm and said, *"Tell him."* My mom turned and faced Gómez.

"I need to talk to you."

"I know." He raised himself from the chair. "Tomorrow; we'll talk tomorrow."

My mom turned abruptly and left, followed by Carmen. The rest of us stood up; the meeting was over. There was no mention of Eddie, or the upcoming duel with Gómez.

But the duel was the first thing I thought of when I woke up Sunday morning. Eddie of course wasn't in bed; his not coming home had become the rule rather than the exception. I went out to the kitchen. My mom was already in full motion, putting away the pots and pans she had cleaned before going to bed the night before.

"Hey mom."

"Hello, dear," she answered, turning her head sideways to me. "Are you hungry?"

"No. I'm going up to Gómez's. I don't even know if the Dodgers won the second game last night."

I approached Gómez's door, but stopped when I heard O.C.'s voice coming from the dining area. He was upset.

"Just tell me this: Have ya lost yer mind?"

"Come on, O.C.," answered Gómez.

"Ya think I'm jokin'? I'm not jokin'. Have ya lost yer mind?"

"O.C., what would you have had me do? The kid was trouble. Someone could have been hurt."

"Someone *is* gonna get hurt, Gómez. *You*! Yer gonna get hurt bad!"

"I can take care of myself."

"No one knows it better'n me. But this kid is strong, 'n fast, 'n he's mean as a rat. 'N yer an old man who's gonna get his butt kicked from here ta Christmas."

"Hell, O.C., I thought it worked out pretty well, considering the circumstances."

O.C. sighed in resignation. "'Gómez the god'; you'll need ta be alla that ta get yersef outta this mess."

"O.C.," Gómez said reassuringly. "I'm already thinking up a plan."

"Tell me now, Gómez, cuz I was also just thinkin'—'bout how I'm gonna miss ya."

Gómez laughed, and I could hear him patting O.C. on the back. "My friend—not so fast! I'm not dead yet! I'll tell you my plan; just let me work out some details first." I heard O.C.'s shuffling feet on the kitchen floor. "But, I can tell you this: last night, when I challenged Eddie, I knew exactly what I was doing. It came to me in a flash—*the whole thing*."

When I saw Gómez enter the living room I pulled the screen door open, and acting as if I had just appeared, I casually said, "Hey."

"Alex! Come on in!"

Gómez had his arm around O.C. "Did you hear about the game last night?"

"No."

"We beat the Padres again!"

"How'd we do it?"

"Gibson knocked in the winning run in the eleventh inning!"

"Wow, eleven innings!"

O.C. pulled away from Gómez and passed me on his way to the door. "Can't stand it," he mumbled. "Need a smoke."

"What?" said Gómez. O.C. let the slam of the screen door answer for him.

Gómez looked at me apologetically. "O.C.'s a little upset about Eddie."

I didn't really want to say anything about it, having eavesdropped on their conversation, so I just said, "Oh," and let it drop. "So, what's going on today?"

"Just cleaning up."

"My mom's already at it. She's trying to get it all done before church."

"I bet. I suppose we should return the dance floor today."

"Sure. So, Gómez, I guess you'll be going to church today, huh?"

He cocked his head. "What?"

"I guess you'll be going to church today."

"Why would I do that?"

"Because you're going to need all the help you can get next Saturday."

"*E tu,* Alex? First O.C., now you?"

I was about to reply when Mr. Sánchez walked in the door. "*Hola*, señors," he said. "So, Gómez, would you like to come to church with us today?"

Gómez raised his eyebrows. "Did I miss the big meeting this morning?"

"Meeting? What meeting?"

"Never mind," answered Gómez.

"Señor, it wouldn't hurt to put the Lord on your side."

"I think the Lord might have more important things to manage; and not just here on earth, but among the *billions* of other planets. I'll spare him this small inconvenience."

"It's your funeral."

"Funeral," repeated Gómez. "I'm starting to notice a lack of confidence, my friends."

"I have lots of confidence in you, Gómez," I said. "It's not that; it's Eddie. Eddie's been fighting his whole life. Even if you beat him, then you gotta fight his friends."

Mr. Sánchez nodded. "Yes, that's the way it is."

"Don't worry, men, I have a plan. It's going to be fine, really. Now, do you mind? I have much to do today."

We walked outside. My mom stepped out of the house and yelled up to me, "Alex, we're leaving for church soon. Come on in and get dressed." Then, seeing Gómez, she added, "Gómez, would you like to join us today?"

Gómez smiled and shook his head. "Thank you, Maria, but I'll just clean up a bit around here."

My mom was about to say something when Carmen stepped onto her porch and yelled, "Is he going?"

"No."

"Ayyy! Has he lost his mind?"

"I think so," answered my mom.

Gómez turned to Mr. Sánchez and said, "Such confidence. I really don't know what to say."

My mom, Carmen, Rosa and I went off to church. On the way my mom and Carmen talked about nothing but the duel.

"It's not going to happen, Carmen. A duel? On our street? Between Gómez and my son? Not on your life."

"How are you going to stop it? Sit down with Eddie and tell him it was a joke?"

"No, I'll talk to Gómez. Surely he understands there can be no duel. A duel! Listen to this conversation, Carmen. We're talking about a duel!—on our street!"

"Yes, you talk to him, Maria. Meanwhile, drive faster. I want to light a candle before God gets swamped by all those whiners."

"Okay. And make it a *big* candle, Carmen."

When we arrived home Gómez and O.C. were loading the dance floor into Mr. Aguilar's van. My mom walked right up to Gómez and said, "We need to talk. It's tomorrow."

"I know," answered Gómez. "Would it be okay if we spoke when I get back?"

"Just knock on the door."

At about one o'clock Gómez knocked. We were in the kitchen: my mom, Carmen and me. My mom stopped me as I stood to get the door. "*Mijo,* permit me, please."

When Gómez was seated my mom offered coffee, which he accepted. We waited, no one speaking, while Gómez sweetened his coffee and added milk. Finally, there was nothing to say but the matter at hand. Gómez broke the silence.

"Señora, you are concerned, yes?"

"Yes, very concerned."

"*Comprendo.* Tell me what you are concerned about."

An exasperated look flashed onto my mom's face. "*What* am I concerned about? Isn't a duel enough?"

"Yes Maria, I understand," Gómez said calmly, "but what worries you about that?"

Their eyes met and held. “I don’t want to lose my son.”

“Maria, Eddie’s *already* gone. He’s in a gang. Just a few days ago he was in a fight—not a scuffle, Maria, but a real fight, the kind where sometimes only one man walks away.”

My mom said nothing. My tía stood up to refill her coffee cup and poured more into Gómez’s without asking.

“Maria, the road he’s on has only two destinations: a prison yard or a graveyard.” Gómez propped up his chin with his right thumb and pressed the forefinger into his upper lip. “I think I’m qualified to speak on this subject.”

Still my mom said nothing. What Gómez had said was true; Eddie *was* already gone. We were only now confronting the fact.

“So, what can I do?”

“I don’t know, Maria.”

“Then why did you challenge him to a duel?”

“It seemed like a good idea at the time.”

“Gómez, is there something here I don’t understand? I fail to see how a duel is going to help the situation. Can you explain that to me?” My mom’s voice was beginning to crack.

“Maria, for reasons you know and reasons you don’t, I have a pretty good idea what it’s like to be Eddie Morales. I don’t believe anyone will be hurt—seriously hurt that is—at the duel. I have a plan. It’s possible that something good may come of this.”

“So, I’m just supposed to trust you, Gómez?”

“I know it’s a lot to ask, Maria. But yes, trust me on this. Not because of any particular confidence you may have in me, but because it’s already a desperate situation with Eddie. It could hardly get worse, and I think there's a chance it'll get better."

My mom dropped her head into her hands. My tía reached over and stroked her hair lightly. *"Manita,"* Carmen said softly, "let's go with it, and if it gets out of hand I'll jump in and kick both their asses."

My mom laughed—ruefully—but it was laughter nevertheless. She lifted her eyes to Gómez. There were large tears suspended in her dark lashes. "Is there anything you need from me?"

"Can you sew?"

"Can I sew?" Laughing despite herself she answered, "Of course I can sew."

"Good!" said Gómez, rubbing his Hemingway, a glint in his gray wolf-eyes. "Because I was thinking I might need a cape."

*****

The Dodgers were on TV against the Braves, and Gómez, Mr. Sánchez, O.C. and I were on Gómez's floor, gobbling leftover *carne asada* tacos. Man, they were just as good as the day before. The fourth inning just ended and the Dodgers were beating the Braves 5-0. "Gómez," said Mr. Sánchez, "why don't you go to church?"

"Don't," interrupted O.C. flatly. "Ya don't know what yer gettin' inta."

"Was he asking you, dirt farmer?"

O.C. ignored Gómez. "Sánchez, ya don't wanna get him started on religion. Trust me."

Mr. Sánchez considered O.C.'s words, then looked at Gómez and said, "So?"

"Well, I'll tell you what. I'm going to get me another couple of tacos and then I'll answer your question." Gómez got up and O.C. said, "Well, if I'm gonna have ta suffer, might as well suffer with more tacos." He started to get up too, but Gómez extended his hand to take O.C.'s plate. "Let me get that for you, former friend."

O.C. flashed his gap-toothed smile. "Gracias, señor."

When Gómez returned he handed O.C. his plate and then plopped back down cross-legged on the floor. He took a large bite, and pointing the taco at Mr. Sánchez, said, "The answer is because there's religious wisdom and there's religious conviction: don't confuse the two. 'Religious wisdom'—what does it mean? The word 'religion' comes from two words. 'Re' means 'again,' and 'ligere' means 'to bind.' You've heard the word 'ligament': same meaning. So, religion means 'to bind again' or 'to connect again.'"

Gómez looked at each of us briefly, and satisfied, he continued. "Wisdom means 'knowledge'—but with an emphasis on the ability to apply what one knows. That's what 'religious wisdom' means."

He took another bite of his taco. "Religious conviction is different. 'Conviction' is a firmly held opinion. It comes from a Latin word, 'convincere,' which means 'to prove wrong.' So you have religious wisdom and religious conviction, and they are two completely different things."

Even I was tracking.

"Man's been lost for a long time; that's obvious. Religion tries to help him find his way back home. The question is: 'Where's home?'" Gómez stopped for a bite; we waited.

"In the West, particularly from a Christian point of view, the purpose of religion is to reconnect one to God. One achieves this through study, prayer, and various rituals.

"In the East—at least in the old days—'home' meant back to *who* you really are, or maybe more precisely, *what* you really are. To that end, one studied and applied various techniques." Another bite. I looked at Sánchez; his eyes were fixed on Gómez. Even the jaded O.C. was into it.

"You might be wondering where you might find religious wisdom: it's in books; most of them ancient books. The Christian Bible is one of those books, but it's only a small part of the wisdom that's been recorded over the last 10,000 years. If you are looking for religious wisdom, you begin in India, with the Vedic Hymns. Coming forward you have Siddhartha—we call him Buddha, Lao Tze in China, Plato, Jesus, Mohammad, and hundreds of others, possibly even greater than those I've mentioned. After all, not every great teacher was recorded in books. No doubt a great many have been forgotten altogether."

Gómez stopped. He put his back to the wall and pulled his legs up, dangling his hands over his knees. "Tremendous, isn't it? Man's search to discover who he is and what he is—it's the greatest story ever told, and, next to serving others, is probably the only really important activity in our lives."

Mr. Sánchez nodded his head thoughtfully. "So, why don't you go to church?"

"Because it doesn't matter if the earth was made in six days or six seconds. What do rosary beads have to do with wisdom? Or Buddhist prayer wheels? Or 'Hail Mary' or 'Our Father'? Nothing, that's what. The path of wisdom is strenuous—that's what Buddha said. *Strenuous.* You can't buy it with gold, and it isn't granted because you plead loud enough or long enough. Religious wisdom is earned."

Mr. Sánchez began to speak, but Gómez interrupted him. "So, to answer your question, I'm interested in religious wisdom, not religious conviction. I'm interested in knowing, not believing. If there was a church that could help me become more of who I really am—why, I'd go to church every day and *twice* on Sundays."

Mr. Sánchez considered that for a moment and then said, "Me too."

We were all silent, contemplating our navels I guess, but after a minute or two our attention drifted to the game. The Dodgers were threatening to score, but Gibson popped out to end the rally. During the commercial O.C. blurted, "That's it? That's all yer gonna say 'bout religion?"

Gómez looked at him slyly. "Why yes, O.C., but if there is something you would like to add, please, go ahead."

O.C. shook his head. "Christ, ya must be slowin' down, Gómez. Ya usta be good fer 'n hour on religion."

Gómez crawled over and put a headlock on him. "Don't make me hurt you, dirt farmer," he laughed. "Like you could!" replied O.C. as Gómez tried vainly to turn him over on his back. Then Gómez broke out into a coughing fit and all play stopped.

"You might wanna see a doctor," said O.C.

"No, it's almost run its course."

Around ten o'clock the game ended with another Dodger win. When I got home my mom and Rosa were already in bed, so I put my head on the pillow and waited for "Hallelujah." Not a bad day. Then I started thinking about the duel.

*****

The week passed slowly. Eddie dropped in a few times, but always late at night. He would flop onto his bed, sleep until the afternoon, then head out again.

On Friday night my mom and my tía put on a barbecue for our villa. Gómez brought out his record player and we heard some classical music, as well as Lalo Guerrero and Django Reinhardt, of course. Rosa picked up Gómez's flute and tried to follow along. It was pretty funny.

Other than Rosa there wasn't much to smile about. My mom and Carmen tried to create a festive mood, but we all were a little subdued, except for Mrs. Cortez.

"When's the big duel?" she asked Gómez.

"It's tomorrow, Mrs. Cortez."

"After he kills you, can I have your record player?"

There were shocked expressions all around, except for Gómez, who laughed. "No, I'm sorry. The record player has chosen someone else."

Mrs. Cortez grunted a *hrrrumph*. "Do you have any other crap?"

"Mrs. Cortez, you deserve more crap than I can give you."

Mrs. Cortez gave Gómez a crooked look, grunted again and then said, "Well, I better go to bed. Need to rest up for the big duel." At that, she stood up abruptly and walked away, not a "so long" for anyone.

"Well, I'm about to turn in too," said Gómez. "I've some last minute preparations."

"What, you gonna start boxing lessons tonight?" said Carmen.

Gómez seemed to laugh at everything. "No, nothing like that. But if you could show me some wrestling moves I'd be grateful."

"Funny man," replied my tía.

"Gómez," said my mom, standing up, "you asked for a cape." She went inside and came back with a gift box, tied with a red bow. Inserted in the bow was a card.

"Well, well! I guess I don't have to wonder what it is!" said Gómez.

"Open the card, señor," said Mrs. Sánchez. We were all so surprised to hear her speak that we turned to her en masse. "I will, Isabella," answered Gómez, "with pleasure."

On the outside of the card was a drawing of an old man in a white suit, a white cape over his shoulder, with a Panama hat on his head and a red scarf around his neck. Standing about him were vague stick figures sketched in black, clapping hands. Gómez looked at the drawing for several seconds. "Wow." He lifted his head and looked at each of us. "Who drew this?"

"Isabella did," answered my mom.

Gómez looked at Mrs. Sánchez, but before he could speak she said, "Open it, señor."

He opened it and silently read the message. Then he turned to Mrs. Sánchez. "Isabella, thank you. From the bottom of my heart, thank you." Facing all of us, he added, "Each of you; you could not have made me happier." He handed the card to me. It read: "To Gómez, our friend."

Gómez pulled the ribbon off the box and slowly extracted the cape. With a flourish he swung it above his head. "Olé!" he exclaimed. It billowed out and settled on his shoulders.

"*Bravo*!" yelled Mr. Sánchez.

Gómez stood and turned, modeling his white satin cape.

"Maria, you did a great job!" said Carmen.

My mom beamed. "I like it too."

"Now," said Gómez, posing like a Don, "I can present myself as a gentleman."

"Si, un hombre magnifico!" said Carmen.

"Thank you, Maria. This cape," he took it off his shoulders and held it at arms' length, "this is—well, it's possibly the most beautiful thing I've ever owned. I will treasure it. Thank you, again." He walked over to my mom and kissed her on the cheek. Addressing all of us, he said, "And now I must say goodnight. *Hasta mañana!*"

Silently we watched Gómez walk up the stairs.

"Damn," said O.C.

*****

I awoke on Saturday morning with an anticipation equal to the previous Saturday, except that this anticipation was accompanied by dread rather than joy. The day passed with all of the speed of a funeral.

I went up to see Gómez around ten that morning, but he was engrossed in a book, "Pillars of the Earth." Without lifting his eyes, he said, "Now that you have some spare time, tell me what you think." He felt for a book at his side, found it, and extended it towards me. It was The Last Unicorn.

I came back around one o'clock, but he was still reading, and at three it was the same. Other than O.C., I didn't see anyone in the villa all day. It reminded me of an old western, with all townspeople staying indoors because a *muy bad hombre* was coming to town.

Around 5:30 I was sitting in my father's chair, reading, when my mom walked into the house. "I don't believe my eyes."

"Mom?"

"There are people setting up chairs on the street. Can you believe that?"

I went outside and looked down onto the street; there *were* people setting up chairs! On the sidewalk in front of Mr. Aguilar's house there were six people, and in front of Carmen's there were maybe ten more. Across the street a fruit vendor was setting up.

I went down to the street and walked up to a kid about twenty-two or so. "What's going on?"

"A duel."

"A duel?" I asked, pretending ignorance.

"Yeah, somebody from Los Toros called out a killer."

"A killer?" This time there was no pretense in my voice.

"That's the word; killed someone with his bare hands." He made a circle with his hands to dramatize choking someone to death.

The guy next to him said, "I heard he killed three people in a bar fight."

"Could be," the first guy replied. "Either way, I wouldn't wanna fight no one from *Los Toros*. Not without an army behind me."

I walked back up the stairs and sat down on the landing. Over the next hour, probably fifty or sixty people set up chairs or sat on the curb, and more were coming. Besides the fruit vendor, there was now a taco stand. Both were busy. Years later when I read about crowds gathering for a hanging, I didn't wonder if it was true.

At 6:30 a black Camaro with wide gray stripes on the hood came down the street. Eddie sat in the back seat, waving to the crowd amid scattered chants of "*Los Toros!*" I stood and walked up to Gómez's; it was almost time. I had a very bad feeling.

"Alex, is that you?" came Gómez's voice from his bedroom. "Come here and tell me what you think!"

The first thing I saw was O.C.—and I almost burst out laughing. He looked like he was wearing a Zorro Halloween costume: pants, shirt, shoes, and cowboy hat—all black. The only thing missing was the Zorro mask.

"O.C., you look—magnificent. A little bit like Zorro, only older."

"I feel more like Bozo than Zorro."

"Stop complaining," Gómez said. I took my eyes off O.C. and looked at Gómez. He was the opposite of O.C., dressed entirely in white. In fact, he was wearing the same suit he wore to The Party, including the red scarf. He looked pretty damn good.

"Not bad, Gómez."

"Don't be bashful, my young apprentice." He was standing in front of a mirror, adjusting his scarf to get it just right. "No reason to withhold your adoration. I know I look—how would you say it in the common tongue?—oh yes, 'dashing' is the word, is it not, O.C.?"

"Ya see what I have ta put up with, Alex?" O.C. said despondently.

"Enough of that, impudent knave. Remember, 'better to be silent and thought a fool, than to speak and remove all doubt!'"

O.C. cast me a pathetic look and nodded his head as if to say, "See what I mean?"

"Gómez, have you seen what's going on down there?"

"Yes, my apprentice, I have observed it through the eyes of my spy—yon toothless knave." He motioned towards O.C. with his chin. "Five score thus far; is it not so, Master Alex?"

"If you say so," I answered, winking at O.C., who pulled his black hat down over his face.

"Alas, *el duelo* doesn't begin for yet half an hour. By then I expect a full house, don't you, *mi segundo por la duelista?"*

"Gómez," said O.C., "ya better hope this duel starts soon or yer gonna be dead 'fore it starts. I'll push yer fat old carcass out there in Sánchez's wheelbarrow 'n drop ya inta the street."

"Exactamente, Sir Bobkin! That's the fighting spirit! Keep it up—for your master's sake!"

O.C. pushed the hat off his head, turned, and banged his forehead against the wall. Gómez ignored the gesture. He looked at me and said: "In the old days, the moments before the duel were called *'El Tiempo de Tranquilo.'* The *duelista*, *el segundo* and *el aprendiz*, they would sequester themselves in a private room, or perhaps, under a shady tree. They spoke not of the upcoming duel—too late for that! Rather, they spoke of simple things. My friends, I would like to do that with you now. *¿De acuerdo,* señors?"

We nodded.

"Bueno." He hung his hat on the chair and plopped his body on the floor, his back against the wall. We followed.

"*Mi aprendiz,* have you ever seen a sight to compare with walking into Dodger Stadium?"

"No, Gómez," I answered, a little too morosely for my own ears.

"Ayyy, that was a special evening. The grass! The lights! The hum of 35,000 voices—and Vin Scully! Imagine that, bumping into Vin Scully!"

"Ya did?" said O.C.

"Can you believe it?" answered Gómez. "Such a thing isn't mere coincidence. The odds are impossible."

"How many times do ya think ya wrote him, Gómez?" asked O.C.

"A hundred; maybe more. And you know what? He *read* those letters!"

"You met Vin Scully. Damn. 'N he read all them letters."

"Yep, he sure did," answered Gómez. "He couldn't write back—because I was in prison, I think. But he read them, by God!"

O.C. shook his head in wonder. "Say, do ya remember the time in Folsom, ya won that game 'gainst the Rebs with a homer in the last inning, 'n as ya went 'round the bases ya pretended ta be Vin Scully 'n ya was announcing yer own home run?"

"I do, *mi amigo,* I remember it like it was yesterday. I'll tell you what, there's damn little in this world as satisfying as putting good wood on a baseball."

Gómez had a far away, dreamy look in his eyes. "When I was a boy I played stickball in the street with my little brother. He'd pitch to me—we used a wadded up sock—and I'd hit with a broom stick. Even then it felt special."

"I didn't know you had a brother, Gómez."

"Yes, a brother and a mother and a father."

"Is anyone still alive?"

"No, just me."

We heard a knock on the door, then the creak of a rusty hinge. "Gómez? Are you here?" It was Mr. Aguilar.

"Well amigos, I think our *'Tiempo de Tranquilo'* is over." Gómez stood up and walked over to the chair on which hung his new white cape. "Señor O.C., please do me the honor." He spread his arms out and O.C. walked behind him, lifting the cape from the chair and setting it upon Gómez's shoulders. Walking around Gómez to face him, he tied the cord around Gómez's neck; then he took the Panama hat and placed it gently on his head.

"How do I look?" beamed Gómez.

"Like a true gentleman," answered O.C.

Gómez nodded with satisfaction. "Then hand me that staff and let's get on with it."

*****

The three of us stood on Gómez's landing and looked down at the street below. It was packed. The curbs on both sides were lined with people, like you'd see them lined up for a parade, coming early to get the good seats. In the street were half a dozen vendors. One vendor was even selling T-shirts that said "The Last Duel" in bold lettering over a silhouette of two *duelistas,* their pistols drawn. I'd have to get one of those.

As we descended the stairs, the buzz from below ceased as if by command and every head turned toward us. I led, followed by O.C., then Gómez. When we reached the second landing we stopped: in front of my door stood my mom and my tía. My mom's face was expressionless, but my tía shook her head slowly in resigned disapproval. Gómez raised his staff in salute and then continued his descent.

Mr. and Mrs. Sánchez met us at the bottom of the stairs. Mr. Sánchez shook Gómez's hand and then kissed him on both cheeks. Mrs. Sánchez simply nodded in that elegant way of hers.

I pushed our way through the crowd and into the street. There might have been three hundred people there to witness The Last Duel.

About thirty yards in front of us was the black Camaro, parked perpendicular to the street, like a barricade. The front door swung open and one of Eddie's hoodlum friends stepped out. I recognized him instantly—the *cholo* that Gómez and I met on the way to Builder's Emporium, the guy who was chipping cement from between the bricks with his knife: Hector.

The crowd cheered and whistled when Eddie pulled himself out of the car. In response, Eddie raised his arms in triumph, and then pulled back the sleeve of his T-shirt to show his *Los Toros* tattoo. When the crowd answered with even more hooting and yipping, Eddie went into a prizefighter's dance.

I looked at him playing to the crowd, dressed in the low slung baggy jeans and T-shirt uniform of the East L.A. gangs, and I couldn't believe it. Eddie. My Eddie. What had happened to him? It seemed like we weren't even brothers anymore. When he looked at me, there was recognition but little else. He had become *Los Toros.*

"It is time, señor," said O.C. to Gómez. Eyes fixed on Eddie, Gómez stepped forward and O.C. followed. When they had come within about fifteen yards of the Camaro, they stopped.

Mr. Sánchez stepped away from Mrs. Sánchez and worked his way through the throng on the left. When Gómez and O.C. stopped, I saw Mr. Sánchez stop too, then push his way through the crowd and into the middle of the street, just a few feet in front of O.C. and Gómez. He acknowledged them with a nod, then turned to Eddie and his second, Hector. "Attention!" he said, turning his head from Eddie and Hector to Gómez and O.C. "Would the *duelistas* and their *segundos* come forward, *por favor!*"

Eddie and Hector sauntered forward.

"Eddie," said Mr. Sánchez, "you have been challenged to a duel by Gómez. The only weapons permitted are those you were born with—your fists, your feet, your mind."

Mr. Sánchez looked at Eddie and Gómez to ensure they understood, then continued. "No other weapons are permitted. No guns, no knives, and *no interference.* This is between Gómez and Eddie, only." Again he paused, this time looking only at Hector. "Is that understood?"

"What's with the cane, then?" answered Eddie.

"Would you deny an old man his walking stick?" replied Mr. Sánchez.

"Sánchez, shut up," said Eddie. "I was talking to this other pathetic old man."

"Eddie," said Gómez calmly, "it's a staff, not a cane, and you needn't worry. I'm not going to beat you with it. I just wanted you to see it."

Eddie began to move towards Gómez, but Mr. Sánchez stepped between them. "There's one more thing: a duel is a serious thing. Once engaged, it is possible that one of you will not be leaving here alive. Even for the victor, triumph may be short-lived. So attend! There will be one last attempt, before the duel is commenced, to address the grievances and reconcile the two parties."

"What are you talking about, Sánchez?" spat Eddie. "What's this bullshit?"

"This is how it is done, Eddie, and it is not open to question. You agreed to the duel; you must follow the rules of the duel—*exactly*!"

"That's crap!" yelled Eddie. He looked at Hector and then scanned the crowd. "That's total bullshit."

"It is nevertheless the way it is done," replied Mr. Sánchez, calmly. "Are you in or are you out?"

"Whatever, man," said Eddie in exasperation. "Let's just get this bullshit over with."

"Very well," answered Mr. Sánchez. Then addressing the crowd, he said, "Honored guests! The terms of the duel have been read to the *duelistas.* Now they must sequester themselves for The Last Discourse—a final attempt to resolve their differences.

"A place has been prepared for them in my villa above this street. My assistant, Mr. Aguilar, will accompany Señor Gómez and Señor Eddie Morales to this villa, waiting outside until the required sixty minutes have elapsed. After sixty minutes, Mr. Aguilar will lead them back here, where the outcome of The Last Discourse shall be made known to first myself, then to you. If they have failed to resolve their differences then the duel shall commence immediately. Mr. Aguilar, please escort the *duelistas* to my villa."

Mr. Aguilar stepped out and Mr. Sánchez motioned to Gómez and Eddie to follow him, which they did, working their way through the murmuring crowd and up the stairs.

I stood in the middle of the street, as stunned as everyone else. Since no one had ever been to a duel, no one knew whether this was normal or not. Most of the crowd swallowed their disappointment, but Eddie's friends yelled "Bullshit!" and "This is crap!"

Gómez wouldn't tell me what transpired between Eddie and him. It was between them, he said. But a few months later Eddie told me. Here's how I remember what he said:

Gómez said nothing as we walked up the stairs. At the top, I remember turning and waving to the street. When I was done clowning around, I turned and looked for Gómez; he was standing about six feet behind me on the walkway. I don't know what I expected to see in his face, but whatever I expected wasn't there. He was smiling, smiling like he was actually pleased with my antics. It knocked me off guard.

When we got inside there were two big chairs. In between the chairs was a small table with a pitcher of water and two glasses. Gómez put his cane in the corner and offered me a chair.

I said, 'So what the fuck is goin' on here?'

Gómez didn't answer. He just slowly took off his hat and untied his cape.

I said, 'Too scared to talk, eh Gómez? Don't be ashamed old man, you should be scared. In an hour I'm gonna kick your ass up and down this street. There'll be nothin' left of you but a grease spot.'

Gómez smiled that weird smile again. He sat down and looked me right in the eye. 'You are a fine adversary, Eddie, and today would be a good day to die. But, first we have work to do.'

'You have work to do, Gómez; I'm just passin' the time. Maybe I should think of a way to stretch it out—not kill you off too quick. After all, a lotta people have come to see me break you up.'

Gómez lifted the water pitcher and filled both glasses, then raised his: 'To Tonali.'

I was about to give him some shit but he cut me off. 'I'm not going to ask you if you know what 'Tonali' means, because I know you don't.'

I said, 'Whatever.'

'There's a lot you don't know,' he said, ignoring my comment. 'In fact, the quantity of what you don't know is so staggering that it raises the question whether you know anything at all.'

'Wake me up when you're done,' I told him. I leaned back and closed my eyes. He started talking.

'As a nation we died on August 13th, 1521, in the battle for what is now called Mexico City. But as a people we died two years before that, on a sandy beach the Spanish called Vera Cruz—the True Cross. That's where our race first sold its soul to the conquistador Cortés.

'Cortés landed in our world with five hundred soldiers. That's all. Plus four priests, sixteen horses, some hounds and an assortment of cannons, guns and crossbows. His goal was the wealth of our nation: gold, silver and gems; and

between him and his prize stood a mighty people, ruled by a weak and vain man, but still an empire, vast and powerful, with warriors numbering well over a half-million.

'Working against our huge advantage were three things—the dreaded small pox; the ancient enmities of our nation; and, let's give the Devil his due, Cortés' indomitable will. Of the three, the small pox was the greatest weapon of the Spanish, far more powerful than their cannons and guns. More than 50% of our warriors died from the pox.

'But for the small pox we would have crushed the Spanish like you step on a cockroach. Even with the pox ravishing the countryside we could have easily defeated the invaders had we hung together, but Cortés exploited the old grudges, and when Tenochtitlan fell at last, the Spanish forces numbered only fifteen hundred, while their native allies numbered over a hundred thousand. That's right: for every fifteen Spanish soldiers there were one thousand native warriors fighting on their side.'

I didn't know that, and for the first time Gómez began to get my attention. I opened my eyes. He said, 'Yes Eddie, it's true. Without the support of our own people the Spaniards could not have defeated us.'

'There must have been a reason,' I told him.

'True. The Mextica had moved south centuries before, defeating the local tribes, making them tributary nations. Perhaps this was our fundamental political weakness. Regardless, this much is certain: the Spaniards were so filthy they were held in contempt by even the lowest of our race. To these loathsome men we traded our honor—and for what? Well, look around you.'

Gómez was standing now. He pointed to the door and said, 'Out there are broken people. They bow to the god of Cortés. They speak a foreign tongue. They fight among themselves for table scraps.' He walked over to the door and touched it with both hands, like he was testing its strength. Then he came back to his chair. He said, 'But, I've drifted. Let's get back to our story.

'When Montezuma heard of Cortés, with his fire sticks and cannons, and worst of all, the armored and terrible horses, he feared that Cortés might be a god. So he sent him gifts—like an offering I suppose—hoping that Cortés would

be appeased and leave the One World. Predictably, the gifts of gold, silver, and gems only whetted Cortés' appetite. When Cortés reached the Heart of the One World, Montezuma actually invited him and his soldiers into the city! Can you believe that, Eddie?

'At any time Montezuma could have driven Cortés into the sea, but instead he invites the wolf into his house. Montezuma rules in name only until his brother Cuitlahuac, the war chief, takes matters into his own hands and, unbeknownst to Montezuma, stages a secret attack to drive the Spaniards from the Heart of the One World—and succeeds! With but a fraction of his army, his men weak from disease, Cuitlahuac does what Montezuma never did—he attacked!'

To tell you the truth, by now I was leaning forward in my chair, hanging on every word. Gómez paused and handed me my glass of water, pouring another for himself.

'The attack began one night in July, 1520, during the Ceremony of the Rain God. It was a proud night for us, Eddie. As the rain god pummeled the five lakes we drove the invaders off our island. Sure, the Spaniards and the traitors who joined them still controlled the countryside, but the Heart of the One World, the sacred city of Tenochtitlan, was ours again!

'Six months later Cortés returned with a thousand Spaniards and over a hundred thousand natives to begin the final assault on the One World. And I'll tell you what Eddie, as wonderful as it was to take back our capital, it is the final battle that flames my Aztec pride. It was a battle to the death: no quarter given or expected. Those brave and loyal warriors understood Cortés' intentions. There was no 'second prize' where the Spanish were concerned. There was liberty or bondage, and nothing in-between.

'There were three causeways that linked Tenochtitlan to the mainland, and the Spanish deployed their overwhelming forces on all three, eliminating any possibility of escape. The Spanish strategy was simple: from the mainland pound the heart of the city with cannon fire. Meanwhile, on each of the causeways the same strategy was employed in microcosm; cannons were deployed with orders to pulverize every building, every defensive position they encountered. Each day, on each causeway, the Spanish would destroy another quarter mile, then send in their horsemen and warriors to overwhelm the survivors. At night the stag hounds were released to drag out and devour the wounded. For three weeks this

is how every day began and ended; each day's rubble simply pushed off the side of the causeway and the process begun again.

'But the Mextica fought on. Jaguar Knights wielding stone clubs against iron clad Castilians; Eagle Knights throwing spears at the fearsome and armored war horses; Arrow Knights firing their bows at the native traitors who, unlike the Spanish, were not protected by armor. These defenders were not just men, Eddie; these were Mextica knights: Proud; Fierce; Loyal.

'Each day the Spaniards bit off and digested each of the three causeways, bite after bite, until at last the three divisions of Cortés' vast army arrived in the ancient center of Tenochtitlan, the 'Heart of the One World.' When the final assault occurred on August 13, 1521, and Mexico fell, she was defended by fewer than one hundred men; men weakened by disease and hunger, who, despite overwhelming odds, had refused to give up. My heart swells when I remember the magnificence of those last defenders of our land; history's forgotten men.

'Eddie, you are probably wondering why I've told you this brief history. Because without this background, you couldn't imagine, much less understand, my surprise to meet again one of my brothers from the One World.'

My mind must have wandered, imagining the final defense of that great city, because what Gómez said made no sense. 'What'd you say?' I asked.

Gómez sat up in his chair and leaned forward. He spoke slowly so that every word hit home. 'I said how surprised I was to meet again, after all these years, one of the last defenders of the One World.'

'You mean I remind you of a Mextica warrior?'

'No, I mean you are a Mextica warrior.' After a long silence he added, 'And those people down there, they are your people.'

This is basically what Eddie told me. There was one more thing he said: as he and Gómez were leaving Mr. Sánchez's house, he suddenly realized that Gómez had a secret. It just hit him, out of the blue, without any hint from Gómez. And as quickly as he thought it, it left his mind. I would learn about the secret later, in a few weeks, but I had no intuition about it, and the revelation floored me.

I was watching the fruit vendor serve someone when the buzzing on the street stopped—suddenly and completely. The *duelistas* had returned, and like everyone else I looked up the stairs.

Gómez and Eddie stood on Gómez's landing, looking down on us. The seconds ticked by and neither of them moved. Then Gómez extended his right arm, inviting Eddie to go first. As they passed the second landing, Gómez stopped briefly to tip his hat to my mom and my tía. It could've been either a greeting or a farewell.

The crowd parted when they reached the street. Gómez and Eddie walked directly to Mr. Sánchez, who was standing in the same spot he was in when Gómez and Eddie departed. The three of them conferred for about thirty seconds, Mr. Sánchez intently listening to Gómez first, then listening just as intently to Eddie, then speaking briefly to both of them and acknowledging their replies. Finally, he turned to the crowd on our side of the street and raised an old megaphone someone had given him. "Ladies and Gentlemen, may I have your attention?" Turning slowly so as to address everyone, he repeated, "*¡Atención, por favor!* Your attention please!"

The humming died down to a faint buzz. One of Eddie's pals yelled out, "Kick his ass, Eddie!" Another revved the black Camaro. Mr. Sánchez ignored it all, simply standing there with his hands at his sides, waiting until he had total silence. When he got it, he took a breath and said, "'The Last Discourse' is complete. The result shall now be made known. Señor Morales . . . ." He handed the megaphone to Eddie.

Eddie stepped forward. Looking directly at the Camaro, he said, "There ain't gonna be no duel. Something happened." He lowered the megaphone, rubbing his chin while he thought of what to say next. Seconds ticked by. He looked directly at Hector. Twice he started to say something, and twice he stopped. He shook his head and said, "I'll tell you later." Then he turned to the group of spectators in front of my tía's house, raised the megaphone, and said, "Go home." He handed the megaphone back to Mr. Sánchez.

Mr. Sánchez gestured towards Gómez, who nodded his head and accepted the megaphone. "Ladies and Gentleman, Señoras y Señores, thank you for coming here today. With your help, your patience and support, Mr.

Morales and I were able to resolve our differences like men, face to face, using reason instead of fists. 'The Last Discourse' was a success!"

There was utter silence. It was the weirdest thing I've ever seen, like being in the eye of a hurricane: all quiet, but eerie, and ready to blow any second. I looked around at the faces in the crowd; with a little push, just a nudge, that crowd would turn into a mob. Suddenly I heard my mom's voice; it took a second to register, as if she were far away. I looked up and there she was—waving her arms and beckoning the crowd. "Come on up! It's a party! Come! Come celebrate!"

As if it were a single body, the crowd moved, like a giant boulder teetering on a peak, as likely to tumble north as south, when some soul—bless him!—said: *"Let's party!"* With that the balance shifted, and suddenly there was clapping and cheering.

As the crowd made its way up the stairs, I fell in behind. In our yard the food table was already filling with a wild and varied assortment of stuff that could be rounded up *quick*. There were crackers and cheese and chips and our blessed salsa, a salad bowl and cold pinto beans, cookies and canned fruit and watermelon, apples, oranges, various sodas, a too-small supply of Corona and some open wine bottles, peanuts and cold tamales and two boxes of chocolate-covered Macadamia nuts and on and on. Every pantry and refrigerator in the villa had been stripped.

On our patio, Mr. Aguilar already had the barbecue going. From behind me there was a whoop as three men made their way up the stairs, holding two cases of beer each. Right on their heels was one of the *músicos de mariachi* from the week before, carrying in each arm a white package about the size of a football: more *carne*. Behind him was another of the *músicos* carrying tortillas and behind him was the last *mariachi* carrying the instruments. They were back!

My mom and Carmen were dashing in and out of the house. Mrs. Cortez appeared with a shopping bag and began to unload bottles of liquor onto the table. I looked around for Eddie. It occurred to me that I hadn't seen him come up the stairs. I found him on the street, standing in front of the Camaro, listening to Hector, who was leaning against the hood, picking at his nails with the tip of his knife. For a second I wondered if someone—me I guess—should go help him, but it didn't look he needed any help. He looked completely relaxed. Well, fine.

Soon the *mariachis* began playing in Mr. Sánchez's yard. After three or four songs, people began dancing, and though there wasn't a dance floor this time, the number quickly swelled to a dozen or more couples. The *mariachis* sounded even better than before, and after each of the traditional ballads there were cries of *Viva México!* It was an enchanted evening. *"Cómo Quién Pierde," "Por Mujeres Cómo Tu," "Mexico Lindo"*—these and other old songs seemed to pervade the very air, as if each word were a tangible thing. Carlos, the leader of the *mariachis*, would walk through the crowd singing a verse, or playing his horn, or kissing a woman's hand, and I thought that this is how it must've been for Mr. and Mrs. Sánchez during those summer evenings, walking the pond in their village. Indeed, when I found the Sánchezes, the dreamy look in their eyes showed they were again in the world of their youth.

I felt a little poke in my back, and then again, and turned to tell the instigator to knock it off. It was Eddie. "Hey bro," he said, smiling. A torrent of emotion surged and I shoved it back down. "You're back," I said, as cool as I could.

A little while later, Carmen leaned over and whispered in my ear, "Mijo, don't turn around too quick, but take a slow look over to your mom."

I did. She was sitting next to Gómez, her legs tucked beneath her, her left arm wrapped under Gómez's right arm, listening as he spoke softly to her. Geez, my mom was the most beautiful woman on earth. Her dark eyes, flickering in the porch light, had something in them I'd never seen before: contentment.

I was contented, too. Around midnight I was lying in bed when I heard "Hallelujah." A short while later I heard a rustling sound: there was Eddie, slipping out of his clothes and climbing into bed. What a day. What a magnificent, unforgettable, unexpected day. Gómez—he did it.

Romance

Of course my mom denied there was anything happening between her and Gómez. "Just friends," I heard her say to Carmen the next day. My tía, usually so direct and brash, let the subject drop as if it were the most trivial thing. I knew it was killing her, but she was doing the right thing: the low-key approach was best. My mom had ventured out from her safe shell and we didn't want to draw her attention to it and have her think, "My God! What am I doing out here!" But dang! My mom and Gómez.

Gómez was low-key too, his hidden emotions betrayed only by the ever-present grin, the whistling and singing, the dancing in the kitchen and the feet that never touched the ground.

Everything in our world was going great: my mom and Gómez were in that magical sunrise glow of early romance; the Sánchezes were always holding hands and whispering things to each other; Eddie was back—no one knew where he was going, least of all Eddie, but he was back from where he had been and that was enough; and though nothing had improved for Mr. Aguilar, Mrs. Cortez, or my tía, they too were floating on the high-tide of hope. On top of all of that, the Dodgers were in first place, leading the Giants by four-and-a-half games.

But it didn't last. What caused the fallout between my mom and Gómez was something they kept to themselves. My tía tried to gently pull it out of my mom, and when that didn't work she tried to extract it like a dentist pulling on an impacted wisdom tooth; that didn't work either. Then she tried Gómez, and the slamming of his screen door when she walked out left no doubt as to her success. I finally found out what happened from the most obvious source—the proverbial fly on the wall, O.C. Martin.

O.C. knew exactly what had occurred because my mom and Gómez were in Gómez's living room when the breakup occurred, oblivious to O.C. in his room. O.C. wasn't a gossip, and he didn't tell me what happened for any particular power it conferred on him. He told me because he was tortured by it and needed to tell someone. All I did was ask and it burst out of him like pus from a pimple. "You'll wanna sit down," he said, as he crumpled onto the floor. "Gómez'll be back in a coupla hours—he went ta the library. I might need alla that time.

"They was in love, Alex, 'n Gómez ruined it. The best thing he'd ever had 'n he throwed it away. They'd been out all day—Gómez hadn't seen L.A., not really—so they planned out the whole day. It started with breakfast downtown at The Pantry, then they went down Sunset Boulevard ta Beverly Hills, 'n finally ta the beach ta walk off breakfast. Gómez says ya get enough food at The Pantry ta last ya through lunch *and* dinner. Then they went ta Long Beach ta see the Queen Mary, then home.

"Gómez opened a bottle a wine 'n we drank it in the kitchen. They was still too full fer dinner, so we just had cheese 'n crackers. Ya don't know it yet, Alex, but there ain't nothin' in the world better'n wine with cheese 'n crackers, unless it's wine with Italian food 'n sourdough bread.

"Anyway, we was sittin' in the kitchen 'n they was tellin' me 'bout their day. They was holdin' hands, Alex. Gómez would start ta tell me somethin', then yer mom would jump in 'n add ta it, then Gómez would add ta it, 'n pretty soon it was like it was just them two in the room, so I decided ta leave 'em alone 'n went ta m'room. That was 'bout eight or nine.

"After awhile, it's real quiet. Then Gómez puts on one of his records, it's that song I like the most, the guy who wrote it I call Taco Bell cuz it sounds like that. I guess they're slow dancin', 'n I'm figurin' that's it, they've done it, they'z finally together 'n it's about time if ya ask me. If they're not kissin' durin' that song then peel me like a jalapeño chili. The record ends 'n I hear Gómez say, 'Maria, there's somethin' I need ta tell ya.' I almost close my ears—I don't wanna hear nothin' too personal—but I got a bad feelin', so I hold on a second ta see what happens next. Gómez tells her ta sit down, 'n now they're at the kitchen table again. I can hear ev'ry word they're sayin'; can even hear 'em breathin'.

"Gómez tells her the truth. He tells yer mom why he's here, that it warn't no accident. When he's done there's a long silence. Then I hear the worst sound I ever heard—yer mom, like her heart was just torn out. 'What? He was yer brother? My husband was yer brother?' Her voice is risin' 'n she's gettin' mad. I can hear Gómez tryin' ta calm her down, but it ain't workin'.

"'Maria,' he says, 'I wasn't tryin' ta deceive ya.'

"'Imagine what ya could do if ya tried!' she tells him.

"They was quiet, then Maria says, 'What is it with you Morales men? Eduardo said he didn't have any brothers or sisters. Were ya 'shamed a each other? Is there some dark family secret? He said his parents died when he was a boy, 'n he was raised by his uncle. Another lie, Gómez? Why am I askin' you? Of course it's a lie. Morales men are liars. They lie. That's what they do.'

"'I didn't lie, Maria,' Gómez tells her.

"'Don't mince words with me, Gómez!' yer Mom says. 'Ya knew the truth 'n ya hid it. 'N cuz of that I kissed the brother of my dead husband. 'N the worse thing is—I knew it; I knew ya was trouble. Knew first time I saw ya. Congratulations, Gómez. Put it in yer family album—the Morales Boys Strike Again! But now it's my turn.'

"I heard yer mom slap Gómez, 'n then Gómez say, 'Maria! Don't go! Come back!' But the screen door slammed like she wanted to bring down the house 'n ev'ryone in it."

I hadn't interrupted O.C. once. I couldn't; I was numb. Gómez and my father—*brothers*? It was both unbelievable and obvious at the same time. Of course: that's why Gómez came to our villa in the first place. Little things I had ignored came to mind: like on that first day, when he heard the news about my father, he seemed to stagger a bit; and then later, when we unloaded chairs from the truck, he was just a little bit *too* interested in my father; and finally, why he never gave his last name. "It's just Gómez." There was no doubt it was true. Ol' Uncle Gómez.

Finally, I was able to get out one word. "Unbelievable."

"Ya don't know the half of it," answered O.C.

That was an odd thing to say. I looked at O.C. What was he talking about? He gave me a quick look and then averted his eyes. His face flushed. What was this all about?

"O.C., what aren't you telling me?"

"Why do ya ask?" he answered, looking down at his feet.

"Because you said, 'You don't know the half of it.' So, O.C., what don't I know?"

Perspiration beaded his forehead. I was beginning to doubt if I *wanted* to know. Whatever it was, it seemed so dreadful—O.C. was now using his shirt to wipe the sweat from his face—that now I *had* to know. "Tell me, O.C. Tell me now."

"Christ dammit, Alex, I shouldn't. Oh, geez." O.C. wrung his hands. I felt I needed to find out if just for O.C.'s sake; much more of this and he was likely to just break apart right here in Gómez's living room.

"Do ya promise not ta tell anyone?"

"Sure."

"Even Gómez? Ya promise not ta tell Gómez?"

"I said I wouldn't tell anyone. That means Gómez too."

O.C., still seated on the floor with his back to the wall, banged his fist against his forehead and said: "The reason Gómez was in prison is cuz he killed his dad."

O.C. paused, looking at me. He didn't want to go on until it had sunk in, and he was right to do that; it took a few seconds.

"Why?"

"Cuz he beat Gómez's brother."

"His brother—you mean my father?"

"Yep."

"Gómez killed his own father because he beat *my* father?"

"Yep."

I felt myself getting angry. "Is that all the fuck you can say about it, O.C? '*Yep*'?"

"I can say a lot more, but what I say don't change nothin'."

I gave O.C. a hard look. "O.C., tell me the whole story."

Reluctantly, he told me. They were living in El Paso, Texas. Gómez was the older brother, Eduardo about five years younger. Gómez's dad beat the boys: not all the time, but a lot; their mother too. Gómez left home after high school to work on a fishing boat. Coming home a few months later, he found his brother badly beaten. He walked to the bar where his father was playing pool, grabbed a pool cue, and without saying a word, beat him to death.

O.C. stopped. I didn't have the strength to speak. The scene painted itself in my mind. Probably five minutes went by. It seemed like the room had gotten darker. Finally, O.C. continued. "It was voluntary manslaughter.

He coulda been out in ten, but he kept doin' things that stretched 'em. That's how he ended up in Folsom."

I felt sick. "Didn't it matter that his father had beaten my father?"

"It mighta. But his brother didn't testify."

I mulled his over. "How do you know all this, O.C.? Did Gómez tell you?"

"No," answered O.C. quickly. "Gómez don't know I know. A friend of mine found out fer me. All Gómez told me was he had a brother; that was all."

"Did you ask him?"

"Gómez? No, that'd be stupid. Gómez don't talk 'bout stuff like that. Ain't you noticed? Gómez don't have a bad thing ta say 'bout anyone—at least mosta the time. Anyway, if I'da asked him, he'd a said he did it and that was that. Then he woulda made a joke 'bout how all convicts is innocent."

"Any idea why my father didn't testify?"

"Yeah, I got an idea. Sorry, Alex, but it gets worse."

He told me that when their mother—my grandmother—found out what had happened, she raced to the jail to be with Gómez. She ran a red light and her car was hit by a truck, killing her. Turned out she didn't even have a driver's license.

The blood seemed to just drain out of my body. This was more bad news in an hour than I'd known in my whole life.

"So, why didn't my father testify?"

"Well, by the time a the trial, he was livin' with his uncle. They mighta lived far away, or it mighta been cuz he was a minor. But here's the real reason, I think. One day I was in Gómez's cell. He stepped out fer a minute, and fer some reason he was gone a while, so I started ta look around fer somethin' to do. I found a box and there was a picture in it, a picture of yer grandmother. On the back someone'd written a note. It had only four words on it: 'I'll never forgive ya.' It warn't signed, but I think it was from yer dad."

O.C. stopped. I looked at him for a long moment. "So, when Gómez got out he decided to look up his brother?"

"Yep. But he didn't come here right away. The way I figure it, he found out where yer dad lived 'n waited ta get an apartment close by. This place opened up. Just luck."

"Why didn't he just come over and say hello?"

"Dunno, but I think he really wanted ta work things out, 'n one visit might notta done it. But if he lived next door . . . ."

It made sense. I sighed and said conversationally, "Well, O.C., does that cover it? Is there any more bad news? You might as well give it to me now."

O.C.'s face went white. His eyes started to tear. Oh shit, there was more. *I knew it.* Without even asking I knew what it was.

"Gómez is dying."

Thinking Blue

The rest of the summer of 1988 was a blur. Probably I went numb on the day O.C. told me who Gómez was, and have been numb, to some extent, ever since. Only now, as I begin to set down the events of July, do I recall details forgotten since that summer.

The most difficult task I had for the remainder of that summer was to make good on my promise to O.C. and keep Gómez's secret, which meant not letting on that I was devastated. Fortunately, the Dodgers came to the rescue. They began to lose—suddenly, and often, and with a will.

It started after Gómez and my mom broke up. We lost two to the Cardinals, took three of four from the Pirates, but then lost six of the next ten. The last game against the Astros we lost 10-0. *Ten to zero*! Our lead shrank from seven games to only one-and-a-half.

That's when O.C. and Mr. Sánchez pulled me aside; enough was enough. O.C. started in first, subtle-like. "Say Alex, I been so worried 'bout the Dodgers I forgot ta ask ya about yer mom. I haven't seen her since, well, how long has it been? The first doubleheader we took from the Cubs? Yep, that's it. Before Gibson's second homer, yer mom had us all hold hands in a circle. Gómez gimme a wink that said, 'Shhhh.' He hates fairy stuff like that, but he went along cuz it was yer mom. And whattaya know, Gibson hits a homer. Do ya remember that, Sánchez?"

"Yes," answered Mr. Sánchez glumly. "I remember because it started a six-game winning streak."

"Yep. I think yer right 'bout that. Then what happened?"

"They broke up and we lost three in a row," answered Mr. Sánchez without hesitation. "Both Fernando and Hershiser lost—back to back, which is impossible. Shelby gets hit in the eye by a foul ball—bad luck. Then Fernando gets bombed by Houston, at home, and the next day he's put on the Disabled List for the first time in his career."

O.C. muttered, "Now our lead is down to a game 'n a half. Say Sánchez, do ya think one thing had somethin' ta do with the other?"

Mr. Sánchez shrugged. "It doesn't take much to upset a winning streak."

"Yup," agreed O.C. "I reckon yer right 'bout that. It don't take much ta upset a winnin' streak."

I didn't say anything—we all knew how delicate these things were. The breakup probably *did* have something to do with how the Dodgers were playing. Certainly, Gómez's mood wasn't the same. He watched the games of course, but he frequently had a "not there" look in his eyes. Many times he would hear us cheering, or, these days, ranting, and he'd have to ask us what happened. But what was I supposed to do, march him down to my house and squeeze his hand into my mom's clenched fist?

The next evening the Dodgers hit bottom, and marching Gómez down to my house to beg forgiveness suddenly seemed like a good idea. We were in Cincinnati to play the Reds and we got spanked, 6-0. In the post-game show Lasorda said, "We're just not hitting the ball. I wish I knew why." I lifted my head and saw O.C. exchange a knowing look with Mr. Sánchez. Then we all looked over at Gómez, sitting there with his back to the wall, gazing into space.

O.C. lifted his eyebrows in a look that said "*Well?*" and mouthed, "It's up ta us," making a small circle with his right index finger to indicate the three of us. We nodded, then O.C. pointed his finger at me, jabbing it in the air a couple of times. I shook my head "No." I looked at Mr. Sánchez, who mimicked O.C.'s movements. Again I shook my head. Now they both were jabbing their fingers at me.

I decided to do it; I just needed to start. "Gómez?"

He didn't even blink, so I spoke louder. *"GÓMEZ?"* It was like speaking to a rock, but I had an inspiration. I did a roly-poly across the room, right in front of him. When I reached the other side, I glanced at him from my bent-over position. He was looking at me.

"What are you doing, Alex?" he said with a wry smile.

"Just trying to get your attention."

"Why?"

"Cuz ya looked like ya was drownin'," said O.C., "but we wanted ta make sure before I took off m'boots and jumped in ta save ya."

Gómez laughed softly. "That bad, huh?"

Mr. Sánchez said, "Yesterday I saw two vultures circling above the house."

"'N this mornin'," continued O.C., "them two buzzards was flippin' a coin fer first dibs on yer eyes."

Gómez rubbed his forehead with his right hand. "*Two* buzzards, eh? That's a bad omen."

"Yes," replied Mr. Sánchez. "But only one of them was for you. The other one was for the Dodgers."

"They lost again?"

"Yes, but we're getting better. Today we only lost 6-0. Yesterday it was 10-0."

"Well, every team has a losing streak."

"This is more than that," countered O.C. quickly.

"It's a jinx," added Mr. Sánchez.

The room was silent for a minute or two; we had done as much leading as we dared. None of us wanted to come right out and say that the breakup was the reason the Dodgers were losing, but the seconds were ticking by and Gómez looked like he would soon slide back into his shadow world.

Once again those two shameless cowards, O.C. Martin and Humberto Sánchez, gestured at me with their forefingers. Mr. Sánchez began to flick his fingers at me. Well, I buckled.

"Gómez, have you noticed anything strange about the Dodgers' losing streak?"

Gómez roused himself once more and said, "Eh? What's that?"

"The Dodgers, Gómez; have you noticed they started losing when you and my mom broke up?"

Oops—hello wolf-eyes. No wonder those two cowards sent the kid in first.

"What are you saying, Alex? That your mom and I are responsible for the Dodgers losing a few games?"

I shrugged.

Gómez shot a look over to O.C. He shrugged too, meeting Gómez's eyes for only a moment before caving in. Gómez continued to glare at him, then swung his eyes towards his next victim, Mr. Sánchez, where something unexpected happened: Mr. Sánchez stared right back.

"Yes," answered Mr. Sánchez in that unequivocal tone of his, "that is exactly what we are saying."

"You are all full of crap." Gómez stood up and walked toward his room. Before he slammed the door he turned and said to each of us, one at a time, slowly and with emphasis, "Crap . . . CRAP . . . and *CRAP*!"

I looked at O.C. and Mr. Sánchez. "Well, that went good."

"It ain't over," scowled O.C. "Not by a long shot."

Suddenly the bedroom door jerked open. "AND FURTHERMORE," bellowed Gómez, "PEOPLE SHOULD MIND THEIR OWN BUSINESS, DON'T YOU THINK?"

We said nothing, and Gómez's eyes bore into each of us with a look that said, "The first one to speak, dies." Finding no takers, he turned and stepped back into his room, slamming the door again. A moment later we heard him cough. Then cough again. I looked at O.C. and Mr. Sánchez. Both of them were looking down, their steely resolve gone.

"I think we need a different plan," I said.

*****

With O.C.'s permission I went to my tía to tell all, because none of us had the skills needed to navigate these waters. Even if we somehow managed to turn Gómez and get him to try to reconcile things with my mom, he was the easy one! Nobody could carry a grudge like my mom; she was the champ. She would've snapped Gómez like a piece of balsa wood.

"Tía," I said when she opened her door, "I'm in trouble." It wasn't true, of course, but it was the quickest way to get her attention. She took a quick glance behind me and ushered me in. When we sat down at her kitchen table she was the lioness and I was the errant but goodhearted cub: *her cub.*

I got right to the point: "Tía, there are things about Gómez you don't know."

Over the next ten minutes, she didn't interrupt me once. When I was done, she went to the fridge and pulled out a cold Corona. "You want one?"

she asked. She leaned back against the counter, popped off the cap and took a long pull. "Carmen needs to think."

Gómez's living room was empty and dark. There was a light on at Mr. Sánchez's so I knocked on his door. Mrs. Sánchez opened it. Her eyes were red and she had a tissue in her hand. She was about to speak when I heard Mr. Sánchez say from inside the living room, "Come in, Alex."

O.C. was sitting in one of the easy chairs, Mr. Sánchez in the other. Mrs. Sánchez invited me to join her on the couch. It was obvious that O.C. had told them everything, and I wasn't surprised. Once he started it would've been impossible for O.C. to stop; he was too guileless, too transparent and too accommodating—and it was just as well.

"Is there anything else?" asked Mr. Sánchez.

"Nope," replied O.C. "But I feel terrible. I don't know why, but I feel terrible."

Mrs. Sánchez walked over and covered his clasped hands with her own, then kissed him on the cheek. "I know this is hard, O.C., but you've done the right thing. You've been a good friend to Gómez; a *best* friend. And Gómez will know this."

O.C. dropped his eyes.

"What to do," said Mr. Sánchez. "What to do . . . ."

"I told Carmen everything, too," I said. "She's thinking it over."

"Well, let's analyze this thing like any problem. What are the pieces to this problem?"

"They're in love," said Mrs. Sánchez.

Mr. Sánchez smiled. "Yes. They are certainly in love." Then Mr. Sánchez stole a glance at Mrs. Sánchez, who turned to me and said, "Alex, are you okay with this? That Gómez is in love with your mother?"

It was a well-intentioned question, but stupid. There is a notion that kids are weak, vulnerable, and excessively sensitive. Nothing could be further from the truth. When you think about how much kids put up with, being ignored, interrupted, jerked this way and that, yelled at and even criticized right in front of others as if they weren't even there—things that no adult would tolerate for a second—it seems to me that kids are plenty tough. I remember bristling at Mrs. Sánchez's question, although I couldn't put my finger on why.

"Sure," I answered disconcertedly. It was a little too disconcerted, so both Mr. and Mrs. Sánchez gave me that overlong, worried adult look. When I didn't burst out into tears they apparently were satisfied.

"Gómez is stubborner than a mule," stated O.C., answering Mr. Sánchez's question.

"Yes," smiled Mr. Sánchez, "he's a mule all right. What else?"

"My mom can be even more stubborn than Gómez," I answered.

"Yes," answered Mr. Sánchez.

Mrs. Sánchez cleared her throat. "Gómez is dying." After a pause, she continued haltingly, "Time. Not a lot."

There was no acknowledgment from Mr. Sánchez or anyone else; we just lowered our heads. Finally Mr. Sánchez spoke: "Well, that covers it, I guess. I'd like to think it over. It's late; why don't we all think it over and see if we can come up with some ideas."

At home, Rosa was curled up in my mom's arms, watching TV. My mom's eyes were closed, but Rosa's were wide-open, hypnotized by the flickering lights. I walked by unseen and went straight to my room.

I picked up The Last Unicorn and laid down to read. But I couldn't get into it. What to do? What to do? When I awoke in the morning, sleep had provided no answers.

*****

I got up late and walked into the living room where Rosa was watching TV again. I was about to enter the kitchen when I heard my mom's voice.

"What's so important that I need to call in sick? Carmen, are you all right?"

"I'm not telling you anything, *mi hermana*, until you promise me you'll stay. Not all day, just the morning." My ears perked up. Had Carmen come up with an idea? "Or," she continued, "tell them one of your kids is sick and you'll be in later."

"Lie."

"Yes, lie. A white lie, that's all."

"I won't lie, Carmen. But I will take the morning off if it's that important to you."

My mom picked up the phone, called in, and put the receiver back down. "Now what?"

"Come over to my house. This is private; I don't want to be interrupted."

When my mom and Carmen walked into the living room, I was lying on the carpet, my eyes blankly fixed on the TV. It was pretty darn convincing.

"Alex!" my mom said cheerfully. "Good morning. I didn't know you were up." I looked up at her sleepily, catching the wry smile on my tía's face. I never got anything past her.

Later, Carmen told me what happened in that meeting.

Manita, I know about Gómez and you.

No you don't.

Yes I do. O.C. heard you from his bedroom.

No he didn't.

Yes, he did.

He didn't hear everything.

Yes dear, he did.

Then tell me. If you know what was said, then tell me.

Gómez. Eduardo. Brothers.

So—you know.

Maria, he's a good man.

Good man? Do good men lie? Do they lie about things that are important? That was kind of important, don't you think? The son-of-a-bitch is Eduardo's brother. What kind of 'good man' would do that, Carmen?

An honest one.

Haa! He lied, Carmen! He lied!

He told you the truth. When it mattered most, he told the truth.

Nonsense.

Not nonsense. Think about it. He has the woman he loves in his arms. His heart is pounding. His body is getting warm. And just at the moment when his body says, 'Excuse me, señor, I'll take over from here,' what does this man do who hasn't been with a woman in what, forty years? He stops himself and says, 'I have to tell you something.'

It's not that simple.

You're right, but you don't know why you're right.

What does that mean?

I'll tell you what it means after you tell me this—can you imagine Eduardo saying, 'Stop everything. Before you take your clothes off, I need to make a confession.' Can you, Maria?

No.

Damn right you can't. But you've only been with one man; I've been with a few more. And not one of them, Maria, not one of them would've done what Gómez did.

So, what are you saying?

What am I saying? I'm saying you've found the man of your dreams. Hell, you've found the man of <u>*my*</u> *dreams, and if you don't get busy, I might forget you're my big sister and go up there myself. Problem is, he loves you Maria. He'd tap me on the head like a good little girl and send me home. I'd have to hate him, of course, and next week we'd be sitting in* <u>*your*</u> *kitchen, and you'd be telling me what a good man Gómez is . . . .*

Carmen, this is not an easy thing.

Maria dear, compared to what's next, this is the easy part. There's more; much more. Stay here. I'm going to get the Kleenex. We're gonna need it.

Carmen told her everything. It took all morning, and when it was over my mom was in no shape to go to work. When she called in and said she wasn't feeling well, she wasn't lying.

While Mom was at Carmen's I watched cartoons for a short while and then fell asleep on the couch. I was more than asleep: I was unconscious. I had just woken up when my mom opened the front door. She glanced at me and went straight to the kitchen. "Mom, I'm going up to Gómez's." I didn't wait for a reply.

I was surprised to see Eddie seated on the floor opposite Gómez. "Hey bro," he said. "You were sleeping when I walked out. Man, you were gone."

"Long gone. I didn't sleep too well last night."

"Me and Gómez were just talkin' about you. He thinks you're hopeless, says you'll never amount to nothin', but I say you're not *totally* hopeless."

"Eddie . . . ." Gómez cut in.

"What?"

"It was *you* I said was hopeless. Alex I said was a genius, the saving grace of the Morales family. And if you're a good boy Eddie, he might take care of you someday."

"Am I gonna have to whup you after all, Gómez?" Eddie glanced at me and winked.

"Think you could, hard ass?"

"I don't *think*, I *know*."

"Then stop talking. Give it try. Today might be your lucky day."

"Wouldn't take luck, Gómez."

"Well," answered Gómez resolutely as he began to untangle his legs, "I think I've heard enough from *El Torito.*"

"Stay down old man . . . ."

The screen door swung open and Mr. Sánchez and O.C. walked in. Gómez settled back down and wagged a finger at Eddie. "You got lucky, Baby Bull."

Mr. Sánchez cleared his throat, and with O.C. standing beside him, said, "Gómez, we need to talk to you."

"Uh-oh," said Eddie, "this is where I check out. Hangin' with one old man is bad enough, but three?" He stood up and walked over to the front door. "Anyway Gómez, I came over to tell you I'm workin' things out with Hector. Gettin' out is harder than gettin' in."

"That's what I've heard," answered Gómez. "Anything I can do to help?"

"No—well, would you mind if I dumped your dead ass in Hector's yard?"

"You think that would do the trick?"

"If I ran you over a few times first, then dragged you through the street, yeah."

Gómez rubbed his Hemingway. "Tell you what: I have a few more plans for this body, but when I'm done, why the hell not."

"Well, that'll be my backup plan. Actually, Hector surprised me. I told 'em some of the shit we talked about."

Gómez furrowed his eyes. "How much?"

"Just a little. He was listenin'."

Gómez nodded thoughtfully. Eddie said, "I'm back in school."

"That's great!" exclaimed Gómez.

"I hope so. Takin' three classes: English, math, and American history."

"Incredible! English—smart move. Good place to start."

"Yeah, at the bottom. I had grammar in third grade and things've been fuzzy ever since."

"I wasn't kidding Eddie, when I said I'd help you any way I can. I spent a lot of time in the prison library—did you know I was in prison?"

"No, Gómez, I'm the village idiot. Christ, Aguilar's hamster knows you were in prison." Eddie grinned and swung open the door. "Adios."

Gómez was smiling, but the smile disappeared once he looked at O.C. and Mr. Sánchez. "Gentlemen," said Gómez addressing the two stern-faced men, "please, sit down. This looks serious."

"It is serious, Gómez," answered Mr. Sánchez. O.C. nodded.

Gómez looked over at O.C. and frowned. "No. No, you don't. We had this conversation yesterday. Once was enough. I don't like to cover the same real estate twice."

"Fine," answered Mr. Sánchez. "Would you rather talk about El Paso?"

Gómez's wolf-eyes narrowed. "Amigos, what do you think you know about El Paso?"

"I know someone from there who's been *tiempo cómo muerto* for a very long time . . . ."

Gómez's boring eyes stopped drilling.

"And, his people want him back."

Gómez's eyes faltered and he stroked his Hemingway slowly. "Mr. Sánchez, there is much that his people don't know."

"I'm sure. There is much that isn't known about all of us. But, in the case of this one person of whom I speak, much *is* known; at least the main events. They were reported in the El Paso newspapers."

Until then both Mr. Sánchez and O.C. hadn't left the doorway. Now Mr. Sánchez crossed the room and settled down onto the floor in the spot Eddie has just occupied. O.C. just stuck his hands into his pockets and leaned back against the door frame. Gómez looked at each of us, and settling on Mr. Sánchez, asked, "What now?"

"It boils down to one thing," answered Mr. Sánchez.

Gómez waited for him to complete the thought, and when he didn't Gómez said, "Well, what is it?"

"The Dodgers, of course," answered Mr. Sánchez.

A smile appeared on Gómez's face. "Yes, of course; the Dodgers. They're not doing too well, I hear."

"Nope," chipped in O.C. He crossed the room and sat down next to Gómez, his skinny legs stretched out. "Just two weeks ago they was up eight games, now it's only a half a game. The whole season's goin' up in smoke."

"Yes," Gómez smiled grimly, "that is serious. Should we mobilize the National Guard? Give Ronnie Reagan a call?"

"It wouldn't help," answered Mr. Sánchez. "Think cause-and-effect Gómez. What caused the slump? That's the question, and the answer."

"I see: logic; scientific thinking. So, what is the question and answer?"

"Maria."

"No kidding? That's the conclusion to your exhaustive analysis?"

"Finding the answer wasn't hard," replied Mr. Sánchez, "but getting a thick-headed mule like you to see what is obvious to everyone else—that's a challenge."

"Well, you succeeded my friend. Now the question: what to do?"

O.C. let out a howl! "He's back!" He leaped off the floor and bounded over to Mr. Sánchez to exchange "high fives." It was ugly, but funny.

"What does Maria know," asked Gómez.

"Nothing yet," answered Mr. Sánchez.

"Wrong," I interjected.

Until then I'd been pretty much forgotten; now all three of them fixed their eyes on me.

"Speak," Gómez gently commanded.

"Carmen told my mom this morning."

"How much did she tell her?"

"Everything."

Gómez's eyebrows pinched together. "Tell me, amigos, just so I know, what does 'everything' mean?"

"Well, Uncle Gómez. . . ." I just let that hang there a moment. "We know about your dad, how he died."

"And your *madre*," added Mr. Sánchez.

Gómez massaged his Hemingway. "Well, that's a lot." He paused and then said, "Which brings us back to the question: what do we do?"

The answer was interrupted by rapping on the screen door. Mr. Sánchez crossed the room and swung it open. "Hello Carmen."

"Hello Humberto. I'm here on official business. May I speak to *El Segundo de Señor Gómez?*"

"Ahh," said Mr. Sánchez. "That would be Señor O.C. Martin, señorita. I will summon him."

"Then chop-chop, señor. My mistress won't be kept waiting."

Mr. Sánchez turned, and grinning from ear to ear, said, "Señor Martin, at the gate awaits a messenger from Señora Morales. She has asked for an audience with you, concerning a private matter."

O.C. drew himself up and approached the screen door. "Señorita," he said. "What kin I do fer ya?"

Gómez rolled his eyes and shook his head. He leaned over to me. "Never send a dirt farmer to do a herald's work."

"Señor," said Carmen without breaking a smile, "please inform Señor Gómez that my mistress wishes to dine with him this evening. Here, at Casa de Gómez. At eight o'clock sharp."

"Yes ma'am," answered O.C.

"And señor, as the second to Señor Gómez, please see to the needs of my mistress. She prefers wine, not beer. She prefers fish, not meat. And she prefers music to baseball. Is this clear, señor?"

"Yes ma'am," answered O.C.

"Very well." Carmen turned to go and then stopped. "One more thing, señor: they will be spending the evening alone—the *entire* evening. Is this understood?"

I could see the edges of the broad smile that spread across O.C.'s elastic face. "Yes ma'am!"

"Thank you." Carmen curtseyed. "Adios, Señor Martin."

O.C. watched Carmen walk away, her hips no doubt swinging broadly from side to side, and then turned to us. "Oooohweee! That Carmen gets me goin'!"

"Must've been the way she talked, eh, cowboy?" said Gómez.

"Nope, don't think so," replied O.C. matter-of-factly.

"Well," asked Mr. Sánchez, "isn't there a message you want to deliver to Señor Gómez?"

"Oh," answered O.C. simply. He turned to Gómez and in an official tone said, "Señor—"

"Hold on for one moment, Señor Martin," said Gómez. "I need to be standing up when I hear this." Gómez raised himself slowly off the floor. "Ready."

O.C. stretched his throat as if to clear it—a comical sight—and said, "The Honorable Señora Morales has requested ta dine with ya this evenin'." He smiled proudly. Gómez did, too.

Mr. Sánchez hissed, "There's more!" O.C. looked perplexed, so Mr. Sánchez added, "No beer . . . ."

Recognition dawned on O.C.'s face. "'N she don't want no beer, no meat, 'n she wants ta be alone—except fer you." He frowned and scratched his baseball cap. "Somethin' else . . . . Oh! No baseball game!"

Gómez laughed. "Thank you again, Señor Martin. I have understood the lady's message. Would you please deliver my reply forthwith?"

O.C. looked a little confused and mumbled, "Ahhh . . . sure." I think it was the "forthwith" that got him.

"Please tell her that I'm delighted to dine with her this evening, and that my man will arrive promptly at eight p.m. to escort her to my villa."

"Okay!"

"That will be all for now, señor," said Gómez. "Off with you lad, and be lively!" O.C. bolted through the door to deliver his message to my tía, and when the screen door bounced shut, Mr. Sánchez let out a spine-tingling Oaxacan war whoop. "We're back in business!"

"Almost," laughed Gómez, "but there's work to do yet; plenty of work. For instance, do you know anyone who can cook fish?"

Mr. Sánchez snorted. "You insult me, sir."

Gómez smiled mischievously. "I had a feeling. Would you do me the honor?"

"The honor is all mine. I'll take care of everything."

And he did. At five o'clock, he and O.C. brought into Gómez's living room a small round table from Mr. Aguilar's, followed by two wooden chairs, a white table cloth and two candles mounted on silver candleholders.

At six o'clock Mr. Sánchez reappeared with the evening's fare and went right to work in Gómez's kitchen. Meanwhile, Gómez and O.C. adjourned to Gómez's bedroom and I sat down to watch the Dodger game. They were in Cincinnati, and in the top of the fourth inning the Reds were leading our boys 1-0: Rijo vs. Hershiser. In the top of the fifth, we scored four runs, and in the ninth we scored four more, thanks to two Red's errors. We won 8-5. Our luck was back!

O.C. had been ducking in and out to check on the score, but I hadn't seen Gómez for some time. I asked O.C. about it and he came up close to me and whispered, "He's takin' a nap. The boy needs his stren'th."

Finally, at ten minutes to eight the door to Gómez's bedroom swung open. O.C. was dressed in his black duel outfit. Gómez had on the same white suit that I'd seen for the third time now, but this time he was wearing a blue scarf. His hair and beard were neatly trimmed; he looked sharp. O.C. extended his arm back towards Gómez and said, "I present Señor Gómez, cleaned 'n pressed."

Gómez bowed to O.C. and said to me, "You didn't know O.C. was the prison barber, did you?"

"Nope," I laughed. "That one got by me."

"How's dinner coming along?" asked Gómez.

"Why do you ask?" yelled Mr. Sánchez from the kitchen. "Is there a doubt?"

"No doubt, señor!"

"Then don't ask stupid questions."

"These geniuses," said Gómez softly, "they're so sensitive!"

"I heard that!" yelled Mr. Sánchez.

Gómez whispered even softer. "See what I mean?"

End over end, a knife whisked through the air and implanted itself in the dining room wall.

Gómez and O.C. and I looked at each other. "I think," said Gómez, "we'd better leave the cook alone."

"Good idea," agreed O.C. "Think I'll rustle up a pretty woman from down the hill."

Gómez bent to retie his shoelace. I had an inspiration, and as he began to stand I grabbed his right hand and said, "Rise, my fortuitous friend."

He did, and as I shook his hand I said, "Good luck, Gómez."

He leaned forward and hugged me, whispering in my ear, "My dear friend, thank you." He put his hands on my shoulders and kissed me on the forehead. "All right, enough of that," he concluded, and tousled my hair.

I walked outside in time to see my mom finish her ascent up the stairs, her right hand tucked under O.C.'s left arm. Goodness, she was beautiful. She was wearing a long red dress, offset by a white silk sash tied around her waist and falling half way to her knees. Her shiny black hair flowed in long lazy curls to her bare shoulders and a string of pearls glowed against her brown neck. Completing the short distance to Gómez's walkway, they turned left into *Villa de Gómez.* O.C. betrayed not the slightest awareness that I was there, but my mom winked as she passed. Whew.

With nowhere to go, I went down to my house and plopped onto the couch. Carmen was there with Rosa. They had on an old movie: *Harvey*, with James Stewart. We watched it as we ate pizza. Then I went to my room and finished The Last Unicorn. Good book. I've been reading ever since.

The next morning I went over to Mr. Sánchez's. My tía had already cautioned me not to go to Gómez's in the morning—like I was an idiot, I swear. Mr. Sánchez opened the door and let me in. He and Mrs. Sánchez were still laughing over some joke, and I asked them to repeat it. "With pleasure, Alex," he said.

"When your mom arrived, O.C. presented her to Gómez as 'My lady, Mary.' Apparently the error was lost on O.C., because we waited a moment for him to correct himself, but he didn't. He simply dismissed himself by walking backwards until he banged into the door and stumbled onto the patio, tripping over his own feet and landing in West Garden. 'Shit!' we heard him say. O.C., he has a natural gift."

Mrs. Sánchez giggled again.

"Then," continued Mr. Sánchez, "I poured them each a glass of chardonnay—expensive chardonnay I might add. They each took a sip as they looked into each other's eyes, and then Maria said, 'Señor, didn't Carmen tell your man I wanted us to be alone?'

"'Why, yes, Maria,' Gómez answered suavely; 'but we *are* alone. This man,' he motioned to me, 'he's just the cook!'" Mrs. Sánchez laughed again.

"But what came next was one of the most touching things I've ever seen, and I'll swear I didn't say it if you tell anyone."

"Of course, dear."

"Alex?"

"Of course, dear."

Mrs. Sánchez winked playfully at me while Mr. Sánchez gave me a narrow look.

"Gómez put on a record—a gift from Aguilar—and they stood in the middle of the room like two teenage kids on their first date. Gómez opened his arms, inviting Maria to dance, and Maria accepted, placing her head on his shoulder. Then I heard the voice—what a voice! Isabella, it was the most beautiful song I've ever heard. While they danced, I cried. Alone in the kitchen, I cried."

"What was the song, Humberto? Perhaps I know it."

Mr. Sánchez closed his eyes as if in thought, and we waited. Suddenly his chest began to heave. He was crying! Mrs. Sánchez went to his side to console him from whatever it was that had so overwhelmed him.

"It was in Italian." He paused: "'Time to Say Goodbye.'" Tears welled up in my eyes, too.

Mr. Sánchez said, "Poor Maria. I could feel her silent weeping as Gómez held her in his arms. By accident, Mr. Aguilar had chosen an album whose first song stated the exact thing that no one could bring himself to say."

*****

I had just walked out of the Sánchez's house when Gómez's screen door swung open and he stumbled out on his knees. After crawling a few feet, he collapsed altogether. I would've been alarmed had my mom not followed him, laughing and throwing her dish towel at him. "You're not funny, Gómez!" she yelled softly, chiding him and laughing at the same time. "Get back in here! The neighbors are going to see you!"

She looked past Gómez and saw me. "Christ!" she exclaimed, quickly covering her offending mouth. "Hello, Alex! Don't mind Gómez. He's fine." Then she quickly contradicted herself and said, "He's not fine! He's crazy! Gómez, get off the sidewalk and come back in here and help me with the dishes!" She turned and hastily re-entered the house.

Gómez rolled over on his back, laughing. "Please, son, come help me. I don't think I can get up!"

"Leave him there," said O.C. as he ascended the last landing. "I'll roll him inta a trash can later."

"O.C.! Just in time! Pick me up, old friend!"

O.C. shook his head as if to say "pathetic." Then he put his arm on my shoulder and said, "All right, Alex, let's help this bag-a-bullshit onta his feet."

That night the Dodgers lost. Well, that's baseball for you, as Gómez would say. But, even in defeat there was reason to believe we were back. Gibson went 4-5, including three doubles and a homer, and Marshall hit a homer too. Besides that, the Dodgers brought up a young phenom named Ramon Martinez.

We were sitting on Gómez's patio after the game, and despite the loss, Gómez was ecstatic. "It's just the sort of thing that happens in a magical season," he said. "Some young pitcher comes up and bam!—he's the difference. When Fernando came up in nineteen-eighty he didn't allow a run in his first seventeen innings." We all nodded our heads thoughtfully.

The next night we beat the Giants, at home, 7-3. We were back to two-and-a-half up over Houston, three-and-a-half over the Giants. We won the next game too, with Ramon Martinez pitching brilliantly in his major league debut. But the next night we lost so completely as to warrant no comment, except to say that it was Hershiser who lost, and after that he began a streak of spectacular pitching which would include breaking one of baseball's most unbreakable records.

The following night Tim Belcher, a rookie that year, threw seven shutout innings to beat the Giants 1-0, starting a seven-game winning streak. During the streak Guerrero was traded to the Cardinals for John Tudor; Martinez, our new child prodigy, threw another great game to beat the Phillies 2-1; Hershiser pitched a five-hit shutout, and the streak concluded with the ever-heroic Leary, certainly the most underrated Dodger of 1988, pitching a four-hit shutout over the Expos.

The Mets ended our steak, beating us twice in a row, but then we went on another five game winning streak to extend our lead to six-and-a-half games over Houston. More than once Mr. Sánchez, O.C. and I exchanged knowing smiles. We had done right. The season had been on the very brink of failure, and but for emergency action all would have been lost. That we had saved the season we had no doubt. Oh, and by the way, my mom and Gómez were inseparable.

The next five weeks of the season were so remarkable, on and off the ball field, as to warrant another book. For this history, however, hopefully a brief timeline of events will convey the main events, and the spirit, of autumn, 1988.

September 6

Dodgers beat the Astros 4-1. Shelby hits a three-run homer to win it in the eighth.

Bart Giamatti is named Baseball Commissioner, replacing Peter Ueberroth.

Eddie comes home with his first test scores in English; he scored a D. Gómez calls him the "Big D," playing on the nickname for former Dodger pitcher Don Drysdale. Everyone laughs except Eddie. He vows to get a "Big B" next time, or he'll be kicking Gómez's Big A.

September 10

The Dodgers beat the Reds 5-0; Hershiser wins his twentieth. It's his second straight shutout and his fifth straight complete game since getting beaten up by the Giants.

Cuban refugees arrive in Miami. However, the "refugees" are simply criminals. Gómez laughs until he coughs. "Say what you will, but Faithless Fidel has got a sense of humor."

Rosa enters Kindergarten. She was supposed to start Monday, but refused to go. She only relents when Gómez promises to accompany her to class. Gómez calls it one of the most gratifying days of his life, and from then on refers to Rosa as "my Rosa." The feeling is mutual: future references to Gómez are met with Rosa's query, "my Gómez?"

September 11

The Dodgers beat the Reds 5-3. Gibson homers in the fourth; in the ninth he singles, and despite a pulled hamstring, goes from first to third on a throwing error. Gibson's influence doesn't end there. Hamilton, who almost never hits a home run, hits a walk-off homer using Gibson's bat. Since the Guerrero trade, there's no doubt this is Gibson's team.

Ancient gold treasures are discovered in a Peruvian tomb. One of the artifacts is a string of gold showing a fierce-looking god lopping off heads. Gómez laughs, which is pretty much all he seems to do these days. "Those Inca gods were always so hard to please!"

Eddie, after some intensive grammar studies with Gómez, announces he failed again to get a "B," but would anyone accept an "A" instead? After a brief debate among the boys, it's decided that he's not permitted to use big words unless he tells us what they mean. Eddie agrees.

September 14

Orel throws his third straight shutout and sixth straight complete game. Mr. Sánchez figures out that if Orel pitches his last three starts and throws twenty-seven shutout innings, he'll tie Don Drysdale's record of fifty-eight and two-thirds consecutive scoreless innings. Of course, he could beat the record on the first day of the next year, but he'd get an * next to his name. If it wasn't for baseball, would anyone even know what an asterisk is?

Eddie reports in on his two other classes: math—B, American History—A.

September 16

Tim Browning beats the Dodgers 1-0. He gives up no runs, no hits, no walks, and the Reds commit no errors. That's a Perfect Game, folks. Damn, ain't baseball great? In front of tens of thousands of people, you are PERFECT. Oh, by the way, Tim Belcher got the loss, giving up one unearned run on three hits in eight innings; near-perfect just wasn't enough. That's béisbol fer ya. Gómez says the same thing happened to a pitcher named Hendley in the 60's, who gave up one hit against the Dodgers—and lost! *One hit and he lost!* Too bad for Hendley his opponent that day was Sandy Koufax, who was perfect.

Hurricane Gilbert pounds Monterey, Mexico. The resulting flood carries off four buses and almost 200 people die. Gómez says maybe it's time to lop off a few more heads.

September 17

The Dodgers beat the Reds 4-3 on Gibson's ninth inning heroics. The four of us review Gibson's exploits: he's personally scored or driven in the winning run twenty-three times! The man is a Phenomenon.

The Olympics begin in Seoul, South Korea.

September 18

The Dodgers beat the Reds 2-0, putting the Reds eight games back.

It's announced that the Iraqi government used poison gas on Kurd villages last month, killing thousands.

A lab states that the Shroud of Turin dates from 1100-1350 AD, contradicting belief that the shroud is actually the burial cloth of Jesus. Gómez laughs, then brings out Angelo and tortures us with flute music.

September 22

Our man Orel beats the Giants 3-0, extending his streak to 49 scoreless innings and his record to 23-9.

Eight Men Out appears in theaters. Gómez tells us the story of the 1919 Black Sox scandal. A pall settles over the room. After that we go see a *real* baseball movie, *Bull Durham*, released earlier in the summer. I love the part where Kevin Costner teaches the kid pitcher how to talk to reporters: funny stuff.

At the Olympics, Ben Johnson sets the 100 meters record at 9.79 seconds.

September 24

The Dodgers beat the Giants—that's the good news. The bad news is that Gibson didn't play because he still has a sore hamstring; Mike Marshall didn't play because of a sore back; and Mike Scoscia didn't play because of a bruised hip. On top of that, Tudor left the game after four innings because of pain in his left elbow. The Dodgers announce that Fernando will pitch Monday.

Pope John Paul beatifies Father Junipero Serra. The newspaper says Father Serra is now only one miracle away from sainthood. Gómez comments it's unlikely Father Serra will be able to perform that last miracle, considering he's been dead for 250 years. O.C., after thinking that over, concludes that, given those circumstances, almost anything Father Serra does at this point should qualify as a miracle.

George Bush and Michael Dukakis hold a television debate, which we don't watch due to the ballgame. Gómez says that if a news story is important enough, the TV station will interrupt the game. That leaves out quite a bit of news.

September 25

The Giants beat the Dodgers 2-0. Giant rookie Dennis Cook throws a complete game shutout. Belcher loses another tough game, giving up only two earned runs in eight innings. Gibson and Scoscia are still hurting and don't play.

At the Olympics, Carl Lewis wins the Olympic long jump.

September 26

The Dodgers beat the Padres 3-2 and clinch the Pennant!

Ben Johnson is stripped of the 100 meters gold medal for steroid use. Greg Louganis, American diver, wins his second gold.

September 27

The Dodgers lose to the Padres, 8-4. Leary gets rocked, but finishes the year 17-10. Tommy Lasorda takes the night off, providing color commentary on Dodger Radio, turning the team over to Bill Russell. When Russell steals Tommy's job three years later I wonder if Tommy thought back to this night.

September 28

The Dodgers lose to the Padres, 2-1, but Orel Hershiser throws ten scoreless innings and sets the scoreless inning record at fifty-nine. Phenomenal! Good thing the game went ten innings, otherwise Orel would've only tied the record! Fifty-nine scoreless—that's equal to more than six straight shutouts! Gómez says it is comparable to DiMaggio's fifty-six-game hitting streak, and I think he's right. Personally, I'd put Orel in The Baseball Hall of Fame on that achievement alone. Hall of Fame voters insist on career statistics, but some achievements are so great as to warrant inclusion among the greats. I mean, David beat Goliath only once. Hey Orel, for what you did that season you belong with the best of the best.

September 29

The Dodgers have the day off.

The Discovery space shuttle launches—the first launch since the Challenger disaster nearly three years before.

Mikhail Gorbachev ousts several key Communist Party leaders. Gómez tells me to read the article out loud, and as I'm reading he starts playing Angelo the flute.

October 1

The Dodgers beat the Giants 2-1, but Gibson aggravates the hamstring pull. That morning he awoke in so much pain that, when awarded a new Chevy truck that night as the Dodgers Most Valuable Player, he couldn't even walk to home plate to receive it. In the game itself, Belcher goes five scoreless and Fernando goes four scoreless. Problem is, Fernando's in pain and everyone knows it.

The Discovery returns to earth, but the Dodgers are still flying high.

October 2

The Giants beat the Dodgers on the last day of the season. The final standings have Houston trailing by twelve-and-a-half games, the Giants by eleven-and-a-half, the Padres by eleven, and the Reds by seven.

Hallelujah

Once cancer metastasizes, at some point the body realizes it can't win and the end comes fast. When the Dodgers clinched the pennant it was clear that Gómez had lost weight, but by the end of the season, just a week later, he went from thin to *emaciated.* Still, no one spoke of the cancer—at least not to him.

When we beat the Mets in the first game of the playoffs, Gómez slept through the game, except when he was coughing. We lost the next two games and Gómez didn't make it out of his bedroom. The fourth game was magic: losing 4-2, Mike Scoscia hit a two-run homer to tie the game in the top of the ninth inning, sending the game into extra innings. All of us: my mom, Rosa, O.C., Mr. Aguilar, Mr. Sánchez and Mrs. Cortez—everyone except Mrs. Sánchez, Carmen and Eddie—were in Gómez's living room when the bedroom door burst open and there he was, a stick man in overlarge pajamas, bellowing accusatively, "What's the score?"

My mom jumped up and led him gently into the living room. Everyone fixed their eyes on the game, careful not to witness the difficulty Gómez had walking.

"Thank you Maria," he said. "But," he spoke slowly and with effort, "one more thing, please. It is possible I may have to stay in this position for a while—" Before he could finish his sentence, a coughing spasm seized his body. When it subsided, he concluded his thought: "Rally—can't move—jinx."

"I understand, dear," my mom answered. She went into Gómez's bedroom and brought out two pillows, propping them behind him. Still, hardly a glance fell Gómez's way: a dozen eyes fixed on the TV, seeing nothing.

"What—is—the score? Or—" then some coughing, "or—didn't—anyone—hear me?"

"Geez," answered O.C. "Can't ya see we're tryin' ta watch the game?"

Gómez couldn't speak, but he did growl.

"Four to four," answered Mr. Sánchez, casually. "Bottom of the eleventh: the Mets are up, Peña is pitching, two outs—" He was interrupted as Vin Scully said, "There he goes!" as McReynolds stole second. Now everyone actually did forget about Gómez. Peña quickly got ahead of Howie Johnson 0-2, then the count evened at 2-2, and finally, after three foul balls, the next foul ball stayed in the park and was caught by Mike Sharperson. Whew. That was tense. And of course no one moved, including Gómez.

In the top of the twelfth, Sax grounded out and Stubbs, batting for Peña, struck out on three pitches. Not good. Then up came Gibson. On the second pitch—*goodbye*! Gibson hit it a mile, striking the potato chip sign on which were the words, "Simply Delicious." And it was. As Gibson continued his painful journey around the bases—he still had the pulled hamstring—all of us howled except Gómez. I did a roly-poly. Gómez threw me a reproachful glance; in baseball there are degrees of celebration, and the Mets still had one more chance.

I settled back into position, or as close to my original position as I could remember. "Hmmm," said Mr. Sánchez. "With Howell suspended, who do we bring in?"

"Hershiser," grunted Gómez.

It was an absurd thought. Hershiser had already pitched two games in the playoffs—two out of the three games! And, he had pitched seven innings *the day before.* There was no chance Hershiser would pitch, but given Gómez's condition, none of us wished to contradict him. When the commercial ended and the game came back on, the first thing we heard was Vin saying, "And here comes Tim Leary!"

"Wow," said Mr. Sánchez. "Well, it makes sense. Leary hasn't pitched once in this entire series, and he's our second best pitcher."

Sasser, the Mets catcher, immediately singled. Then Lee Mazilli singled too! Now I felt foolish for celebrating too soon. Fortunately, Jeffries flied to left. Jesse Orosco relieved Leary and walked Keith Hernandez, loading the bases for Darryl Strawberry. Yikes! Still, I'd rather face Strawberry than Hernandez. Whew!—Strawberry popped to second base. When Kevin McReynolds strode up to home plate, Lasorda stepped out of the dugout.

Vin Scully's voice rang from the TV: "Here comes Tommy. He's looking to the bullpen, and up goes his right hand. He's bringing in The Bulldog—Orel Hershiser!"

I looked at Gómez, who gave me an almost imperceptible nod.

As Orel strode to the mound, my admiration for him was boundless. Two pitches later McReynolds flied out to center. Game over. The Dodgers win!

That was the last time Gómez saw the Dodgers play. The next day he never got out of bed. My mom's doctor came over, and after meeting with Gómez he declared what everyone already knew—Gómez was dying of lung cancer. He urged Gómez to go to a hospital, but Gómez refused. When he began to write out a prescription for a painkiller, Gómez grabbed the paper and crumpled it. "What would you like me to do?" the doctor asked us.

My mom excused herself and went into Gómez's room. When she came out a minute later, she told the doctor to go ahead and write out a new prescription; Gómez had agreed. Then she turned to us and said, "It's as much for us as for him."

On Wednesday night the usual crowd, plus Eddie, gathered in Gómez's living room to watch game seven, which the Dodgers won 6-0 behind whom else—Orel Hershiser. But there was no celebrating. We were pleased the Dodgers won, of course, and the game was a welcome distraction, but none of us could muster the enthusiasm to celebrate. I looked at Gómez's record player and considered playing "Hallelujah," but quickly dismissed the thought. O.C. went into Gómez's room to report on the game and came out a few minutes later to say that Gómez wanted to see each of us. It was time.

Mr. Sánchez went to get Mrs. Sánchez, and when they returned they entered Gómez's room first. When they walked out, Mr. Sánchez held an envelope that deeded the record player and records to him and Mrs. Sánchez. There was also a note that read, "Music to dance by." Tears were streaming down Mrs. Sánchez's face, but Mr. Sánchez held his ground, only his red eyes and the strain on his face betraying his emotions. He told Mrs. Cortez she was next.

Mrs. Cortez went in, and soon we heard her laughing heartily. I thought I could even hear a wheezy laugh from Gómez. Walking out, she had Gómez's scarves—red, blue and white—woven together and tied by a string from which hung a long slip of paper that said, "HANDS OFF—PROPERTY OF MRS. CORTEZ!"

Mr. Aguilar entered Gómez's room next and came out with Gómez's white Panama hat on his head. Overcome with grief, without lifting his eyes he doffed the hat quickly and exited the house.

My tía was next, and she entered with Rosa holding her hand. Except for the crazy Mrs. Cortez, only Rosa returned from Gómez's room with the same cheerful disposition with which she entered. And why not? She now had a new silver hand mirror. Carmen had put sunglasses on, but nothing could hide her sorrow. An envelope protruded from her purse. In the envelope was a letter, and in the letter was a mystery that read: "November 15th, corner of Broadway and Mission."

Eddie, who was in there awhile, showed no emotion whatsoever when he came out. He walked across the living room, a white staff in his hand, and continued out the front door without a glance at anyone. We didn't see him for three days.

Next was O.C., who was falling to pieces before he even reached Gómez's door and was utterly undone when he returned. He had Gómez's flute, Angelo, in his right hand. He motioned it towards my mom, who was sitting at the kitchen table, watching Rosa admire herself in her new mirror.

My mom was in Gómez's room for maybe ten minutes, and when the door opened she was clutching a white, satin cape against her face. My tía quickly met her and led her out of the house. Her grief tore my heart.

Finally it was my turn. When I entered Gómez's room he lay flat on his bed, a bony figure in pale white pajamas, his left hand lying across his forehead. The fingers of his right hand moved slightly—a gesture to come forward. He handed me an envelope, and then said in a barely audible voice, "Open." I did.

Dear Alex,

What a time we had! I'm sure there has never been a salsa garden to compare with ours! And the Midsummer's Eve Party—what a night! And the Dodger game—meeting Vin Scully! To make so many dear friends so late in the game . . . .

You may wonder why I've asked for you last.

Help them, son; they are worth fighting for. Eddie will do what he can, but it is not enough to fight against something. One must fight for something, too.

There is a package for you in my closet.

Your friend,
Gómez

I looked at Gómez. Tears dripped down my face. I was trying so hard to hold in the grief that my cheeks hurt. He lifted his right hand and touched my arm, then pulled back the sheet slightly. There was his catcher's mitt. He felt for my hand and placed it on the mitt. A moment later he took his hand away. I waited, then went to his closet and took the package. It was about the size of a book, wrapped in brown paper. On the cover, in Gómez's hand, it read: "Open on Graduation Day."

Gómez died the next day, Thursday, October 13th, at 2:47 a.m. I was in bed when I woke up, thinking "Gómez is dead." I got on my pants and went up to his house. I reached the top of the stairs and saw Mr. Sánchez. He knew, too. My mom was sitting by Gómez's bed, holding his hand. It had just happened. His face was peaceful.

The Dodgers were going to the World Series without Gómez. O.C. told me later that when Gómez arrived at our villa he had only hoped to make it through the season, but when the Dodgers seized first place and wouldn't let go, Gómez extended his goal to the playoffs, and if possible, to the World Series. "Imagine that," Gómez had said to O.C., "being here, in Los Angeles, with the Dodgers in the Series."

But it didn't work out that way. "That's baseball," as Gómez would say. "You're in the right place at the right time, the game is on the line, the crowd is going crazy, you get the pitch you want and you hit it—you hit it *hard*, a line drive to deep center, and the centerfielder goes back, back, back, then leaps up, over the wall, and—dada doom, catches it. Yer out."

On Saturday morning Gómez's body was cremated, the ashes placed in O.C.'s care, at O.C.'s insistence. Despite our desire to be cheerful, each effort to raise our collective spirits collapsed beneath the weight of our collective gloom, like the soaring melodies of "Bolero," in reverse. Mr. Sánchez suggested that we meet that night at Gómez's for the first game of the World Series. Everyone was there but my tía and Eddie. Even Mrs. Sánchez came. It was her first, and last, game.

Despite the great start to game one—Mickey Hatcher's two-run homer in the first inning—we all continued in the semi-comatose state we'd been in since Gómez's death. Besides, with Kirk Gibson out of the game—and maybe the Series—with a bad hamstring *and* a bad right knee, there was little reason to believe we could beat the powerful Oakland A's. When Mrs. Cortez declared in the sixth inning that she needed to leave early to wash her hair, none of us even looked up. And when Mr. Aguilar left because he had to get up early for work, no one bothered to tell him that it was Saturday night, not Sunday night.

By the time the ninth inning rolled around, it was just me, O.C., Mr. and Mrs. Sánchez and my mom. When the Dodgers came to the plate in the bottom of the ninth trailing 4-3, they faced the best relief pitcher in baseball, future Hall of Famer, Dennis Eckersley. Our first batter was Scoscia, who popped out to short. The next hitter was Hamilton: he went down in flames. The screen door swung open and there was Carmen.

"¿Que pasa?" she said

"We're losing," I answered, "and there are two out in the bottom of the ninth inning."

"*Mijo,*" she chided, waving her finger at me, "I told you not to talk baseball to me. Make it simple, so even a little girl like me can understand."

"See that guy with the bat in his hand? He's our last hope. And earlier this season he was so bad Lasorda benched him."

"So, I'm just in time," she answered. As Mike Davis walked up to the plate Carmen pulled her purse off her shoulder and extracted two pompoms. She placed them in front of her chest and said, "*Mijo,* what do you think?" Damn my tía.

Carmen tossed her hair to one side and said, "So, what's this guy's name?"

"Mike Davis."

"Go-oooo Davis!" yelled Carmen, waving her pompoms above her head. The umpire signaled ball one. "Is that good?" asked my tía. "Yep," answered O.C.

Then Carmen danced through the living room, chanting, "Do it again, do it again, gooooooo Davis!" Strike one. "Is that bad?" asked Carmen.

Mr. Sánchez smiled wryly and nodded his head.

"*Don't* do it again! *Don't* do it again! Or I'll kick your ass, Davis!"

Ball two. "Yeah!" said O.C., pumping his fist.

My mom began clapping her hands in rhythm to Carmen's chants. Ball three! Now we were all clapping!

"You can do it! You can do it! Go-ooooooooo Davis!" Strike two. But now we weren't going to let minor setbacks like that dampen our enthusiasm.

Carmen did her version of a back-flip, which was as pathetic as it was funny. She bounced up quickly, undaunted by her failure, and flapping her pompoms, chanted: "Don't screw up! Do something good! Come to Carmen with your wood . . . bat."

Davis walked!

Sure, it was only a walk, but sometimes if you can just crack the door open a little bit . . . .

Alejandro Peña, the pitcher, was next up, and of course he wouldn't hit. The camera moved to the dugout, searching for the pinch-hitter. Then we heard the words, "Here comes Kirk Gibson!"

We went crazy. Here he was, limping out of the dugout, the absolute right man at the right time. Now we were all standing; hooting and hollering and dancing and—when he fouled the first pitch—*groaning,* just like Gibson. On the second pitch he dribbled a weak ground ball—foul, then ball one, another foul, ball two, a throw to first, a stolen base, ball three—and then we stopped. *This was the moment: three balls, two strikes, two outs, ninth inning, down 4-3 with a runner on base, their best versus our best.*

Gibson steps out of the box and taps the dirt off his shoes with his bat. Eckersley winds up and throws his famous 'back door slider,' starting inside, then curving back towards the plate. Gibson swings—just a poke, it seems—but the ball leaps off his bat, arcing like a white comet against the black night, over the fence and into eternity.

That's baseball.

Hallelujah

Life moves on, and our little villa was no exception.

Mr. and Mrs. Sánchez opened a dance studio called "The Zoot Suit." Soon they were renting out a restaurant on Saturday nights, cars pulling up to the red carpet one after the next, doors swinging open and spilling out couples dressed in clothes so outrageous as to declare to one and all, "You ain't never seen nothin' like me!"

Mr. Aguilar concluded that he deserved all the accolades he got for his sizzling *carne asada*, so he bought a local taco stand. Last I heard he had six restaurants, each featuring only two salsas: Salsa Gómez and Salsa Sánchez.

Mrs. Cortez achieved notoriety for holding up three liquor stores, each time wearing a different scarf. The police finally captured her when they followed the trail of money thrown out the back of her getaway cab.

Eddie did leave *Los Toros*, though he never told me how he managed it. He also finished high school, went to college and got a Bachelor's Degree in Sociology. He joined the LAPD, where he served for ten years. After that he went into politics. Yep, that's my big brother down there at City Hall, a

Los Toros tattoo under his white shirt, a white staff standing conspicuously in the corner of his office.

O.C. moved back to Oklahoma; he had a brother who owned a farm. For several years we exchanged postcards on holidays, but the last two cards I sent were not acknowledged, and it's been a long time now. I was very fond of O.C, and I miss him.

Remember Gómez's letter to my Tía Carmen? He told her to go to the corner of Broadway and Mission on November 15th. Well, she did; we all did, actually. It was a billboard! A Carmen billboard! It said, "The Beautiful Carmen Salazar." Above the caption was a picture of her from that night at Dodger Stadium. She glowed like an angel.

Apparently Carmen had made a big impression on a certain Dodger player—Dodger star, I should say—Dodger *Latino* Star, to be more precise—who, because of that billboard, was able to track her down. She blew him off at first, but he persisted. Three months later they married, and now they have two boys. Their names? Why, Gómez and O. C., of course. I can't help but smile when I hear her call them.

My mom became involved in almost anything that had to do with helping people, and about ten years ago, frustrated that work got in the way of the really important things, she quit her job and became a nun. No joke. She looks pretty good, too!

That package Gómez left for me was a book. All the pages were blank, but one. On the bottom of the first page, in Gómez's hand, it said, "By Alex Morales."

And Gómez? Hardly a week goes by that I don't wonder whatever became of my friend, Gómez the god.

Acknowledgements

For a Lifetime of Help and Support:
Carolina Loweree
James H. Loweree
Barbara F. Loweree
Elizabeth Loweree
Jimmy Loweree

Editing:
Robert T. Patterson

Proof Readers:
Carol Loweree
Jimmy Loweree
Glenda Rae Bourland
Jessica Pantermuehl
and Steve Loweree

Graphic Artist:
Ed Paiva

Best Friends,
Peter, Tom, and Brad

Bob Dylan,
for showing me I had a voice

LRH,
for countless gifts

About the Author

Little is known about Mark Loweree, and what is known would not suggest he could write a book of any merit, let alone a good book about Mexican-Americans. As the name suggests, Mark is a gringo: a blonde-haired, blue-eyed, raised in Newport Beach white boy. Mark himself evades the subject of authorship, claiming that a Muse gave him the story—the *complete* story, from beginning to end—in the autumn of 2000, while listening to a song by Andrea Bocelli.

Inspecting Mark's prior literary achievements, we see that he was the sports editor for his high school newspaper, and that in the early 70's he anonymously penned bad topical poetry for his college newspaper. That's it. That's the sum total of his prior literary credits.

Therefore, as unlikely as it is that *Gómez the god* was divinely inspired, when the editors inspected all the possibilities, they concluded that supernatural intervention was not only possible, but *necessary.*

We invite you to draw your own conclusions.

Printed in the United States
by Baker & Taylor Publisher Services